...AULD ZIMMERY

...AULD ZIMMERY

Robbie Kydd

THE MARISCAT PRESS
1987

Some of these stories, or versions of them, have appeared in
New Writing Scotland 2 and 3.

The publisher wishes to acknowledge subsidy from the
Scottish Arts Council towards the publication of this volume.

Cover design by James Hutcheson.

Author's Note

In these fictions I have attempted to illustrate the eight 'critical
periods of development' in our human life cycle, as identified by
Erik H. Erikson in *Childhood and Society* and *The Life Cycle
Completed* (both published by W. W. Norton and Company).
They are also intended as a tribute to his humanity and humour.

Published by The Mariscat Press,
3 Mariscat Road, Glasgow G41 4ND.
Typeset by Cordfall Ltd,
Civic House, 26 Civic Street, Glasgow G4 9RH.
Printed by Bell and Bain Ltd,
303 Burnfield Road, Glasgow G46 7UQ.

CONTENTS

This book is for everyone who helped me write it,
wittingly or unwittingly.

Auld Zimmery

She's been in here again, Fiona the Punk, and I've realised at last why she irritates me so much. It's because I can't manipulate her with my tired auld mannie act. She's iron, and rude with it. She makes me find my own clean underpants; and she puts my blessed zimmer out of reach so that I have to make an effort to stand up and get a hold of it; and when she's on duty I have to bath and dress myself, and cut up my own meat (what there is of it) and clamber into bed unaided, while she stands there with her arms folded scornfully and the regulation sulky punk expression, sending the message, 'You could come alive if you tried!' It's a hell of a message to hear from a teenage Care Assistant with a multi-coloured Mohican hair-do, and an ochre-yellow face and clanking heavy-metal ear-rings. I wonder what the craitur wears under that punk-pink overall? Something 'hard-core', I bet. I'll be dead before I find out, I suppose, and serve me right.

She's been reading my diary while I was away at dinner and she takes no notice at all when I complain. She just marches out and I'm left trembling. Wishing someone else dead stops you from wishing yourself dead. Now that I've written that down I won't have to kill her. I'll just die. That'll show you. And I don't care if you read this either. I'll be dead. Aye, deid.

The besom has disappeared and I wonder if my wishes have killed her, but she re-appears. She's had a coupla days aff (why can't I have a day off?) an a couple mair in loo o workin on bank holidays. She explains this to me off-handedly and adds, 'Ma boy-friend says I dinnae have tae work, but I'm no gaun on the broo, no when I kin get mair breid jist lookin efter auld wankers like you in a fine warm place.'

'Doesn't anyone complain about your language?'

'Naw.'

'How do you get away with it?'

'I dinnae sweir at clypes, that's hoo I get awaa wi it.'

So I'm some kind of honorary punk, or at least not a clype. She has her insights. I can't tell her to her face that I've missed her, my counter-irritant to dying, but if I write it down she'll probably read it. I missed you when you were off-duty. Got it? Now nick two *plain* chocolate home-wheat biscuits from the boss's tray in the office. You know the milk ones we auld zimmeries are given make me sick. Just two of them, instead of love. Who's a clever wee girl, then?

She's off-duty again, and the Wraiths have taken over. I can't stand them. They're not real. Come back, Fiona! Come clumping along the lobby and sweir at me and roll up your sleeves and bully me and sneer at me and make me so mad I'll 'come alive, start up, tick, hum, work juice, summon spunk, unglue spirit, melt wax soul . . .' I shudder to think what you'd say if I quoted old Illustrated Bradbury out loud to you. What you'll blurt out when you read it will be bad enough. But maybe you'll never read it. Maybe you'll never come back on duty. Nobody ever tells me anything about anything, least of all the duty-roster. Mind you, if they did, I'd forget, wouldn't I, so what would be the point? Yes, Mrs Scott, or whatever your name is, I'd be better off dead, obviously.

They've taken Andy away, so the other bed is empty. Yet again. Poor chap. He had a rotten life and he never got used to the rottenness or found a way of overcoming it. Which Andy am I writing about? There have been so many, and I'm one of them myself. Sometimes I think my bed must be empty too, for my own life is a meaningless blank when I try to look back. It may have been a rotten life, I have no evidence one way or the other. (I'm sneakily glad I'm on my own again, though. I can have my reading lamp on all night, except when that Night Woman, a Wraith on silent slippered feet, tries to interfere and make me sleep.) No, I was writing, confused old fool, about Andrew MacPhail, my recently deceased room-mate, victim of Crichton Smith's 'poor ruined Scotland' — child neglect, unemployment, alcoholism, violence, List D School, Borstal, Barlinnie, bad housing, bad teeth, bad sex, bad lungs, bad. Perhaps I should have called someone to call the priest to salve the rotten loneliness of his end with his little bottle of oil. But I did hold his hand and he returned my grip to the last, when the dark came. And that's what I want when I lose hope altogether. When Fiona goes. A hand to grip.

I glimpsed her boy-friend today, from the hallway, threateningly clanking and cockscombing in the street outside the front gate. He was standing in the middle of the busy road, living dangerously. He does it on principle, Fiona says. I'm glad I don't have to meet him though. I detect a twinge of jealously in myself when I think of her ordering him to change into clean underpants. If he wears underpants, that is. I wonder if they've got round to cod-pieces yet? I predict the return of cod-pieces before I shuffle off.

Where is the pattern that was to be a comfort? 'You examine where you're at and where you're going and it makes no sense, but when you look back at where you've come from a pattern seems to emerge ... If you use that pattern to look forward with then you can sometimes come up with something.' Someone said that, or something like it, sitting in a pool of his own urine. Phaedrus? Pissing? Pirsig? What *was* his name? I've always meant to test his idea, omitting the urine and the motor-bikes (from what vasty abyss have they appeared?) but looking back now I see no pattern, none at all, only disenchanted/disconnected happenings dreichly/drably happening, and not too many of them either. As for looking to the future, it seems 'liable, like the past, to have no destination'. T.S.Eliot. Silly auld fart, to use Fiona's terms. No one like him for pushing you further down when you're down. 'Do not let me hear of the wisdom of old men, but rather of their folly.' Maybe the pool of urine is a prerequisite for 'coming up with something'. No problem to provide it. Just let go. But if I let go, I'd die. And that's too much of a temptation.

When will Mother Hen (Matron, Depute Officer-in-Charge, what's in a name?) when will she move another Andy into the other bed? I'd give anything for his noise, for the clicking and rattling and muttering and coughing, and for the assurance that Scotland is still out there. Even the stenches from his socks and his fags and his 'special privilege' commode . . .

These lonely nights are getting worse and worse. I always refuse tablets, just to be politely awkward, but the price I have to pay is pain. Not a grand overwhelming pain, the stuff of tragedy, but a collection of little pains. My joints ache, not just in my mysteriously malfunctioning legs, but everywhere; my eczema patches itch and sting and itch; sudden pin-pricks stab my lungs and my eyeballs and my bladder and my tongue and my ear-canals and my testicles (what's left of them); disturbing twitches occur all over me, the worst on the back of my neck and in my crutch; my teeth feel ready to fall out. It's no use telling any of them — Mother or Fiona or Mother Hen or what's-her-name, that craitur, Punkie. One of them might make sympathetic noises, but on the other hand she might not. She might tell me there's no cure for a myriad of tiny ailments. When I haven't a pain I can identify, I have irritations. I see flashing lights and black worms writhing across my field of vision, while a distant Niagara sounds in my ears and an ambulance siren wails, always coming nearer and never arriving. Even my piles, blast them, are only an inconvenience at wiping-up time; they don't hurt. The doctor, if I complained to him, would say I'm mildly depressed (i.e., none of his business) and suggest Diversional Therapy to Mother Hen. I know his kind.

Why did Fiona leave me? What did I do to deserve it? I have this dreadful emptiness as I try to remember. I can't describe my terror as the hostile blankness envelopes me and the grey miasma fills my skull to bursting point. 'Remember!' I hear myself shouting as sweat pours off me and the stupid duvet traps my legs and the light from my reading-lamp sears my eyelids. Then I come fully awake and discover there's no Gletkin turning up the brightness. It's still the same hundred-watt bulb that Fiona nicked from the store for me. I must remember to take it out and hide it. Andy's commode would be a handy place now that he'll not be needing it any more.

Koestler was wrong. Gletkin doesn't turn *up* the lights. She gradually turns them down, replacing sixties with forties, forties with twenty-fives, and twenty-fives with nursery night lights, all to save money she says, her starched cuffs creaking and crackling. Gletkin has a shiny leather revolver belt; it creaks too. 'The Cuts, Mr. Robb, The Cuts,' she intones, and I see someone at a power-station wielding huge levers like they used to have in railway signal-boxes.

Perhaps there are sinister purposes behind The Cuts. Perhaps we're being conditioned to the coming of the dark, the inevitable dark, 'the vacant into the vacant'. (Auld fart Eliot, yet again.) If it came on us suddenly when the lights were bright, we wouldn't be ready for it, would we? Koestler though, he turned the lights from bright to dark, all with one flick of the switch. His own decision. Darkness at his command. I envy him, most of the time. I hope the Night Wraith doesn't clype about this hundred-watt bulb. I saw her looking at it.

Writing all that, whatever it was about, has calmed me down and I've slept for a few nights. Writing as Diversional Therapy. Writing about death diverts me from the thought of death. It's logical. I don't want to read it over, all the same, as the words might be unfamiliar and upset me again, but I *must,* because I'm sure I wrote something that was for Fiona to read and remind me about. Go on, you old fearty, read it over. Nothing's killed you yet.

Fiona was my wife before she deserted me. Hold on to that, even though it doesn't quite make sense. Fionas don't desert. It's more likely I deserted her. Then it would be my fault, wouldn't it, and explain why I feel so bad? 'Grampa! Grampa!' I hear her screaming across the airport concourse in her Californian accent, the multi-coloured Los Angeles faces crowding me as I'm herded towards the gate, 'Grampa! I wanna go *with* you!'

Of course she wanted to go *with* me. I had given her more attention than she had ever had in her life. I had been available to her night and day for three months while her mother was in Hawaii recovering from an abortion (or so she said) and the Mexican nurse-

13

maid had yet another unterminated pregnancy. The kindergarten/nursery-school/whatever was closed, so we were on our own. We loved each other from the moment she woke me in the morning, the smoggy morning, for our ritual visit to the bountiful ice-cold mother-provider of a fridge, till I sang the dear wee madam to sleep with 'Coulter's Candy'.

We loved each other with a passion that frightened me, shot through as it was with intimations of inevitable loss and pain. We knew, yes, we *both* knew that I was going home to Scotland and Granma and love, while she was staying where there was no home, where 'home' means 'house' and love is a sick slick joke. My daughter Jenny — yes, God forgive me, my daughter — holds her high and she screams and screams, waving her sweet little limbs as if in agony. 'As if' in agony? She *was* in agony and I left her. Right in that sad new world, poor ruined California, where everything is disposable, nothing indispensable, even love. Especially love.

Yes, I did the deserting. When I heard 'Coulter's Candy' from some radio the other day I shed fountains of tears, not knowing why. I know now. I hope I remember.

Old fool, I tell myself, you mustn't entertain the idea that you were ever indispensable: 'Unless you are,' someone, not a Californian obviously, whispers in my ear, disturbingly. So I could still be Grampa, far away in Scattlan, and indispensable. Fiona, remind me to write. Jenny is capable of anything. Right. She could have left poor heart-rending wee Fiona with any one of the husbands she has discarded in the interests of personal growth. Right. And he might have left her with one of his subsequent wives, also into personal growth. Right. Right. Right.

The doctor says my heart is sound and very strong — 'I hope mine's like that when I reach your age' — but it's thumping so hard just now that I'm afraid it will cause a blow-out somewhere else. In my brain, most likely, and it would serve me right. What have I got to get excited about? I'm dead, aren't I? If I'm not, I ought to be.

'Still writing rubbish?' asks Fiona, when she finds me dozing upright in my bed, my A4 pad in my lap and my trusty 0.7mm Pentel still in my hand, implying that writing is a poor way of coming alive, but better than nothing. I could try harder.

'Aye,' I reply, wide awake at her challenge.

'Kin I read it?'

'Well. Yes. I suppose so,' I temporise, thinking she may be growing up, actually asking my permission, but there's dynamite in some of the complaints I've made about this place and its denizens. Could she handle all that and not clype? I look into her face uncertainly and its expression is unfamiliar. Something must have happened to her. She's a shade less hard and sulky, almost vulnerable. Her ears look naked with her hair shaved away at the sides like that, but they are shapely ears; worth showing off, but vulnerable. I hand her the pad, after flipping back the pages to the place where I want her to start. She reads my scrawl rather slowly, moving her lips. She looks up.

'Ye're dottled. I'm no yer wife.'

I concentrate on her eyes, her dark dark eyes, glowing in the midst of her magenta and tangerine and black eye-shadow, and feel as if I'm drowning.

'My wife's name was Fiona,' I say in a precise, controlled and entirely false voice.

'Ye're kiddin.'

'No,' I say, still holding on to her eyes, for the rest of her, the warm pulsing fragrant rest of her, is shimmering and dissolving. Tears fill my eyes and stream down my face. Sobs shake me.

Fiona sits down on the bed, close to me. Our eyes lose contact. I *am* drowning.

'Ya silly auld soad,' she says, putting her arms round me. I go on sobbing and she presses my face to her bosom, savagely tattooed but amply available above today's tight and garish, but not too metallic, sweater. How her overall got itself unbuttoned I can't remember.

'Go on, bubble,' she murmurs in my ear, 'I didnae ken ye had a wife.'

'I was married for fifty years.'

'Goad, an I thought ye were a horny auld bachelor.'

'No, I was . . .' We are quiet for a while, while I try to remember what I was going to say. Darkness, suddenly lit by a searchlight from Fiona.

'Ye've wrote it doon here that yer wife deserted ye.'

'Yes, she . . .' It won't come out, so I bury my face deeper in the sweet punk-scented warmth, experiencing pain like an orgasm. I'm coming alive, I think, just let me die again.

'My boyfriend's deserted me an I'm no greetin.' So something *has* happened to her. She's in pain too. I lift my face.

'Tell me.' If she does, maybe my pain will go away.

'Naw. It's you that's greetin, stupit.'

So out it comes. The glory that was my Fiona. My plump and faithful childhood friend; my passionate spring-time lover; the mother of our two beautiful and successful children; the talented artist; the resourceful helper; the companion of our sweet autumnal re-flowering. I wax poetical and a part of my mind insists that Fiona slips right under the duvet and holds me close. But she rumbles me. She would, wouldn't she, being her.

'An efter aa that, she left ye?'

At that, it's back to where the comfort is, and more wet tears. But there's iron in Fiona, as well as comfort. There always was, since our sandpit days.

'She left ye?'

I feel a kind of swaying motion. I think Fiona has picked me up in her arms and is rocking me like a baby. I wet myself, warmly. You-know-who won't like that. Andy is a bad boy.

I don't know if I can write the next bit, but I must, for at last I've 'come up with something', with Fiona's help. I'm sure of it. Wet with tears as well as urine. I must pin it down on paper.

'We lived in a top floor flat.' The tremors in my voice are more than just senile. My hand trembles as I write. Fiona won't be able to read a word of this. 'A wee studio. After the children had gone. We stayed in it longer than we should have. The stairs. They were too much for me.'

'I ken aboot thae kinda stairs.'

'Fiona had to help me up and down. And carry the messages. She was always so strong. I stopped going out. One day I had to go to the doctor. When we came back she was carrying the messages. And helping me. We stopped half-way up for a rest. She fell down. Just dropped to the stone floor. She was breathing. No one answered when I rang the bells on the landing. Everyone was out at work. I shouted. No one came.'

'Aw jeeze!' She strokes my hair.

'I went down on my hands and knees. I couldn't tell if she was still breathing. I couldn't feel her heart. I couldn't move her. I started to crawl up the stairs to our own door. I was going to phone for help. I only reached half-way.'

'I cannae bear it. I'll have tae, noo. Whit happened?'

'I don't know. Next thing I was in hospital. They were dressing me up to come here. Nobody's ever told me what happened . . . Nobody's ever mentioned . . . Till you said . . . wife . . .'

'Whaur the hell are yer kids, then?'

'Wee Andy's in Australia. Very busy. Jennifer's in California. Into personal growth.'

'D'they ken their mither's deid?'

'They must,' I say, feeling the word 'deid' like a stone in my belly. Yet it is a kind of lightening too, for I now know what the stone in my belly is. Fiona deid. Dead. And it was my fault. That's the stone. 'Oh, Fiona, I didn't have to go to the doctor. You wanted to fetch him up to see me, but I insisted on going. I wanted out, a little escape. And it was only one of my usual pains. The paracetamol kind. It killed you.'

'I wouldnae hae let ye "insist". I'd hae lockit up yer troosers and phoned fir the doctor.'

'You bitch! I'll go out without them and freeze to death. That'll show you!' My feelings change so fast these days that they confuse me. I am ready to bite her, right on those tattoos, but I daren't. Mother is too strong, she'd smack me. She's had enough of me, anyway. She dumps me on the bed and stands up.

'I'm richt sorry fir yer wife. Ye're a hell of an auld nuisance when ye're ready. Here, lemme gie yer face a dicht.'

She has to use a big bunch of tissues on my resentful face, and then several more to wipe my tears off that tattooing. I refuse to help her change my wet pants. She sweirs at me, poètically.

'Time passes. Listen. Time passes.' Curly-headed what's-his-name, died of drink, I can't remember. No matter how hard I listen I can't keep track of time passing. Sometimes it goes fast, sometimes slow. Sometimes it seems to stop altogether, but I don't die. I just exist, taking a minimal part in the routine of living, if 'living' is the word. When I write down a happening in this diary I can't place it on any kind of time-scale, so I've given up putting in dates. They're meaningless. When Fiona says 'last week' she might as well say 'last year'.

I don't know how we got this way, sitting with our arms round each other, but that's what we're doing, Fiona and I.

'Punkie,' I ask, 'your boy-friend?'

'Wha're ye cryin Punkie?'

'I used to call my wife Tankie. She was your shape.'

'Ye're a right scholar and gentleman, aren't ye?'

'If you say so, Punkie.'

'Okay, it's Punkie then. But thae bitches'll complain if I dinnae get on wi ma work.' She makes a move to go, but I hold her.

'Your boyfriend? You said he deserted you . . .'

'Ach! Him! He didnae desert me. I gied him the push. He wisnae a real punk. He's gaun tae College in the back-end an he nivver tellt me. That shows ye whit he wis.' She curses him freely.

'I'm sorry. I'm awful sorry.'

'I'm no. Good riddance. It was just dressin up an easy lays fir him. He wisnae a man fir real.' Two enormous tears form on her eyelashes and roll slowly down her eye-shadow. 'He wisnae a man like you. I wish ye . . .'

We hold each other quietly for what seems like a long time.

'I'm just an old . . .' I whisper.

'Och, I ken that . . .'

I think there's another silence at this point. More cuddles too, I'm sure. Then Punkie sighs and straightens her back. Female problem faced. Female decision made. I know it. I can still read the signs after all these years. It must be like riding a bicycle. I look into her face and, sure enough, she is smiling a wise old female smile. The tears have dried.

'Aye-aye,' she whispers, rubbing noses briskly, just like Wee Fiona, 'I ken whit I'm lookin fir noo,' she strokes my face, really quite tenderly, I suppose, 'a fella that'll haud ma bum the way you're haudin it, and no the way he did. He wis aye jist coorse.'

'Oh, Punkie,' I whisper, for my poor old hands, which had been round her substantial waist, have tired and slipped and are now resting on her rearward roundnesses (neutralising words!). I squeeze gently — as if I was capable of anything more energetic!

'Ye're makkin it oabvious that ye're better.'

Better? From what? Oh yes, of course, I remember. The pain, I've found out what it's about, and it stops, now and again.

'Aye, I'm better. And you?'

'I'm okay,' and she kisses me on the forehead. I lift my face and make a kissing motion with my mouth, my dry withered old unkissed mouth.

'Ach, y'auld soad, I love ya!' she says, and is giving me a long warm more-or-less motherly kiss with her moist prune-coloured lips when the door bursts open and Mrs Scott, every inch the Senior Care Assistant, barges in, steel hair aglint and great bosom ready for aggro.

Just writing about that woman makes my heart pump to overload, so I stop and lie down under my duvet and fall asleep like a good boy. A more-or-less good boy. A bad boy, to be honest, But bad boys sleep as soundly as good boys, so I sleep well.

'Dear me!' says Mrs Scott with an elaborate phoney double-take, Bette Davis fashion, 'I'm just bringing your new room-mate.'

She ushers in an auld auld mannie in a neat brown suit. He is the spitting image of all the other Andies who have occupied the bed and he doesn't look as if he'll last long either. But then I've belonged to Count Zimmer's Walking Undead for years and I'm still coming alive. He could be too, I suppose.

'I haven't been informed,' I protest loudly, 'and you didn't knock.'

'You're not yourself, Mr Robb,' she says, a little shocked by a raised voice from the Undead, 'You were told three days ago. *And* yesterday. *And* this morning. And I *did* knock, but you must have been too busy to hear.' She introduces us. 'Mr Wah-wah-wah. Mr Robb. He's a wee bit forgetful, but I'm sure you'll understand and be friends. And this,' with a thumb at Fiona, 'is one of the other Care Assistants. I don't know how long she'll be working here.' Menace, menace.

So Punkie buttons up her overall and helps to settle in the new Andy. Usual all-too-familiar routine. She gives a two-finger sign to Mrs Scott as she follows her out; blows me a kiss; and makes an ambiguous throat-cutting gesture as she shuts the door. I don't know whose throat is to be cut. Fiona's, I should think, if I read the power-structure correctly. But I wouldn't underestimate a Fiona if I were Mrs Scott.

I know I should make an effort and get to know the new Andy, but I haven't summoned up the energy yet. He's the grateful type, pleased with everything and snuggling up to Mother Hen. 'Cheep-cheep!' he quavers, and she scratches about and gives him biscuits. When he isn't with her he's in the lounge with the auld wifies, so I still have the bedroom to myself for my scribbling. But I'm not writing anything like as much as I used to. I've taken to weeping instead, thinking about my very own Fiona, or Phimister as I used to call her when she was in one of her managing moods. Every so often I think of those stone stairs, but they are too hard to contemplate for long and I think of her softness again, and weep. It's out of character, but a relief.

I seem to have lost Fiona again and I'm lonely. Why has she left me? I haven't seen her to speak to since our little weep together, only her back, once or twice, disappearing down the passages to the auld wifies' department and taking no notice of my yearning after her. She's never in the dining room either though I think I've heard her dear hoarse voice through the hatch-way and then lost it again. If she's been transferred to the auld wifies' end, I'd be the last to be told. I'd just forget, so what would be the point? What, in heaven's name, would be the point?

It's no use asking Mrs Scott what has happened to Fiona, so I've waited till Mrs Blaikie comes on duty, perspiringly parading her marital problems along the lobby like tattered banners. She'll never be promoted to Senior, that's for sure. I lean hard on my zimmer and listen and listen and listen until my joints ache and I deserve something in return.

'What's happened to Fiona?'

She blushes a dirty red. 'Oh, I kent ye'd ask that!'

'Well?'

She helps me into my room and draws the door to. 'She's been baad.'

Fiona bad? The woman's crazy. 'What do you mean?'

'Oh, Mr Robb, she's been wicked!'

Definitely crazy. 'Tell me.'

'Oh, I couldnae!' Red splotches disfigure her neck and I realise, don't ask how, that she's talking about that unfaithful Punkie, while I've been longing to know what happened to my poor old Tankie while I was in hospital. Was I at the funeral? I know she's dead. Deid.

I re-arrange my thoughts as best I can. Mrs Blaikie wouldn't know about Tankie. Why did I ask her?

'Has she been stealing then?' I ask, thinking of the pilfering the little so-and-so has so blithely done on my behalf.

'Oh no, Mr Robb.'

'Hitting folk?' Punkie *did* have a hard fist.

'Naethin like that. It's much worse!'

It can only be the one thing, the serpent. 'Seducing the old men?'

Mrs Blaikie goes a sickly white. 'That's whit they're sayin.'

'Precisely what are they saying?'

'Oh, Mr Robb . . . I cannae say it . . . provokin . . . arousin . . . oh, it's shamefu . . . '

'Which old men?'

'I dinnae ken, quite a few, they're sayin.'

'Including me?'

'Oh no sir, Mr Robb! No a gentleman like you!'

Mrs Scott has talked, the bitch. In hints and whispers, in the highest tradition of bitchery. I lie down under my duvet with my Pentel in my hand like a dagger. My adrenalin drains away and I fall asleep. But I keep my hatred in reserve.

I've woken up with this need to zimmer off creakily to the office to beard the Cock o the North (Officer-in-Charge, Big Charlie, Matron's hen-pecked 'Old Man' — what's in a name?). I'm not sure what I want to ask him about, but he always knows everything, every single thing, without taking any part in decision-making. Castrated by his knowledge as well as by his wife, as Fiona would have said. Unfortunately, I zimmer past the office door without noticing it, out of the front door, down the short drive, and into the street. I am half-way to the first corner when I hear Phimister's voice, with its sardonic edge. 'Running away again?' she calls clearly and I stop, my heart at it again. A bus, a strange and unfamiliar bus, whooshes past, a row of wondering faces goggling at me, and the wind of it nearly knocks me over. I haven't seen a bus in years — they must have changed — but this may be another town. Or another country. Where is Scotland?

I get a grip of myself and my zimmer and turn to go back, suddenly re-living all sorts of fights I had with Phimister, especially the ones when she accused me of avoiding problems by running off. I resented her and her ability to control me. I resented the effect she had on other men — provoking and arousing them, to use Mrs Blaikie's words. I am resenting her now and wishing there were motorised zimmers, with wheels, so that I could whizz off to the airport and book a seat to — What would be the use? Wherever I found myself would still be nothing but a metaphor for my predicament, just as this place is. Death closing around me. Four drab walls. No one to hold my hand.

I am guiltily remembering that Fiona's birthday is round about now, for I think I saw snowdrops on my way down the drive. With all her charm and verve and poise she was not at all easy to give presents to. It was as if they, and the giver, had to prove themselves. Sometimes, years later, she would kiss me and say, 'You gave me that. Clever you!' Sometimes a present never evoked a response at all.

Once, when we were poor, I gave her a bunch of snowdrops for her birthday and she just grunted and went on painting. The next morning, though, there was a little water-colour of them by my shaving things; a subtly ambiguous statement about the joys of spring and their inevitable death. I wonder who's looking at it now? I hope they deserve such a treasure. By predicting death it postpones death.

The cold is biting me in my cardigan and slippers and my scalp is shrivelling on my skull, so I set off for 'home' (you *must* regard this as your *home*) and reach the door, my absence un-noticed, as the bell goes for tea. In the hall, amongst the pot-plants, is a huge calendar I haven't seen before. Maybe I've seen it, but I certainly haven't taken it in. Anyway, it is telling me plainly that it *is* Fiona's birthday. I am so pleased with myself for remembering that I actually start the conversation at the table I share with the current Andy and two other ancients.

'It's my wife's birthday today. She'd have been . . .' I try to remember how old she'd have been, but I've taken on board only the day and the month from the calendar. The year, in letters a foot high, escapes me. My cronies are interested, though. They didnae ken I'd been mairrit. Of course they didnae ken; I'd never exchanged more than two words at a meal before. Andy — the other two call him Willie, I must try to remember — volunteers that he is a bachelor, but the other two are widowers like me and we have a long crack, over the baked beans, about wives and their queer ways. Andy — Willie, I mean — adds a few reminiscences about his Mither so we talk about oor Mithers too, as if they are still alive and no deid thae thirty year. When the staff come to clear away the table, and us, oor eyes are weet wi sorra and camaraderie. Silly auld soads! Aye, but still leevin.

My doddery old cronies and I are making a habit of this reminiscing at the dining-table. Today it was our schooldays — grey slates and squeaky slate-pencils and oak-and-iron desks and steel pens and blue-black ink and iron teachers and thick leather belts. It all comes back to me so crystal-clear and urgent that I have to leave aside this diary and pin down that day when Miss Wood belted me for the first time. Every morning I find I have forgotten what I wrote yesterday, so I have to start at the beginning and re-read everything before I can carry on with putting down the story. I could weep with frustration. I could weep too for the lack of the masochistic thrill I was hoping for. I must be too old, or perhaps I never was a masochist. I can't remember. Fiona would know. She always *knew*.

I'm zimmering, millimetre by bloody millimetre, along the passage when I meet Mrs Scott and remember the other Fiona, the faithless one.

'Where's Fiona?' I screech.

'Come, come, Mr Robb, you're not yourself these days.'

'Where is she?'

'Why ask me?'

'You didn't clype on us?'

'What *can* you mean?'

'You saw us kissing and you clyped.'

'I saw more than that, as you well know, Mr Robb, but it was a very long time ago . . .'

I interrupt. 'What do you mean by "more than that"?'

'Really, Mr Robb, you know what you were doing and I was surprised at you, a respectable man like you.'

For a second or two I see what she saw — a little shrunken tremulous old man fondling a punk girl's bum with his skeletal hands. Yuck! Then I remember what the craitur and I were trying to do — share our views on life and love and loss and gentleness and understanding and pain and integrity and loyalty and helping each other . . . and the cuddles were helping us to do it. My heart goes right beyond overload and I blow a fuse and fall over. I gather Mrs Scott tried to grab me and fell too, lacerating her shins on my zimmer. Serve her right. It's possible I hit her with the thing. I seem to remember a convulsive movement before I fell. That would serve her right too. If there's industrial injury compensation to be had, she'll have it. She could take me to court, of course. Assault to her severe injury. My mind went blank, said the accused.

I've had quite a few days in bed to cool me off and I've spent the time making resolutions. The first was to be sociable, now that I've wept myself into a happier frame of mind, and visit the Hen Run, the lounge that is. I've just been there and I'm wabbit; worn out, in English. First, they had to find a chair and put it in the latest comer's place, just inside the door and next to the TV, where I could see nothing of the thing, though it was blasting away right at my ear. Then the old hens started to become hyper-active and invent excuses for hirpling out of the lounge and tripping over my feet. Most were intent on hacking my ankle-bones, but one plonked her zimmer on my foot, leaned on it with all her weight and fixed me with a glittering eye until Willie, peacemaker Willie, wheedled her off. A few painted old harridans wanted to flirt, or draw me into a game of cards, or whatever. I was miserable, but I stuck to my resolution manfully till a racketty music programme came on. Then, when they wouldn't turn it down, I escaped to my room and peace, wetting my pants on the way back. I weep, yet again, because I went to the Hen Run in the hope that Fiona would be there. Silly auld soad, you should have gone there years ago, while Fiona was alive and you could still control your sphincters. It's too late now.

Needless to say, I've forgotten what my other resolutions were.

'Willie, you'll hold my hand, won't you?'

'Whit d'ye mean, Andra?'

'When I'm for off.'

'Ye mean . . . Oh aye, I'll dae that. An I'll say a prayer fir ye. But ye're no fir off the noo?'

'No, but it won't be long.'

'Ye'll tell me, eh?'

'Aye, I'll call you,' I answer, but Willie has begun to snore companionably. He doesn't seem to want a reciprocal arrangement, but then he has The Lord to hold *his* hand, or maybe at eighty-three he's too young to be thinking that far ahead. This letter from Fiona, she says I'm about to become a great-grandfather, which is likely enough, I suppose. She hopes it will be a boy, so that she can christen it Andrew after me. She doesn't say anything about the Father. I'll write to her in the morning when I have a little energy.

Memories float to the surface, nagging me to sort out what they mean. I see a triple-headed sculpture of Fiona and two children. What is it? I think I commissioned her to do a self-portrait and this was what she came up with. The children were clearly family, but whether they were our children or our grandchildren or even ourselves in childhood she wouldn't say. Or perhaps she did say and I just can't remember. Where is that sculpture now? Maybe Jennifer looted it and took it to California? No, Phimister destroyed it herself. Too jejune, she said. But Wee Andy was home from Australia and had photographed it for me and I might just still have a copy - in that deep bottom drawer I can't possibly kneel down to open. Willie's still souple enough. I'll ask him.

It's the middle of the night again and I'm able to switch on my reading lamp, for they've taken Willie away to hospital. His heart, of course, not his lungs or his liver — he didn't smoke or drink ever. It won't be him who'll hold my hand. He'll never call me 'Andra' again. I need a hand, a human hand, preferably a Fiona's, with a firm skeleton beneath the warmth and softness. I'm going to die here. I'll never be ill enough to be sent away to hospital, where I'll be properly looked after but no one will hold my hand. I'm not allowed to be ill. I'm wonderful for my age, considering. I'm not allowed to talk about my 'zimmer' any more, I must call it a 'walking aid'. The poetry has gone. One day I'll quietly pack it in and Fiona won't have to bother with my dirty pants. Yes, my dear, I know they're soiled. *You* smell nice, though, don't you? You're strong, too.

Fiona said something fierce about takkin ma troosers awaa. I don't think she ever actually did it, but she was certainly capable of such an action. I'm confused. How did we settle that argument? I wasn't going to the doctor, she was. She'd mentioned a pain, which was unheard of, and said she'd better go. I was so upset that she agreed to my going with her. In fact she was pleased to have me go. She didn't know what she was going to hear. She needed me. It's hard for me to believe, but Fiona Phimister needed me. That would do for my epitaph.

I remember more. We were holding hands when she fell. She'd laid down the messages and taken my hand. She usually held my elbow. I weep tears of relief as well as sorrow. She was holding my hand. I was holding hers.

Tools, Skills
and Feeling Small

Andy tries to copy the figure 7 from the blackboard on to the clean new page of his jotter. It is Friday, so it is jotters instead of slates, and he has to be specially careful, Miss Wood says. His pencil wobbles and the 7 looks like a worm. He tries again and it looks a worm that someone has almost bitten in half.

Andy looks to his left. Fiona, at the next oak-and-iron desk, has drawn a whole line of beautiful 7s, almost as good as Miss Wood's on the blackboard. Miss Wood isn't looking, she is bending over someone at the front of the class, so Andy finishes his line of 7s in a rush. They look like a fence that is falling down.

He glances to his left again. Fiona is sitting up 'properly', holding her pencil 'properly' in her plump fingers. She is half-way through her second line of 7s, all of them perfect.

He looks to his right. Geordie, who shares his desk, is working hard. His short legs are twisted together and his head is almost on the desk and his tongue is sticking out. He has drawn two careful 7s, almost as perfect as Fiona's. He untwists his legs, twists them again the other way round, licks his pencil, and starts on his third 7. MacMillan is slow but sure, Miss Wood says, but she'll be cross if she sees him licking his pencil.

My big brother, Andy thinks, writes his figures *very very* fast and they come out like Miss Wood's, so he does his second line *very very* fast. They come out like a line of telegraph poles getting bigger and bigger and more and more uneven. He looks up and Miss Wood is arriving at his desk, smelling of peppermints and leather shoes. Her black gown is dusty with chalk. She has a 'lady' smell too, so Andy tries to hold his breath .

'You must be more careful, Robb,' she says, bending down from her great height and putting his fingers round his pencil 'properly'. She guides his hand to make the first 7 of his third row. It is, of course, nearly perfect.

'Now, try that yourself,' says Miss Wood. Andy tries, still holding his breath. He breaks the point of his pencil. He is too frightened to look up, and tries to breathe without breathing.

'Careless boy!' he hears Miss Wood saying crossly. She is not really angry, though. She reaches into the deep flying pocket of her gown for her shiny pen-knife, sharpens Andy's pencil, and moves away to someone else, after pleased glances at Fiona and Geordie. Andy takes several deep breaths, as quietly as he can. His big brother can sharpen a pencil, but he can't.

Andy needs to go to the bathroom, but he doesn't want to ask Miss Wood if he may leave the room. She will still be cross with him, after the broken pencil. He presses his legs together and hopes for the best. He tries another 7 and it looks like a squashed worm. The next he tries is better but much too big. The next is almost perfect, but even bigger.

Fiona, Andy can see, has finished a whole neat page of proper 7s, all the same height. Her finger-nails are round at the top, a much nicer shape than his blunt ones. They are spotless underneath too, while his are black. His big sister says, 'Your nails are going to a funeral'. Andy wishes he could hide them. The pleats in Fiona's kilt are perfect.

The playtime bell, it must ring soon. Andy breaks his pencil again, but pretends to go on writing. Fiona turns to him, half closes her eyes and puts out the tip of her pink tongue. Then she looks at the mess in his jotter, opens her eyes wide, and makes an O of her mouth. She has noticed! She *always* notices. Why does he have to sit in the row next the girls? None of the boys want to sit there. It was Miss Wood who made him. Andy wishes with all his heart that he was right at the other end of the room. Not that he wants to leave Geordie, who is his friend.

His friend is sighing and straightening out his legs. He is wearing a khaki jersey several sizes too large for him and which would fit a very wee soldier, ragged tweed shorts, odd stockings with holes in them which are draped right down round his ankles, and gym-shoes without laces, but he doesn't care. He doesn't care a bit. His legs are short and thick and dirty and sun-burned. Andy glances down at his own scrawny, warty, clean, pale knees sticking out between his clean flannel shorts and his clean grey carefully-darned stockings. His tackety boots are shiny. Father cleans them, laughing about Lloyd George and Mother getting the vote. Grown-ups have boring secrets. Andy can't run as fast as Geordie, or kick a ball as cleverly and fiercely, and he never gets sunburned. He wants to go to the bathroom — it is called the 'lavvy' at school.

The playtime bell goes at last, but Miss Wood is slow about letting the class out. Andy thinks he is going to wet his pants, but she goes on fussing about passing forward and counting the pencils. Pencils are precious, because of the War to End War. So are jotters. Then everybody has to sit up straight enough to please Miss Wood, which is very straight indeed. After she is satisfied that everyone is like a poker, she gives the magic signal and Andy marches out with the others.

He runs across the playground, weaving and dodging to avoid the crowds of other boys, all weaving and dodging too. He reaches the outside 'lavvy', but stops dead when he meets the smells of fresh pee and disinfectant and old pee. They seem to be pouring out of the door. To make things worse, there is a lot of shouting and giggling going on inside. The big boys from Standard Five, they will be showing each other how high they can pee. They were doing it yesterday. They are always doing it. Sometimes the Jannie shouts at them, but as soon as he's gone they start again.

Andy has *got* to pee, so he rushes through the big urinal where the game is going on, opens the door of the first w.c. and manages to lock himself in. Sometimes the locks are too stiff for him. Sometimes the locks have been torn off. A big boy must be peeing really high for a fine spray is coming over the partition, but Andy is in too much of a hurry to be bothered about it. He unbuttons his trousers and looks into the lavvy. The water is brown and it has a lot of other boys' froth on it. He can't pee. Oh dear. He pulls the chain and the noise of rushing water makes his thingie sore. The water stops rushing and his pee comes spouting out and splashes over the seat and the floor and everything. He manages to point his pee at the water in the lavvy, where it makes a few bubbles, which quickly disappear. Why doesn't his pee make a froth? Andy is sure that Geordie's pee makes a froth.

He buttons up his trousers, opens the door of the w.c. and makes a dash for the playground. Free at last! He runs round and round, giving a small yelp every so often. I can run. I can run. I can run. He changes to a gallop, slapping his behind. I'm a cowboy on his horse. Giddy-up! Giddy-up! Giddy-up! Andy is not allowed to go to the pictures but Geordie has told him all about Tom Mix and the other cowboys there, kindly explaining the still photos in their glass cases outside the Grand Cinema.

Andy gallops in and out of the big boys' football game but they take no notice of him. He gallops right to the front of the playground. He has to be careful here, for just across the road is the Catholic school. The playground over there is rough gravel and some of the big Catholic boys can throw stones right across. Catholics are even rougher than the rough boys here, and the priest forgives them right away if they do anything bad. 'I can fight papes,' says Geordie, 'they're jist a lotta tattie-howkers.' Mother would be very angry if she caught Andy fighting. She doesn't even let him shove his big brother when his big brother has just shoved him.

Andy gallops away to where Geordie is kicking a very old tennis ball furiously against the school wall, all by himself. Geordie is too small for the big boys' game, and nobody his own age wants to play with him because he is too good. Geordie takes no notice of Andy so he gallops on, but he has to stop suddenly when he sees Fiona in the girls' playground on the other side of the spiked iron railings. She is stotting a ball cleverly and singing a stotting song, watched by a group of girls, who see Andy looking and turn to each other and smile as if they know a secret. Fiona sees him too, half-closes her eyes, thrusts out her pink lower lip and turns her stotting into a kind of dare. Andy knows it's a dare because Fiona used to be his friend before they started school and he met Geordie. They played together every day. It's a silly dare, because he couldn't stot a ball in the boys' playground even if he had one. Balls are for kicking. He wants to shout 'fatty!' at her. Instead, he runs away and finds a quiet spot round the corner of the building.

There is a haipny in the right hand pocket of his trousers. Where did it come from? Maybe Mother put it there. Maybe it was left over from his Saturday penny and he forgot about it. It is his to spend, anyway. He decides to buy a poke of toffee at Beardie Jean's dark wee shop on his way back to school after dinner. Mother doesn't like him going there because Beardie Jean smears her toffee-tins with beef-dripping and she never washes her hands and she puts vinegar in her toffee. Mother can smell vinegar a mile off, whether from forbidden chips or from forbidden toffee. The toffee is nice, though, sweet and sharp and greasy, in big splinters like brown glass, and you can chew it for a long time.

Beardie Jean's pokes are made of newspaper, usually the Glasgow Bulletin, and Andy isn't too happy about them. 'Where has that newspaper been?' asks Mother. She tears newspapers into squares and threads a piece of string through them with a big needle and hangs them up beside the lavvy. Fiona has toilet paper in her house because her Dad works in a bank. Beardie Jean's toffee is really nice, all the same.

Playtime seems to have lasted for ever, so it must be nearly over. Andy remembers that it will be reading and writing next, so he runs to the boys' door to be first in the line when the bell goes. The Jannie comes out in his shiny-peaked hat and clangs his big brass bell and Andy has to fight for his place at the head of the line. Geordie pushes and elbows him and he has to take second place. He would cry if it wasn't Geordie. Mr Calder, who teaches the Qualifying, appears at the top of the steps and the boys go silent and still, for he was gassed in the War, has a nasty tongue, and belts very hard when he does belt. He marches the boys in, class by class. Andy swings his arms very stiffly and as high as everyone else.

At the class-room door Andy breaks into a run and makes for his desk. He sits down and opens his reading-book happily. He has reached the very last story in the book although it is only two weeks since school re-started after the summer holidays. Mother likes that. She was hearing his reading homework last night and he showed her that he could read the first page of the last story. She hugged him, but he wasn't sure he liked being babied.

Father, who had put down his Glasgow Herald, saw the hug and said, 'Don't get too brainy, will you? We don't go in for geniuses in our family.' Then he laughed, even though he hadn't said anything funny.

His big brother said, 'Swot! Swot! Swot!'

Hig big sister said, 'You're soft on Fiona Phimister.'

'No, I'm not!' protested Andy. 'I bet she can't read.' 'She can so!' 'She's got a tide-mark round her neck.' 'No, she has not!' 'See! You're soft on her.'

Miss Wood tells everyone to open their books and find 'the place'. Andy finds the right page, puts his finger on 'the place' and turns the pages over his finger until he reaches the last story, but he can't start reading it until he has looked at Fiona's neck. She is sitting up properly with her finger at 'the place' and her neck does *not* have a mark at all. He can see it all because she has an 'Eton Crop' which is very fashionable and short. It is a round smooth clean neck, as plump as the rest of Fiona, and the more he looks at it the funnier he feels, so he turns away.

Andy sits up as properly as he can and starts to read the last story. At his side Geordie is lounging easily, with only an eye on 'the place'. Miss Wood will tell him to sit up in a minute, but Geordie doesn't care. Every time Andy has to turn a page he looks up at Miss Wood, to make sure she isn't looking, but the story is so interesting that he forgets to keep his finger on 'the place'.

Miss Wood usually starts with the worst readers at the front and 'under her eye' (and there are twenty-five of them); goes on to the middle readers (and there are twenty-five of them too); and ends with the good readers at the back (and there are 'only' twelve of them, including Andy and Geordie and, of course, Fiona). About once a year she starts at the back, but never in the middle. The worst readers have to read one sentence, the middle ones two sentences, and the good ones three sentences. This is the second year that the class have had Miss Wood and Andy feels safe enough in her routine to lose himself in his story, which is a long one about King Arthur and His Knights. He is so lost that he doesn't notice that Miss Wood has started at the back and that Geordie is standing up to read his three sentences in his hoarse bellow. As Geordie sits down he gives Andy a dig with his elbow at the exact moment that Miss Wood says, 'Wake up, Robb!'

Andy stands up, but he has of course lost 'the place'. He looks at Fiona's book, but she immediately shuts it on her finger, just to stop him from seeing. She isn't his friend any more. Geordie pushes his book across the desk, his finger tapping the place, like the good friend he is. Andy starts to read, but not very well. He is much better at reading 'to himself' or to Mother. Miss Wood says, 'Speak up!' and he stumbles and has to start again. He reads two sentences and Miss Wood says, 'That will do'. He isn't a good reader any more, he's only a middle reader, and what's worse, Miss Wood may move him down among the middle readers and away from Geordie.

'Now, Fiona,' Miss Wood says and Fiona stands up, holds her book in her two hands 'properly' and reads her three sentences in her clear, 'nice', almost English, voice. She sits down, arranges her kilt neatly over her fat knees, and put her finger back at the 'the place'. Andy knows what she's doing, but he can't bear to look or listen.

Everyone else in the class has their finger at 'the place'. Miss Wood has a strap and she uses it too. She will have her eye on Andy because he lost the place and did not read as well as she knows he can.

Fiona is sitting up with a serious face and seems to be paying attention to Miss Wood and the reading that is still going on. Quietly, she lifts her foot and kicks the girl in front of her, right on her behind. The girl is the tallest and slimmest and prettiest in the class, with fair hair in long pigtails and big blue eyes. Her name is Pamela and she is Miss Wood's pet, always going messages and helping with the register. She has rows of medals for Highland dancing and Geordie says she is stuck-up but Andy secretly worships her. He wouldn't dare to speak to her. Fiona hates her and tells everybody. She kicks Pamela again. Pamela jumps and looks as if she is going to hold up her hand and clype, but she doesn't. Miss Wood will catch Fiona one day, but she won't get the strap. Girls are lucky, not getting the strap.

Andy forgets the girls and the strap and goes back to the last story, remembering this time to put his finger firmly in a pretend 'place'. When he has finished the story he tries to read the tiny print at the bottom of the page which says, 'Printed in Great Britain by . . .' but it is too difficult. He looks back at the other stories and pictures, but he knows them all too well to read them again. Geordie is dribbling a pretend ball under the desk. Fiona is gazing at Miss Wood and then at Pamela and then back at Miss Wood. Andy drifts off into a day-dream about King Arthur.

He is roused by the end of the reading lesson. Miss Wood has gone back to her desk and is looking round the class. Her long face seems quite kind. She is going to say, 'Take out your writing jotters.' She says it.

Andy is good at writing — not as good as Fiona, but better than almost anyone else. Letters have nice friendly shapes, unlike figures, which are used for sums. Horrible sums. He sits 'properly' and puts his left hand 'properly' half on the desk and half on the jotter. He grips his pencil properly and does exactly what Miss Wood says. He writes a lovely round capital A. A for Andy. A for Apple. He writes a second one and then a third. He has written a whole line, all the same size, just as Miss Wood says he should. He could write capital As for ever. He likes Miss Wood and everybody in the whole world.

Andy knows that there has been trouble over that capital A. Miss Wood prefers the capital A that looks like a witch's hat with a squiggle across it, but the Rector came in one day to change things. He said that in future capital As would be the round kind, like a small a. It was something to do with the League of Nations and the new world after the War. Miss Wood made a face behind the Rector's back. Everyone had to learn to write the round A, but Miss Wood turns a blind eye to witch's hats and everyone but Andy has gone back to them. They are in the copy-books and on the wall-charts.

Miss Wood says things like, 'That's a baby kind of capital A.' So does Andy's big brother. His big sister says, 'I bet Fiona Phimister can't write,' but Andy takes no notice. Mother says, 'The Rector must know what's right.' Father, who is a teacher himself, says, 'Miss Wood should be boss in her own classroom.' Andy just carries on writing it, for it is his own very special A now, his very

very own. Miss Wood can't stop him, for the Rector is on his side.

He and Fiona finish their pages of As so quickly that Miss Wood says, 'Go on to the capital Bs.' Fiona's first line of Bs is a work of art. She goes on to her second calmly. Andy also starts on his Bs, which are nice, but not so nice as As. Geordie is nearly half-way through his page of As and his witch's hats manage to look nearly as fierce as he is. It's nice to have a fierce friend, Andy thinks, getting fed up with writing single letters. He seems to have been doing it for months and months. Miss Wood is far away and not looking, so he turns to the back page of his jotter and writes 'Andy'. He does it again and again until he has written it ten times. He sneaks a look at Miss Wood, but she is still far away. Fiona and Geordie are busy and have not noticed what he is up to. He writes 'Andy is a good boy' right across the page from one side to the other.

The class is beginning to be restless because the children are wanting their dinners. They are sniffling and coughing and shifting about in their seats — but quietly, of course, because of the strap. Andy isn't noticing that he's hungry and writes his sentence again and again until the page is full. He does not hear Miss Wood approaching.

'What are you doing, Robb?' she demands, tall and frightening in her black gown, 'that jotter is for *work*, not scribbling. Haven't I told you how precious paper is? Men have *died* so that you can have jotters. Go out and stand on the floor.'

Andy goes out and stands by her desk. It is taller than him and the strap's inside it, coiled like a snake. He puts his hand in his pocket and holds his haipny tight. Miss Wood gave Geordie the strap for standing on his desk and shouting, 'Come on, the wee blue devil! Come on, the Rangers!' just as she was coming into the room. Now she is fussing about passing forward and counting the pencils. Andy knows from her 'strict' voice that she is going to give him the strap. Now she marches the class out and follows them. Fiona, as she goes past, looks at Andy with wide-open eyes. Is she glad or sorry? He can't tell. Once she held his head when he hurt it falling off a forbidden wall and daren't run home to Mother. Her hands were softer than Mother's. Will the strap be as sore as that bang on his head? Now he can hear the children yelling as they run through the playground on their way home to dinner. Miss Wood is taking her time about coming back. Maybe she's gone to tell the Rector about him. Andy goes blind and deaf with terror.

Miss Wood returns, goes straight to her desk, opens it and takes out her strap. Andy can now see and hear everything much too clearly.

'Hold out your hand,' she says. He lets go of his haipny and holds out his hand.

'Not like that! Straight out!' He stretches his hand right out.

The strap is thick, like the sole of a boot, and has a long slit at the end. It comes down out of the sky and a terrible soreness fills the world, the whole universe, and then rushes to his fingers. They've suddenly become ten times as big as they ought to be. There is an enormous slamming noise and Andy nearly faints, but it is only Miss Wood dropping the lid of her desk.

'You can tell your mother *why* I gave you the strap,' she says, shooing him out.

His arm will never be able to carry the weight of the soreness in his hand, his enormous hand. His arm feels as if it might come out of its socket. His eyes are ready to water. Mother wouldn't like him to hate Miss Wood, so he doesn't. Not now, anyway.

Geordie and one or two of the other boys have waited for him at the school gate. Fiona is nowhere to be seen — she must have run home.

'Wis it sair?' the boys ask. He daren't cry now.

'Aye, it wis sair,' he answers. Mother wouldn't like to hear him talk like that, but he must. He is now one of the bad boys who have had the strap, and that is the way they all talk. He shows the boys his fingers and is surprised they are not swollen, only red. Geordie puts a friendly arm round his shoulders.

'When she gied me the strap,' he says, 'she missed ma haun an hut me on the wrist an it swellt richt up. Did she hut yer thumb?'

'Naw, she didnae.'

'Ye're aa richt, then. When she huts that bane in yer thumb, then ye'll greet. Ye should try blawin on yer fingers.'

Just talking about them makes Andy's fingers seem smaller, but they are just as sore in a different way. They feel like bare bones. He blows into them as Geordie had suggested, but it doesn't help much. The other boys drift away.

Geordie turns and runs and Andy runs after him, the pain almost forgotten. Geordie starts to hop and skip and Andy copies him, the pain just a nuisance. At the corner of the road to the council houses, where Geordie lives, some big Catholic boys are hanging about with their hands in their pockets, looking at a coalman's big Clydesdale. Catholics often don't eat dinner, especially on a Friday, Fiona's Mum explained once, in a kind voice. Geordie runs past the loiterers as fast as he can, towards home, though the coalman's horse is a special favourite of his. Andy runs as fast as *he* can, up the main road to his corner, by the sweetie-shop. He turns and looks back, but the Catholic boys have vanished. His fingers still hurt, he finds, now that he has nothing else to think about. They are hot, like four chips straight out of the pan. He tries sucking them, but they don't cool down.

The bright window of the sweetie-shop attracts Andy's attention and he forgets his fingers. There are aniseed balls and black-strippit balls and sugar-elly straps and sherbet bags. He looks them over hungrily and decides he prefers Beardie Jean's toffee — you get more of it for a haipny. He'll go to school the back way after dinner and buy some. Bars of chocolate are tuppence so he tries not to think about them.

He has a last look at the shop window. At the back, beside the pencils and rubbers and envelopes, there is a little note-book. He can read NOTE-BOOK in smudgy print on the front cover. What's more, it has '$\frac{1}{2}$d' written on in pencil in the top corner. Andy gets excited, for he realises that it could be his. He could have his own writing-book, his very own. Where would he find a pencil? Forgetting the pencil, he fondles his haipny and thinks about Beardie Jean's sticky-sweet toffee. Then his fingers start to sting again and he has to suck them. He remembers that Mother will be wondering where he is. He should have been home by now. He runs towards home as fast as he can, but has to stop suddenly when he sees a car he hasn't seen before parked outside somebody's house. Andy likes cars much better than horses, which are smelly and dangerous. This car is shaped and varnished like a boat at the back, and the badge on the radiator says 'Swift'. It smells of petrol and oil and leather and rubber. He wishes he could climb over the side and sit in it. He remembers Mother.

When he arrives home, she is fussing, as usual.

'Where have you been?' she asks, 'You're late.' Not answering is the best plan. 'Hurry up and wash your hands.'

Dinner is mince and tatties, his favourite. They are almost cold, so he can eat them very quickly, thinking about the note-book. He feels for his haipny. It is safe.

'Why are you smelling so horrid?' asks Mother, 'You haven't wet yourself, have you?' Not answering is still the best plan.

His big brother sniffs loudly. His big sister giggles. 'He sits next Geordie MacMillan and he plays with him all the time,' she says. 'No wonder he smells.' She giggles again. Clype!

'Go upstairs and change your underpants!' says Mother. Andy goes upstairs and sits on his bed for a while. Then he comes back down.

'That feels better, doesn't it?' asks Mother. Not answering again works. She gives Andy stewed apples and Creamola, another of his favourites. He is in the middle of gobbling it when Mother gets anxious again.

'You'll be late for school!' she says. Andy rushes off, one hand in the pocket where his haipny is.

He runs fast till he reaches the end of the narrow lane that leads to Beardie Jean's. He stops. He must decide. It is either down that way and buy a poke of toffee, or straight on and buy the note-book. His fingers are still telling him that he was belted. He hops up and down. He 'runs on the spot' with his knees right up. He says 'Eanie-meanie-mynie-moe' and the note-book wins, much to his relief. He would have to give Geordie a bit of the toffee and Fiona would see it — she always *sees* — and pester him for some and it would be finished by the end of the afternoon playtime. The note-book he can keep for ever. He can take it to bed with him.

The lady in the shop is neat and clean, not like Beardie Jean at all. She takes Andy's haipny and gives him the note-book without changing her expression or saying anything, but Andy doesn't care. The note-book is his. It has a pale green paper cover and the lines on the pages inside are really close together. He will write like his big brother, really small, and as neatly as Fiona. Where can he get a pencil? The note-book smells delicious — like nothing else on earth. It is properly stitched together, too, like a school jotter. Andy dawdles along, opening it and sniffing it and stroking the smooth pages.

He reaches school just in time to be last in the line and for once he doesn't care. He hides his note-book under his jersey, which is not a very safe place, so he grips it through the jersey, as firmly as he can. When he reaches his desk, he decides to put it in his school-bag. Geordie sees him putting it away.

'Ye bocht that? ' he asks.

'Yes,' Andy has to answer.

'Ye're stupit! Ye could a saved yer money fir the fitbaa the morn. Rangers is gaun tae smash Kilmarnock,' says Geordie, but he is not really cross. He is still a friend. Andy hasn't dared to tell him he's a Kilmarnock supporter.

Miss Wood calls for silence, and gets it. She calls for Pamela to help her hand out the tins of crayons and the drawing books. She reminds the children that they must not waste the crayons, which are even more precious than pencils, or the six-inch-square coloured paper drawing books.

Andy looks at the drawing he did last week. It is on a green page and it is supposed to be a flower. It doesn't look like a flower at all, never mind the flower that Miss Wood told them to draw. It looks like a baby's drawing, all scrawly.

Fiona's flower is really wonderful and makes the green page look greener. He'll never draw like Fiona.

Geordie's flower looks like a red-white-and-blue Rangers rosette and his green page looks like a football pitch after a muddy game.

Miss Wood announces that today's page is the brown one and that they are to draw an apple. She puts an apple on the top of her desk where they can all see it. It is a red Canadian apple, just like the ones Mother buys, with a yellow streak and a long stalk.

Andy opens the dusty little crayon box. None of the crayons are more than an inch long and they have all lost their paper covering, so he knows he will get his hands dirty. Mother won't like that. He chooses a scrap of red crayon and, without thinking, writes a huge round capital A, right in the middle of the page. He is terrified when he sees what he has done, for it isn't an apple. It has *two* little stalks, little *red* stalks, at one side instead of just one at the top. He puts his hand on it to hide it but realises that his hand will smudge the crayon, so he lifts it a little, and looks at Fiona.

Fiona has outlined a perfect red heart and, as Andy watches, writes A L P right across it. A L P means 'Andy Loves Pamela'. Girls are always writing stupid things like that. Geordie wouldn't ever write that.

Fiona smiles as if she knows a secret. She looks up at Miss Wood and Pamela, who are doing the register. She 'shades in' her heart, covering up the A L P, then adds a neat black stalk at the top. Then she fattens it until it becomes an apple. Pamela returns to her seat, looks at Fiona's book, and sniffs. Fiona looks at Miss Wood with a sweet expression and returns to her drawing. She picks up a yellow crayon and puts in the yellow streak. With the tip of her pinkie she carefully smudges the yellow until it looks exactly like the streak on the apple. She licks the crayon off her pinkie, sits up properly and gazes at Miss Wood. Then she kicks Pamela. Pamela turns round with a swing of her pig-tails and makes a horrible face.

'Fiona! Behave!' says Miss Wood, and Pamela 'faces the front' again. Watching her, Andy notices that her long thin neck has a line on it, just above the collar of her blouse. Above the line her skin is as clean and white as Fiona's, but below the line it is a greyish colour. So that's what a tide-mark is! Andy's feelings are confused. (They are still confused seventy years later. Goddesses stay goddesses, even with dirty necks. She'll be somebody's great-granny now.) Andy is glad to remember his note-book and forget everything else for a while.

Geordie's head is down, as usual, and his tongue is out. His apple is a good shape, but it is smudged round the edges. It has a long black stalk which looks like the smoke coming out of a factory chimney. Geordie sighs. He smells of vinegar.

Andy lifts his hand off the brown page. He fattens up his apple just as Fiona has done, covering up the two little stalks at the side. He shades it all in and puts in the yellow streak. Daintily, again copying Fiona, he smudges the yellow with the tip of his pinkie. He then licks his pinkie clean, but wishes he hadn't, for the crayon tastes dusty and nasty. Miss Wood comes round just as he is finishing off his apple with a dark green stalk.

'Would you like to write "apple" underneath?' she asks.

Andy is not happy about this, the others might think he was Miss Wood's pet, but the thought of the big capital A is too tempting. He picks up an orange crayon and writes a lovely A. He follows with two fat ps, a very very straight l, and a cheeky e. When he lifts his head he sees that the word is wobbly, because he had no line to guide him. He looks round fearfully. Miss Wood is coming. She looks at his brown page. It is spoilt.

'Go out to the floor and hold it up so that everyone can see it,' she says. Andy can't tell how angry she is. His fingers are still sore, but she might belt him on the other hand. He goes out to the floor, not daring to look at Fiona or Geordie or anyone else.

'Children,' Miss Wood says, 'look at Robb's drawing. It is by far the best today. He is the only one who saw that the stalk is green.'

Andy stands there, unable to think until he remembers his notebook, safe in his school-bag. He will write in it after school if he can find a pencil, or borrow one from his big brother. He won't tell him about the notebook, which he will hide under the mattress.

Miss Wood sends Andy back to his seat. Fiona is looking straight at him with a sweet smile on her face. Andy knows that it is not a nice smile at all.

'Copy-cat!' whispers Fiona. Andy sits down.

'That's guid!' says Geordie, looking at Andy's apple and dribbling his pretend ball under the desk.

At playtime Andy puts his note-book under his jersey and gets a good grip of it from the outside. He runs round and round the playground. As he passes the girls' railings Fiona sticks her head through and shouts 'Andy Robb is no good, chop him up for firewood!' She shouts it again and again and half-a-dozen other girls join in, so Andy runs to the front of the playground. There are no children in the Catholic school playground. They will be saying prayers to the statues you can see through the windows. They have to bow down and pray to the statues six times a day. It will be safe for Andy to walk up and down, fondling his note-book.

After playtime Miss Woods reads a story. It isn't a real story. It is about the soldiers who died for us and Miss Wood reads it in a sad and trembly voice. It is even sadder than the Sunday School stories about Jesus dying for us. Andy is not good at listening to these kind of stories. He isn't sure if the soldiers and Jesus are the same and has a picture in his head of a man in armour dying on a cross. He prefers King Arthur or Robert the Bruce. The picture of the man on the cross goes away and Andy goes on thinking about his notebook and where to get a pencil and what secrets he will write about.

Geordie nudges him under the desk and he wakes up and looks down. Geordie is offering him half a cold chip from the pocket in his khaki jersey. Andy takes it. It smells nice and vinegary. He manages to squeeze it round his mouth with his tongue and then swallow it without chewing. If Miss Wood saw him chewing during her sad story it would be the strap again, and Mother would be told. Mother would then tell Father, and Father would laugh at him again, and he couldn't bear that. Geordie is watching Miss Wood and chewing openly. He will be caught one day, but he doesn't care.

The story ends and it's home time and Andy straps up his school-bag and swings it on to his back. His notebook is still under his jersey and he holds it tight. Once out of the play-ground he tries to run after Geordie, but Geordie is dribbling his tennis-ball faster than Andy can run, weaving in and out of the gutter and round the people in the street. Once for a dare, Geordie dribbled a ball under a cart-horse, when the man wasn't looking.

Andy gives up the chase and thinks about his notebook. He is wandering along, half in a dream and half keeping an eye open for big Catholic boys, when Fiona overtakes him, running. Her school-bag is bouncing on her back. He can run faster than Fiona, for she's fat and he's skinny, so he starts to run after her . He starts to catch up with her and she stops. He has to stop, too.

They played together nearly every day before they went to school, and they still do in the holidays, but now he's not sure if he really wants to catch up with her. After all, he knows that he can run faster than her. Fiona starts to run again, her fat legs moving fast. Andy runs too; he can't help it. She stops. He stops. She runs again and this time she doesn't stop. She goes on running until she reaches her house and disappears through the gate in the privet hedge. Andy slows to a walk. That silly girl hasn't made him forget his notebook, for he is still holding it tight.

As he wanders past Fiona's gate she comes out. He stops. She comes up close to him. She smells as she always does, clean. Really clean. She could be his friend if she wasn't a girl. Why does she have to be a girl? And why does she have to be called a daft name like 'Fiona'? There isn't another girl in the whole world who is called that. It is almost as bad as her little sister's name, which is Morag. In the summer holidays Fiona's Mum lets her wear khaki shorts to play in the garden and with her Eton Crop she looks like Billy Bunter. But she's so fat and the shorts are so tight you can see she hasn't got a thingie. Why can't she be a boy?

'What have you got under your jersey?' she asks. She has noticed. She always notices.

'I'm not telling.'

'Is it a secret?' With Fiona it's no use pretending.

'Yes.'

'I won't tell. Cross my heart.' Andy is forced to tell.

'It's just a wee notebook.' He shows it to her.

'Oo! Its nice! Have you got a pencil for it?'

'No.'

'I'll get you one.' She runs into her house and comes out in a minute with an inch-long stub, properly sharpened. Andy takes it, not looking at Fiona. He tries to say, 'I'll give you a shottie of my notebook,' but half-way through he has to run away. If he gave her a shottie it wouldn't be his *very very* own any more.

Running away, he tries to tell himself that he is really running away from Fiona's mother, who is always coming out and asking him, 'Where did you get that red curly hair? And those freckles?' He hates that, but it's even worse when she asks to feel his muscles, for he has no muscles, compared to Geordie.

'Copy-cat! Copy-cat!' Fiona is shouting after him.

When he reaches home Mother asks, 'Well, what happened in school today?' He can't think of anything to say, so he doesn't answer. He drops his school-bag in the hall and runs up to the bedroom he shares with his big brother. He hides his notebook and pencil under the mattress on his side of the double bed. I will be writing in it soon, he thinks, very soon.

He didn't go to the lavvy at school, so he's bursting. He rushes to the bathroom and pees properly, without splashing, but he forgets to wash his hands.

'Do you want a rock-bun?' calls Mother from downstairs.

'Yes!' he shouts, rushing down headlong.

'Have you washed your hands?'

'Yes, Mother,' he says, and has to stop where he is, just inside the kitchen door. He puts his hands behind his back. They are dirty from the crayons and half-a-dozen other things, never mind the bathroom.

'Here's your rock-bun.' He daren't take it.

'Show me your hands!' Mother is like Fiona, she *always* notices. He shows her his hands.

'Who's been teaching you to tell lies? If it's that Geordie MacMillan, I'll go and see the Rector.' Saying nothing is the best plan. 'No bun! Go up to your room!'

Andy climbs the first few steps slowly, swallowing the spit that the rock-bun has made in his mouth. Then he remembers his notebook and runs up the rest. He shuts the door of the bedroom, takes out the notebook and pencil from under the mattress, and lies on the floor. He has half-an-hour until his big brother comes home and he's going to write for the whole time.

To start with, he writes very very small, but that is tiring and the pencil gets blunt too, so he decides that his letters will be two lines high. What he writes is a secret. He has trouble spelling Fiona's secret name, which is Greek. Only he and Fiona know about it. He has a secret name too, but it's easy to spell. Andy is lost in his secret world.

His big brother bursts into the room and, quick as lightning, grabs his notebook. He doesn't bother to read it, just flips roughly through the pages and throws it into the air.

'That's a waste of a good notebook,' he shouts, 'scribbling on it like a baby. You should learn to write properly.'

Andy snatches it back and crawls under the bed. His big brother reaches to pull him out, but he screams in the hope that Mother will hear. She doesn't seem to hear but she shouts 'Rock-buns!' which takes his big brother away much quicker.

Andy sees a gap under the skirting-board. It's a good hidey-hole so he slides his notebook into it. Then he lies under the bed and cries for quite a while for he hasn't got a nice new notebook any more, only a scribbled-on one. The secrets don't seem like secrets any more now that he has written them down. They're just scribbles, and for scribbles you get the strap. *And* deserve it, according to Father, who would laugh, even though he was really serious. Mother would frown and ask if he had clean underpants.

Andy remembers his Saturday penny and cheers up. He could spend a haipny of it on another notebook and write proper stories in it and not secrets. With the other haipny he could buy a rubber to rub out mistakes. On Sunday he could spend half of his Sunday School penny at Beardie Jean's and put the other haipny in the plate. No one would notice, and there's no strap at Sunday School.

Andy sees the pencil Fiona gave him lying where he dropped it. He comes out from under the bed and picks it up. It is blunt. He hides it under the mattress. He *must* learn to sharpen a pencil, he thinks, he really must.

'Selfies'

'Selfies!' shouts Andy, grabbing the plastic potty and trying to pull it out of Mother's hand. 'Jobbie in big potty selfies!'

Mother is too strong, though. She smacks his hand and makes him let go. 'You're not going to spill that filthy stuff all over the floor again. I've had enough of your dirty ways!'

Andy puts the smacked hand to his mouth, sits down on his nappy-clad bottom with a furious bump and glares up at Mother. 'You job!' he says, his blue eyes squinting.

Mother hears him, but decides to take no notice. He swears again, more quietly, 'You job!'

Mother goes off towards the downstairs loo, still taking no notice. Andy mutters the archetypical obscenity a third time, sees the set of Mother's head on her neck and says no more.

Mother empties the contents of the potty into the loo. 'Little job yourself!' she says under her breath, 'Oh, I shouldn't say things like that.' She cleans the inside of the potty with loo paper. 'But wait till I tell Father, he'll make you ashamed of yourself.' She puts the loo-paper into the loo and reaches for the handle.

Andy, who has been watching intently, starts to scream like a herring-gull, and scrambles to his feet. Startled, Mother holds on to the handle while Andy rushes at her as fast as his skinny little toddler's legs can carry him. He tries to take her hand away, still screaming wordlessly. She gets the point.

'Okay, selfies then,' she says, letting go of the handle.

Andy stops screaming, reaches up and rattles the handle until he gets his breath back. He peers into the water, where two tiny lumps are visible amongst the loo paper.

'Bye-bye, jobbies!' he says quietly, as if to himself. He uses both hands to pull the handle down and watches the rushing water solemnly. 'Bye-bye!' he whispers.

When the water is calm again, and nothing at all is to be seen in it, Andy lifts his head and toddles through to the kitchen, where Mother is at the sink. He wraps his arms round her leg and rubs his face against the denim, the sweet-smelling motherly tenderness of the denim.

'Nasty sexy little b.' she murmurs, disengaging her leg. Andy makes a half-hearted attempt to take hold of her leg again, but doesn't persist when Mother pushes him away abruptly; he's had messages about this kind of behaviour before. He steps back and looks up at Mother's face.

'Biccy, Ma-ma,' he announces. 'Jobbie gone. Biccy time.'

'My hands are wet. Get a biccy yourself.'

Andy doesn't understand. He knows where the biscuits are, of course, but he has never had the chance to open the tin himself.

'Ma-ma, biccy.' He is polite but firm. Laws, such as biccy following 'jobbie-gone', exist to be obeyed.

'Open. Tin. Selfies,' says Mother.

Andy seems to ponder for a moment or two, his mouth open and his blue eyes staring. Then he realises what Mother means, toddles to the cupboard under the work-top, opens the door and lifts out the precious tin. He sits down, lays the tin on the floor and tries to open it, but his hands aren't quite big or strong enough. He tries again and again. He bangs the tin on the floor without effect and starts to whimper. Mother dries her hands, kneels down, and offers to help him. His whimpers turn into a wail. Mother tries to take the tin from him, but Andy wraps his arms tightly round it and turns away from her, tears streaming down his purple face and his nose running like two rivers. Between wails he cries, 'Selfies! Selfies! Selfies!'

'I've had enough of this "Selfies" business,' says Mother impatiently, wrenching the tin from Andy's grasp and putting it back into the cupboard. She shuts the door with a bang. 'No biccy today. I'm not having you screaming at me like that. You're supposed to be a quiet child. You *are* a quiet child.'

Andy's wailing crescendoes to a peak and Mother puts her hands over her ears. It diminuendoes slowly, wail by wail, into snuffles and then into silence. Mother returns to the sink. Andy puts his left thumb in his mouth and sucks it.

His face reverts to its normal pallor and his tears dry, but his nose stays messy.

Suddenly, and very quietly, he takes off on all fours. He goes through the hall and into the sitting-room, obviously searching for something. He looks under various pieces of furniture without success and then, under a sofa cushion, he finds it, his armless faceless doll.

'Daddy-long-legs' is the polite name Andy's parents and older brother and sister have for this creature. If Andy has a name for it, no one has heard him use it. 'The Thing', as it is less politely called, is knitted from dark grey and khaki wool and is of unmistakably phallic aspect. Nobody, and certainly not Mother, admits to knowing where it came from, though Father, laughing in his exaggerated fashion, has been heard telling Andy that it must have been found hanging on a wall in 'Alloway's auld haunted kirk', or that maybe the Witches in *Macbeth* knitted it in one of their tea-breaks. Andy doesn't understand the jokes, of course, but he surely understands the tone of voice and hunches his shoulders and clutches The Thing even more tightly.

Mother hides it when people call, and is probably guilty of hiding it under the cushion, but can't quite bring herself to throw away the insanitary and obscene object. Andy never shows it any attention that could be called affectionate, but he is never parted from it for long without becoming querulous and even tearful. Older brother and sister have nice teddy-bears, known as Claude and Baby Bear respectively. They are rather battered, but still *nice*, and can be displayed on their owners' beds while they are at school.

Andy retires behind the sofa, clutching The Thing under his right arm and sucking his left thumb again. He sits there for a long time, his blue eyes squinting inwardly. Whether he is bothering to listen to Mother moving about in the kitchen is not at all clear.

Eventually, Mother comes into the room with Andy's outdoor clothes.

'Come on, we're going to see your little friend Fiona.'

Andy lets himself be dressed without comment or complaint, but when Mother offers to pick him up and carry him he screams, 'Walk selfies!' and struggles and kicks until she has to put him down again. He toddles to the front door and waits quietly for her to open it. As soon as she does, he is through it and toddling away down the garden path. Before she can close the door he is out of the garden gate, which someone has left open, and is toddling away in the direction of Fiona's house, gripping Daddy-long-legs firmly under one arm. Mother wastes time shutting the gate, so that Andy is well past Fiona's house by the time she catches up with him. Just as she thinks she has him he breaks into a run, his head up and his little stick-like legs flashing beneath the bundle of his nappy-filled pants. Startled, for he has not really tried to run before, Mother breaks into a run too, but before she can lay hands on him he trips and falls and bangs his head and his knees on the pavement and starts to cry, not loudly, but loudly enough to embarrass Mother, out there in the public street. She picks him up and holds his face close to her shoulder so that his crying is muffled. She pats his back gently and it stops.

Mother inspects Andy's head and knees for damage, but finds nothing to alarm her. She sets off for Fiona's house but is halted by yet more screams from Andy. He is trying to wrench himself out of her arms and she realises that The Thing has been left lying on the pavement. She picks it up and gives it to Andy and the screams stop as if they had been switched off. Andy brushes his lips across the place where The Thing's face would be, if it had a face.

'I'll have to do something about all this noise,' she says, giving him a few shakes. Andy continues to kiss the face that isn't a face, though perhaps the kiss isn't a kiss either. His nose is red and his blue eyes are opaque, even to his Mother. Perhaps especially to his Mother.

At Fiona's house her Mum is standing in the doorway with Fiona clamped to her leg. Both have obviously seen at least some of the happenings in the street, but Fiona's round little face and dark eyes register more concern than Mum's long face and grey eyes. As Mother arrives at the door carrying Andy, Fiona turns her head with a swing of her straight black hair and presses her face against Mum's leg. She manages to walk sideways and maintain this pose as they all proceed in embarrassed silence to the sitting-room.

Mum has set out coffee-mugs and juice-beakers and biscuits as usual and everyone is looking at them awkwardly when Fiona lets go of her Mum's leg, runs to one of the armchairs, clambers into it, turns round and bounces up and down, giggling. When she has had enough of this she turns on to her tummy, slides down off the chair and runs across the hearth-rug with a joyful shriek to the other chair, where she climbs in and bounces again, her giggles even louder.

Released by this unembarrassed behaviour, Mum goes off to fetch the coffee and juice while Mother sits Andy firmly on the floor. He watches Fiona intently, his squint barely evident. Almost certainly, he doesn't notice that his plump little 'friend' is out of nappies, having reached that milestone before him; he looks more interested in playing the chair game too. He doesn't have the chance, for Mum arrives with the drinks and decides that Fiona must be calmed down with the offer of a bisuit. Fiona takes no notice at first, but eventually accepts the biscuit and toddles out to the hall, returning with her rag-doll, which is known as Beastie.

Beastie, despite her name, is an attractive female creature run up by Dad — yes, rugby-playing Dad — out of lace and Laura Ashley fabric and other oddments. She has kept her freshness well, despite a fair amount of non-accidental injury from Fiona. Dad christened her 'Bridget', as suggested in the colour supplement where he found the pattern, but Fiona altered the name, instantly and unnervingly, to 'Bastard'. Then, without pressure from anyone, she decided that she liked 'Beastie' best. The creature's face, to adults, has a sexy leer, which is the subject of much sharp-edged teasing of Dad by Mum. She says it shows what he was thinking about as he sat there meekly embroidering it.

Fiona sits down on the floor and offers her biscuit to Beastie, who responds with her usual leer. Fiona seems satisfied, slobbers the biscuit for a while, then offers it to Beastie again. As she continues quietly with this game, Andy is glowering fixedly at her. He has gobbled down his biscuit quickly without offering it to Daddy-long-legs, who hasn't a mouth anyway. In the comparative peace the two mothers start chatting. They are intimate friends, having trained together in the same hospital. They quite like each other too.

'Jeans are terribly expensive. Good jeans, I mean,' says Mother.

'I haven't bought a new pair in years,' says Mum. 'They're never comfortable when they're new.'

'Oh, I like my old ones too, but there are limits... Andy, how dare you? Give it back to Fiona at once!'

Andy refuses to part with the uneaten half of Fiona's biscuit, which he has snatched. He holds on grimly as Mother prises open his fingers one by one. Fiona watches quietly. She doesn't seem too bothered by the outcome. The silent battle ends with the slimy half-chewed biscuit in Mother's hand.

'Yeuch!' she says, 'shall I give it back to Fiona?'

'Of course!' giggles Mum.

Fiona accepts the half-biscuit and offers it to Beastie before re-starting her steady slobbering of it. Andy sits and glowers at her again, the squint in his narrow blue eyes even more pronounced than usual.

'He's getting to be a bit of a handful,' complains Mother. 'I wouldn't let him have his biscuit this morning because he was noisy and rude. And now he's snatching. Just wait till Fathers hears about it!'

'Smack-smack!' says Fiona, smiling a Queen Mother smile which is improved, or perhaps not, by a surround of biscuit crumbs and slime.

Andy's glower becomes inward. He picks up Daddy-long-legs, hugs him close and turns his back.

'Father doesn't smack Andy,' says Mother hastily. 'He just laughs and laughs when I tell him what he's been up to. It was much easier with the other two. Mind you, Andy doesn't like being laughed at. He doesn't like it at all.'

'I don't know where Fiona gets that "smack-smack" from,' says Mum. 'I do wish I liked her. Dad worships her, the little trouble-maker.'

'Smack-smack!' repeats Fiona. Andy's shoulders can be seen to hunch themselves a fraction.

'You little liar!' replies Mum and turns to Mother again. 'These old jeans are getting tight.'

'They couldn't be much tighter.'

'I'll need to buy one of those bib-and brace-things.'

'You mean ... ?'

There is a pause. Nobody moves.

'Prrreg-nant,' announces Fiona, her Elizabeth of Glamis smile at its sugariest and slimiest.

Mum laughs delightedly, but Mother's face shows alarm. She even goes a little pale.

'Not really?' she asks.

'Well, Fiona seems to think so. She's usually first with the news *and* she's usually right.'

'You'd think she'd been here before. I thought you were going back to work?'

'Mum-mum prrreg-nant.' says Fiona, still smiling royally. 'Fi-o-na prrreg-nant. And-ee prrreg-nant.' She picks up Beastie and giggles. 'Beastie prrreg-nant.'

The two mothers look at Andy's back, which conveys to them eloquently that he is still glowering inwardly. Has he heard, and if he has, has he understood? (Many people are going to ask themselves these kinds of questions about Andy, and not all of them are going to find answers.)

'You'll be wanting a boy?' asks Mother.

'I've never wanted anything else. You know that.'

'But I'd have thought you'd want a recruit to your cause, you know, Women's Lib.'

'Oh, I'm all for the cause, but if it's another girl I'll swop the little b. for Andy the day she's born. Or give her away and go back to my job. I have a right to a job.'

'Mum-mum jobbie,' says Fiona. 'Da-da prrreg-nant.' She is removing Beastie's lacy knickers.

Andy crawls behind the sofa, puts his thumb in his mouth and grips Daddy-long-legs even more firmly.

'These bib-and-brace things make everything so obvious,' says Mother. 'It's like carrying your tummy in a shopping bag. Or a sling.'

'I'm not bothered.'

'I wasn't either, really. I just liked the excuse to wear a skirt again. Father prefers me in a skirt anyway.'

'Dad's not fussy, but he prefers me in nothing at all.'

'You're boasting. What'll you call him?'

'Murray, after his Dad. Murray the maniac.'

'And-ee suck thumb,' says Fiona, without looking up.

She is busy trying to tie Beastie's bright yellow pigtails together.

'Oh Andy, do you have to?' complains Mother, for Andy's rhythmical sucking can be heard behind the sofa.

'Perhaps we'll spell Murray M-o-r-a-y.'

'And if it's a girl?'

'I've told you. I'll swop her for Andy.'

'And-ee do jobbie, comments Fiona, lifting Beastie's skirt and pulling her knickers on again.

'OH NO!' shouts Mother, for Andy's stink is indeed filling the room. 'I should have known he was holding out on me.' She picks up Andy round the waist, holds him well away from herself, and makes for the door. 'You should be ashamed of yourself,' she tells him.

'Change the darling here, if you want,' offers Mum, but Mother is running down the hallway.

'No, no, the other two will be home soon. I have to be ready for them.' She opens the front door.

'Don't smack the poor wee mannie,' pleads Mum. 'Just this once. For me.'

Mother turns. 'I don't smack him,' she says, 'I wait for Dad to make him *really* ashamed of himself.'

There is an awkward silence. Mum looks at Mother with eyebrows raised.

'Little liar!' comes Fiona's voice.

Startled, the mothers look round and see her smiling plumply, her head on one side and dimples showing on her cheeks and on her fat little knees. She is holding Beastie upside-down by one leg.

Andy creates a diversion. He throws Daddy-long-legs down on the doorstep and instantly decides he wants him back again.

'Want Longley!' he shouts. 'Want Longley! Want Longley!'

Mum rushes forward, picks up the newly christened Thing and gives it to Andy, who goes quiet. She strokes the scanty ginger fuzz on his head and elicits a tiny sly smile, which quickly vanishes.

Enchanted, she strokes him again, but this time he turns his head away and clutches Longley even more tightly.

Fiona interrupts. 'Beastie liar!' she says, smacking the upside-down creature on her lacy bottom. 'Bad, bad Beastie!'

Mother runs away home, still holding Andy away from her, as if he had a dangerous infection. Mum watches them out of sight, then closes the door thoughtfully.

'He actually looks pleased with himself,' she says to herself, 'getting his own back like that. Oh I could *eat* him!'

Meanwhile, Fiona has vanished. Mum looks for her, probably with a view to a brief lecture on the rudeness of calling people 'liar', but can't find her in any of the obvious places. Eventually she discovers that the door of the downstairs loo is locked. This is a new development. Fiona's parents have assumed that she can't reach the snib.

'Fiona, what are you doing in there?'

Silence.

'Answer me!'

'Wee-wee *selfies* in big potty.'

Another new development.

'I hope you can let yourself out,' says Mum, deciding not to be one of those over-anxious mothers. She goes off to clear the coffee things into the sink. After a few minutes comes the noise of the loo flushing, followed immediately by a shriek from Fiona.

'Beastie jump in potty! Beastie jump in potty!'

'This is it!' mutters Mum, rushing to the loo door. 'This is definitely *it*. I don't care if I'm pregnant, they'll have to have me back.' She rattles the door. 'Open up this minute.' The shrieks intensify. 'I'm warning you, somebody else is going to have to stay home and look after you and that loathsome Beastie creature. What a horrible child you are!'

The shrieks modulate to a heart-rending cry, 'Can't open door! Can't open door!'

The Princess
and the Stick
Insect

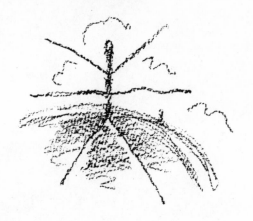

My daddy says I'm plump and cuddly, but Mummy says I'm just a fat wee blether. Nobody says that Beastie is fat because she isn't. She's my Baby and she's long and thin and she has frills on her knickers. I want knickers with frills, just like hers, so that I can show them to My Daddy. My Daddy is a big black horse with a big black moustache. He smells of pennies and pound-notes because he works in the Bank of Scotland. Mummy won't *ever* give me frilly knickers. I asked her today and she said 'no', so I cried and she said, 'not at your age'. Mummy is a pest, and she's nearly as long and thin as Beastie. I don't know why My Daddy-horse cuddles her.

Mummy is upstairs putting Morag to bed for her little sleep. She has left me alone in the sitting-room. I'm glad Beastie is here with me. We could switch on the telly if we wanted to, but we don't want to. Me and Beastie are fed up with the telly. We don't want to read my Ladybird book either. It's the one about the Princess and her bright golden ball and we know already about me being the Princess.

What the Princess really wants to do is play at 'Mummies' and suck one of Mummy's ciggies. Mummy likes her ciggies. Beastie likes them too. She tells me so with her big round eyes and her red red lips.

We saw Mummy putting her bright golden packet of ciggies and her bright golden lighter behind that jar on the mantelpiece. I can't reach them there. Me and Beastie put on our thinking caps. Maybe I could climb up and reach them if I put my stool, my own special stool, in front of the stereo.

I sit Beastie up against the settee so that she can watch me. She never shuts her eyes and she always watches me if I tell her to. I fetch my stool and put it in front of the stereo. Then I climb up, right on to the lid. I stand up and hold on the mantelpiece with both hands. I can see Mummy's bright golden packet of ciggies and her bright golden lighter. I reach out for them and soon I have them in my hands, but I don't feel safe. In fact, I'm very very wobbly. I try to kneel down on the lid of the stereo. Something goes wrong and I fall right down to the floor. I bang my knee on my own special stool and land — bump! — on my b.t.m.

I take a deep breath. I am going to cry for Mummy, but I don't because nothing is really really sore. I'm not really hurting anywhere and Mummy would be cross at being called away from Morag. She likes Morag a lot, I don't know why. I pick up Beastie and give her a nice hug just to show that neither of us is really hurting.

Mummy's bright golden ciggie packet is lying on the carpet. Some of the ciggies are squashed but we find one that isn't. I put it in my mouth and Baby Beastie says she wants it. I tell her not to be a greedy pig, I'll give her a suck later when I've lit it. I look around for Mummy's bright golden lighter and I find it hiding under the stereo. I'm the bestest in the family at finding things that are hiding.

The lighter is a bad lighter and it won't light for me. I give it a good smack and it lights up for a little. I smack it again but it still won't stay alight for long enough. I give the silly thing a good talking to and it lights properly with a nice bright flame. I put the end of my ciggie into the flame and give a suck. I get some smoke into my mouth and the ciggie goes red at the end. I watch the pretty blue smoke coming out of the red end of the ciggie. The lady at my play-group says I'm a quick learner and she is right.

I let Beastie have a suck and she watches the pretty blue smoke too. Then I suck again, just a wee bit harder, and blow out the smoke the way Mummy does. It doesn't taste nice.

Maybe the smoke will taste nicer if I have a real suck, like a grown-up Princess. I suck really hard and the smoke goes all the way down inside me and it hurts. I cough and cough and cough and my throat is very very sore. The inside of my nose is very sore too. In between my coughs I scream and scream for Mummy. I run to the bottom of the stairs and meet Mummy rushing down. She picks me up and turns me upside down and shakes me and thumps me on my back and I think I'm going to die. I stop coughing and Mummy stands me on my feet and I sit down again on the floor with a bump and cry like that Baby Morag. She is *always* crying. When I cry it is for a reason.

'This is worse than working in casualty,' I can hear Mummy

saying. I go on crying like a baby because my back is sore after all the thumps she gave me. In fact, it's sorer than the sore throat I got while I was smoking. Mummy didn't really mean to hurt me. She can't help it if she's been a nurse and has to thump people. In fact, I can see that she's really very worried about me. She picks me up in her arms and walks me up and down the hall. She smells nice and she talks to me the way she talks to Morag and I snuggle into her soft bitties and put my arms round her neck and all the sorenesses get better. I love my Mummy sometimes. I stop crying, so she takes me into the kitchen and gives me a glass of water.

'What happened?' she asks me.

I can see that she is still worried about me but I know she's going to be angry when she finds out that me and Beastie have helped ourselves to a ciggie. She is not going to laugh about it at all. I suddenly remember that I have left my Baby Beastie all alone in the sitting-room. Maybe she's been coughing too. I put down the glass and run through and pick her up. She hasn't been coughing, the lucky thing. Mummy has followed me and there is a smell of smoke. It isn't ciggie smoke, but a much horrider smoke.

Mummy starts to stamp on the carpet where smoke is coming from a black hole. Her face is very red and I think she is going to be really angry so me and Beastie quietly leave the room. We go through the kitchen and out into the garden. We have almost reached the sandpit when Mummy catches us and picks us up very roughly. She starts to carry us back to the house and I get very cross and try to kick her and Beastie falls to the ground.

'Beastie's fallen!' I shout, but Mummy takes no notice.

'My Baby's hurt!' I scream, but Mummy just dumps me on the sitting-room floor. She grabs my arms very tightly and shouts at me, right in my face.

'Listen to me for once, you horrible little girl! Look at that hole in the carpet! We might all have been burned to death and it would have been *your* fault. You must never ever play with my lighter again, or steal my cigarettes. Look, you've squashed the whole packet, every single one of them. And look at the things you've broken, just look at them . . .'

67

I stop listening. It isn't *my* fault that Beastie is a baby and wanted a ciggie. And Mummy is still shouting and her *spit* is going into my *face*. That's not the way anyone should speak to a Princess.

'I want Beastie,' I say.

Mummy stops shouting and breathes in and out through her teeth. I think she is going to say something really naughty, but she stops herself. I can see her stopping herself.

'I want my Baby,' I say, 'and you're hurting my arms.'

'You're forgetting what I'm going to tell Daddy, aren't you?'

I never forget my Daddy. He never shouts at me or spits in my face, so I look Mummy straight in her eyes. They are a nasty grey, not soft and brown like My Daddy's and mine.

'Maybe,' Mummy says, 'you won't be his spoilt little Princess this time. That stereo lid can't be mended and that 'Boys of the Lough' record is ruined . . .'

Well, I didn't know about the stereo lid and it isn't *my* fault that it's shiny and slippery and breaks easily. My Daddy is always telling Mummy to put away the records properly so it isn't *my* fault that 'Boys of the Lough' got itself ruined. But nothing like this has happened before. My Daddy *might* be angry. He told me once that 'Boys of the Lough' was *deleted*, which means precious. He is very very strong because he plays rugby in scrums and mauls.

'I can see what you're thinking,' says Mummy, 'you're going to try and wind him round your little finger again, you little manipulator!'

'I'm not a little manipulator,' I say in my firmest Princess voice.

'Oh yes you are, brat. But if you say you're sorry I'll let you go, and you can fetch your Baby.'

I am not very good at saying 'sorry' to Mummy, even when I want to. It's much nicer to say it to My Daddy-horse. I just wind my arms round his big thick hairy neck and breathe 'Sorry!' into his big furry ear and then it's all over and I'm his deleted little Princess again.

'Say sorry!' says Mummy in *her* firmest voice.

I wriggle and try to slip out of her grip, but Mummy is very strong, even though her arms aren't half as thick as My Daddy's. They aren't nice and hairy either. When My Daddy-horse carries me I can touch the top of Mummy's head.

'Say sorry!' she says again, squeezing my arms even tighter. She never gives in.

'Sorry,' I mumble, but she won't let go.

'Don't mumble!' she says.

'Sorry! Sorry! Sorry!' I shout, and she lets me go. I run out into the garden and pick up my Baby Beastie and give her a special hug and tell her she isn't a little manipulator either. Babies can't be manipulators. I don't care what Mummy calls us.

I hurry to my sandpit, where I keep some of my toys. Sometimes I allow Morag to play in it, but I don't let her keep her toys there. I throw them out if I find them. Sometimes Mummy *makes* me take Morag to play there, but usually the horrible thing cries so much I just take her hand and lead her back to Mummy.

Mummy is watching me crossly from the window so I turn my back on her and start to build a palace for me and Beastie, with a nice warm stable for My Daddy-horse. I dig the foundations and find a horrible plastic frog buried in the sand. Its arms and legs are long and thin and yellow and green and spongy and it looks like Mummy. I'm sure it's a Mummy-frog so I throw it over the fence into old Mrs Linkletter's garden. I don't care if she goes geriatric about it. I'm not afraid of witches.

I finish the palace and put Beastie in the middle of it to sit quietly. Then I put a roof over the stable to stop My Daddy-horse from jumping out.

Mummy says I'm very hardy, for I never catch cold, but I'm feeling the cold now and my nose is running. The silly old sun is hiding himself behind the clouds. I begin to think about Mummy. She'll be warm and smelling nice in the house. Maybe she'll let me use one of her scented hankies to blow my nose. She'll have stopped being cross by now, surely. Some of that botheration *was* my fault, even though most of it was Beastie's. I take the Baby Queen of Horror out of her palace and make her say 'sorry' properly. Then we go into the house. This is one of the times I *love* Mummy.

I can hear her upstairs talking to Morag. She is speaking in her wish-I-was-back-at-the-hospital voice, which means that Messy

Morag has soiled her nappy. Dirty thing!

'Shall I bring a clean nappy?' I shout from the bottom of the stairs.

'Yes, thank you, nurse, and bring the bucket too,' calls Mummy. She is calling me 'nurse' because we used to play at hospitals. I think I had an apron and a cap with red crosses on them. I must have lost them in the garden because I now want to be a stable-girl and wear riding britches and a hard hat.

I'm a very quick stable-girl when I want to be. I put Beastie under the radiator in the hall, fetch the nappy and the bucket and climb the stairs like a big girl. Mummy is in the bathroom, wiping Messy Morag's b.t.m. She says, 'Thank you, nurse.' She is still going to tell My Daddy about the botheration. I can hear it in her voice.

'I'm really sorry, Mummy,' I say, 'and so is Beastie. We won't steal any more ciggies.'

'Good for Beastie,' says Mummy, but she's still busy with Messy Morag and not really listening. She hasn't noticed my runny nose either, so I just take a piece of toilet paper and blow it myself. Will she *ever* forget?

I carry the nappy downstairs in the bucket and put it beside the washing-machine. Mummy has followed me, carrying Morag, who could walk if she wanted to. Mummy opens her very special tin of biscuits. She hands one straight to Morag, but she holds my biscuit right under my nose and waves it back and forwards with a frown on her face. This means that me and Beastie don't deserve our biscuit. Why didn't she wave Messy Morag's biscuit under *her* nose. She didn't deserve it either, making a smell like that. Mummy gives me the biscuit and I gobble it down quick, forgetting poor Baby Beastie. I'm a greedy girl sometimes, but I try very hard to love Mummy.

Mummy says she's going to make chili-con-carne for tea and will I look after Morag Mouse in the sitting-room? I *never* call that messy thing Mouse, but she's not difficult to be a nurse to. I just switch on the telly and she goggles at it without moving, nibbling her biscuit. It doesn't matter what programme is on, she just goggles. Me and Beastie only like *some* programmes. We sit quietly and hope that one we like will come on soon. The chili-con-carne is smelling nice, but when we look around the room we notice the black hole in the carpet and my stool with its leg broken and the stereo lid smashed to pieces. We stand on tiptoe and we see a scratch right across the record. My Daddy will be home soon. Oh deary me, I wish I was at my Grannie's.

Me and Beastie have the sharpestest ears in the house and we listen very very hard for My Daddy opening the front gate. At last we hear him and we're out of the room and behind the front door before Mummy or Morag notice anything.

When he opens the door I shriek 'Daddy! Daddy! ' and fling myself at him, dropping Beastie on the floor. My Daddy swings me up and kisses me with his soft lips, but his moustache and his bristly chin tickle me and I have to squeal. With My Daddy, I like squealing. He gives me a 'beardie' and I squeal again. He settles me on his hip and I see that Mummy-frog has arrived and is looking at him.

Mummy-frog and My Daddy-horse are always talking to each other with their eyes. Most of the time I know perfectly well what they are saying. Just now Mummy-frog is telling My Daddy that I have been very naughty while he was at his work. In fact, she is saying that I have been *wicked*. I look at my Daddy's eyes and he is telling Mummy-frog that he doesn't care if I've been wicked, I'm still his Princess. He gives me a little squeeze and I can feel all the horsy muscles in his arm, but I don't squeal because Mummy-frog is cross.

I put my arm round My Daddy's neck and rest my head on his shoulder. This makes Mummy even crosser, I can see her saying, 'I'm fed up with minding children, especially that little bitch! Pick up Morag Mouse too, she's been *good*!'

Messy Morag is hanging on to My Daddy's leg, of course, and wailing 'Da-da! Da-da!' She is always doing that. He bends down to pick her up and settles her on his other hip. I manage to kick her *three* times, though. I'd have kicked her *twelve* times if My Daddy wasn't so clever at stopping me. I can count up to twelve but Morag can't even count up to two.

Mummy is now telling My Daddy something else. Her eyes are

very bright and shiny and she is putting the tip of her tongue out a little. Before I can look to see what My Daddy is saying back to her there is a funny little sound at the front door. It could be Mrs Linkletter's geriatric doggie scratching. He does that sometimes. Mummy pushes past us and opens the door. My friend from down the street, Andy the Stick Insect, is standing there. He has nothing on but his vest. I can see his thingie. He is looking down at the doorstep and he is shivery and blue all over. He must have run away again. He would be much happier at my play-group, living in a jar and eating leaves.

'Oh, you must be frozen!' says Mummy. She picks him up and wraps her arms round him. She likes Andy and wants to steal him. I like him too, but I don't want to steal him. He belongs to his Mother and stealing is wrong.

I know exactly what the Stick Insect is going to do and he does it. He wriggles and wriggles and kicks and kicks until Mummy simply has to put him down. He doesn't make a sound. I knew he wouldn't. He rushes off down the garden path with Mummy after him. I am beginning to be unhappy.

The bad Stick Insect should run to his own house, but he runs the other way instead, past Mrs Linkletter's gate. If Mummy doesn't catch him soon he'll be away round the corner and the people at the bus-stop will see him. Nobody will be happy about that.

My Daddy is holding me tight. If he wasn't I might slip down and run after Andy too. He is dodging and dodging and Mummy still hasn't caught him. I had no idea the Insect could run like that.

'He'll make a scrum-half!' says My Daddy, who is laughing loudly in his deep voice. My Daddy shouldn't laugh when I'm not laughing. After all, I *am* his Princess and I'm not happy at all now.

At last Mummy catches Andy and carries him past our gate. His face is *purple* and he is stiff all over.

'He's nearly catatonic,' Mummy calls out, and My Daddy shuts the door cleverly with his heel. He doesn't want me to see Andy any more.

I don't know what 'catatonic' means, but it sounds *awful,* as if Andy was going to die. His face was really really purple. I am very

very unhappy. I *must* see Andy. I throw myself out of My Daddy's arms and thump and thump and thump on the door. He is still smiling so I hit his legs with my fists.

'I want Andy!' I shout. 'I want Andy! I want Andy!'

I can hear My Daddy talking to me. He is saying, 'That's not my Princess, is it?' and 'But you can't see Andy, he's being a bad boy.' Morag is looking at me with her pinkie in her mouth. I don't stop shouting.

Then My Daddy stops smiling and starts to be angry. He's never been angry with me before. 'Don't be ridiculous!' he shouts at me. 'Shut up, Fiona! Do you hear me? Shut up!'

I can hear My Daddy being angry, but I can't stop shouting. Messy Morag has her arms round his neck and is snuggling in. I shout even louder.

There is a bang on the door and My Daddy opens it to let Mummy-frog in and I'm knocked against the wall and sit down with a bump but nobody notices except Morag. She smiles her silly smile at me over My Daddy's shoulder. I stop shouting and puff my breath in and out as quietly as I can because I want to hear what Mummy is saying.

'Would you believe it?' she is telling My Daddy, 'the front door was open and they were having a fight about who should go and chase Andy. They were so angry with each other they couldn't see me standing there holding him. And the other two kids were leaning over the bannisters and listening to it all. I just dumped the poor wee fella in Mother's arms and walked away.'

'No wonder he runs away,' says My Daddy, and I think he's talking very sensibly. I am just going to say so when I see that they're at it again, talking to each other with their eyes about something I don't understand.

'I want Andy,' I say quietly, but loud enough for everyone to hear. I still don't know if he has really gone catatonic. Mummy said 'nearly'. I *know* he was purple because I *saw* him.

'You'll have to wait your turn,' says Mummy-frog to me. Then she turns back to My Daddy again. 'A boy feels so different in your arms, all wiry and springy and bony. . .'

'Two's enough!' says My Daddy, putting Messy Morag down and unbuttoning his coat.

Mummy-frog is putting out the tip of her tongue at My Daddy again. She is going to kiss him, I know. A Princess always knows. Everyone seems to have forgotten about me. I haven't forgotten about me. Princesses don't forget about being Princesses. I haven't forgotten about Andy either. I start to shout again and bang the door with my fists even harder than I did before. I won't let My Daddy take his coat off. I shout and shout and shout and they don't kiss each other because I stopped them.

'I can't stand these tantrums,' says My Daddy to Mummy-frog. 'I'll just take her along to see how Andy is. Okay?'

'Give in to her then. You always do,' says Mummy-frog very crossly. 'Don't be long. I mean that.'

So I grab My Daddy-horse's coat and pull him along the street to the Insect's house. He tries to walk very slowly. He should have reins and a bit in his mouth so that I could pull him faster. He is walking so slowly I know that he doesn't want to talk to the Insect's Father, who is an authoritarian bastard. That's a big black father-bird with long legs and sharp claws and a long hard beak for pecking people with. I've never seen one, even on the telly, but I know I could draw one with my felt pen. Then I could cover it up with lots of the black paint we have at my play-group.

We ring the door-bell and the Insect's Father answers. He looks at us with horrible staring eyes, exactly like the authoritarian bastard in my picture. I move a little behind My Daddy. I wish I had Beastie with me too. Father-bird doesn't ask us to come in.

'This little pest,' says My Daddy, 'wants to know if Andy is all right now.'

'As you well know, Andy has been misbehaving, ha-ha-ha! He has just had his bottom warmed and is proceeding upstairs, ha-ha-ha!'

I am hanging on to My Daddy's hand with both of mine. I know about bottom-warming, but I don't know what *proceeding* means. It sounds as bad as *catatonic*.

Now I see the Stick Insect. He is in his blue pyjamas and his ginger curls are brushed flat. He is walking very slowly and stiffly to the foot of the stairs and his Mother is following him. He is looking down, as if his neck was so stiff it was sore. He knows that me and My Daddy can see him but he is pretending he can't look up. Maybe he is catatonic *and* proceeding. I am very unhappy. In fact, I want to cry. Then I see that Andy has Longley under his arm. That makes me feel a wee bit better. Longley's proper name is Daddy-long-legs, but Andy pretends he can't say that. He never calls his Father 'Daddy' either. As a matter of fact, he never calls him anything.

I want to ask My Daddy what 'proceeding' means, but he is in a hurry.

'There's your old Andy then,' he says, trying to push me past Father-bird. 'You wanted him, have him!'

I won't let My Daddy push me and I won't look at the Insect. I only want My Daddy. I grab his leg where his knee is bony.

'Say goodnight to Fiona,' says Andy's Mother, 'be a good boy.'

I take one last peep through my hair. I know the Insect. He won't say anything to me. I knew he wouldn't. Instead he holds up his arms to his Mother, wanting to be lifted. She frowns at the Father-bird's back and picks up Andy quite roughly, but she doesn't make him throw away Longley. She usually *hates* Longley. I *like* Longley and I am glad for him that he is going to bed with Andy. I really truly wish I had Beastie with me. She likes Longley too, because they are both long and thin.

I want My Daddy even more. I let go of his knee and hold up my arms to be lifted. He scoops me up and I grab him round his neck.

'Is Andy catatonic?' I whisper.

'Of course he's not. That was a joke,' says My Daddy. 'Say goodnight to him.'

'Is 'proceeding' a joke too?' I ask.

'Of course it is. It's a jokey way of saying "going". Say goodnight and you and I will *proceed* towards home.'

I won't even pretend to look at the Stick Insect. I know what he is doing. He is looking over his mother's shoulder and sucking his thumb. Sucking your thumb is naughty but not nasty. That's what

I think, and what a Princess thinks is important.

The authoritarian bastard shuts the door on us and My Daddy turns away quickly and we're on our way home.

Riding My Daddy-horse along the street is lovely. I want to kiss him on the mouth, so I pull his face round a bit. He doesn't seem to mind, but then he stops proceeding very suddenly. He sniffs at my mouth.

'You've been smoking!' he says.

'No, it was Baby Beastie who was smoking.'

'*You* have been smoking. I knew you'd been naughty.'

'*Morag Mouse* has been smoking."

'If she has, and I doubt it, *you* have been smoking too. Smoking is not a joke, Fiona.'

'Mummy . . .'

'I know Mummy smokes, but she's a grown-up. Little girls are not allowed to smoke.'

'I didn't really mean to, Daddy, but Beastie . . .'

'I know you, Fiona. If you were smoking, you meant to. I'm having a conference with Mummy about this . . .'

I don't like Mummy-frog and My Daddy having conferences. Sometimes I can stop them if I want to.

'I said I was sorry to Mummy already, and me and Beastie *promised* we wouldn't ever steal a ciggie again, or play with her lighter, or smoke . . .'

'Will you promise me too?'

'Oh yes, Daddy, I promise . . .' and I give him a big hug.

'That's it then,' he says, and he gives me a little hug, with a little smack in it at the end. He starts proceeding again and I see our garden gate and remember all those things that got broken.

'Daddy, stop!'

He stops like a good Daddy-horse.

'I'm *very very* sorry.'

He lifts me off his hip and holds me out in front of him.

'Yes?' he says, looking straight into my eyes.

I don't really want to tell him.

'Out with it, young lady.'

I remember that conference.

'Beastie broke the lid of the stereo, and she burnt the carpet . . .'

My Daddy's eyes open very wide.

'. . . and she scratched "Boys of the Lough". We were climbing up for the ciggies and Beastie . . .'

'Cut out the Beastie. Does Mummy know?'

'I've said sorry to her already.'

My daddy is staring into my eyes without blinking.

'And *are* you sorry?'

'Yes. Beastie is very sorry.'

My Daddy is just going to say something really nasty about Beastie, but I can see him stopping himself.

'Fiona,' he says, 'Beastie's proper name is Bridget and she is a rag-doll, as you well know. What I want to know is whether you, Fiona, are sorry.'

He won't let me whisper it into his big furry ear. He is gripping me harder than Mummy-frog did, and his eyes are not soft at all. They look like authoritarian bastard eyes. His hands feel like claws too.

'*Are* you sorry, Fiona?'

I am starting to cry. I don't want to be pecked by a long hard beak.

'*Are* you?'

'Yes, Daddy,' I sob, 'I'm sorry.'

He puts me on his shoulder and gives me another of those hugs with a smack at the end. It is quite a hard smack this time. I make his shirt-collar wet with my crying, but he doesn't mind, even though it's his Bank of Scotland shirt-collar. He proceeds slowly home, gently patting my back. I keep on crying. I am a bad little baby-girl really, but I don't mind. I am my very own Daddy-horse's bad little baby-girl, and that's nice.

When we get home I see Mummy-frog rushing about getting the tea, so I stop crying. I run to pick up Baby-Beastie, who is lying where I dropped her. I am giving her a good hug when I remember how naughty she has been. I give her bottom a good warming instead. Poor Daddy-horse is taking off his coat at last.

Suddenly Mummy-frog rushes out of the kitchen with a glass of orange-juice.

'Nurse Fiona,' she says, 'look after Morag Mouse.'

She pushes me into the sitting-room and gives me the juice. Then she turns to My Daddy.

'I want a word in your private ear,' she says, pushing him along the hall and up the stairs. My Daddy is pretending that he doesn't want to go, but I can see that he likes Mummy pushing him. They are going to have a Mummy-and-Daddy conference, but it's not about me, they're giggling too much. I leave Messy Morag by herself and creep to the bottom of the stairs to see if I can hear anything else.

'Fiona's priceless!' I hear My Daddy laughing, 'Do you know what she said to me?'

'She blethers so much I've given up listening to her,' Mummy-frog is saying back. She is laughing too.

Their bedroom door slams. I don't like that at all. It's bad manners. They are both very keen on that private ear of My Daddy's. Once when we were at the beach I caught Mummy-frog whistling very quietly into My Daddy's tummy-button. She glared at me like a dragon when she saw me looking at them instead of digging with my spade. Maybe My Daddy's tummy-button is his private ear. I don't know anything about Mummy-frog's private ear and I don't want to know.

I creep back into the sitting-room. Daddy-horse would be angry with me if I tried to stop *that* conference. Me and Beastie sit down in front of the telly alongside Morag. We are sad and puzzled and thirsty. We have a long drink of juice between us. We feel a little better.

'Your Mummy is a frog,' I tell Morag, 'and My Daddy is a shiny black horse.'

Morag doesn't listen. She never does when she's watching the telly. I speak louder to make her listen.

'Your Mummy is the kitchen maid and My Daddy is a rugby forward.'

Morag still doesn't listen. Me and Beastie have another drink of juice so that we can speak louder still.

'My Daddy is *not* an authoritarian bastard. He's a Prince. He's *allowed* to stop people from doing things.' Morag turns to me. She seems to be listening. 'Your Mummy is *not* a Princess. *I'm* the Princess and she's a manipulator.'

'F-ona baad!' says Messy Morag. I don't listen to her. She doesn't know what she's talking about. I'm not really feeling any happier inside myself. I tell Beastie about it but she won't listen. She just smiles her silly little baby smile. I remember how bad she has been and put her in the baddest place I can think of, which is right under the big long cushion on the settee. Then I sit on top of the cushion. Maybe I'll throw her away.

Mummy-frog and My Daddy-horse and other grown-up people laugh at me and call me a wee blether when I talk to them about all these important things. They don't seem to realise that I am *not* joking. If they listened properly they would realise that I'm perfectly serious, the way a Princess ought to be. When I'm a Mummy I'm going to *listen* to my little Princesses when they are talking about important things and they will be much happier than I am.

I am not happy either when I remember the Stick Insect proceeding to his bed. I wish he was happier. If I drew him a nice picture I could run along to his house and give it to him. Then I would be happier too. I'll draw it after tea while Morag Mouse is having her bath.

Talking of tea, I can smell the chili-con-carne burning. Now Mummy and My Daddy will *have* to listen to me when I shout up the stairs, even if they did slam the door. I have the sharpestest nose in the family and I always smell things first.

Caught in
the Rye

I was sure I was going mad . . . Otherwise, why was I standing there on the verge of the by-pass, with the rain soaking my tee-shirt and jeans and filling up my 'training' shoes, and my mind inter-galactically empty, except for senseless phrases orbiting round and round? My father's wrath broke upon me . . . nuclear conflict . . . teacher of guidance . . . my father's wrath . . . guidance . . . conflict . . .

Cars and lorries were rushing past with headlights glaring, throwing up fountains of spray which wet me even more. If you were Holden Caulfield, I said to myself, you'd have a few dollars to call a taxi and check in at a hotel and get drunk. But you're not Holden, and it's Friday, and all the small change you've got is $3^1/2$p from last Saturday's pocket money. So you can't even afford a bus home, if that's where you want to go. . .

The phrases went on orbiting relentlessly. . . I forced myself to think about them, in case there was some sense in them which would give me a lifeline back to sanity. Okay, my father and I really had had a quarrel just before I left. It was to do with being more regular about church on Sundays and settling down to swot for more Highers than I want to bother with. He also had a side-swipe or two at my Scottish Nationalist and C.N.D. friends, who exist entirely in his imagination. I'm a loner. I have no friends. I'm sure the pressure he was exerting wasn't so much to do with my welfare as with his own positions as Elder of the Kirk and (not, thank god, in my school) Principal Teacher of Guidance. There it was again, the senselessness. . . How could he teach 'guidance' to children? He could maybe teach guidance *of* children to other teachers, but *to* children, I can't see it. Yet if sane people have decided on that title, I must be insane not to understand it. . . Perhaps I've inherited some tendency, some taint, from my father. . . He did seem mad when his wrath broke upon me. . . Taint? Tendency?

A heavy lump of spray thrown up by a thundering lorry hit me, cold, in the crutch and the animal in me demanded that I find shelter before it shrivelled away altogether. I hunched my shoulders and turned away from the insistent wind and the threatening headlights on the nearer carriageway, the phrases echoing yet again in the black hole that was my brain . . . wrath broke . . . nuclear. . . teacher. . . wrath . . .

I'm writing this in a real black hole with a contraband ball-point in a contraband jotter. Normally I churn out vast quantities of fantasy (phantasy?) stuff — science fiction, horror film scripts, spy stories and sic-like rubbish, but this is more difficult. I'm trying to record realities. . . things that I've really actually positively done and happenings that have in actuality happened. . . This style I'm using doesn't seem right at all. 'Wrath broke dot-dot-dot' etc., etc., etc. It's not really *me*. If only I was (were?) Holden Caulfield! Then all my experiences would come out in gritty muscular American teenage talk. 'Gritty muscular' — that's a mixed metaphor, Robb. But I still wish I was Holden, with a big allowance in dollars.

(I'm a madman. Holden doesn't exist. He didn't write *The Catcher in the Rye*. He's the creature of the author, what's-his-name, Salinger, who's probably a smooth phoney middle-aged New Yorker who wears those square-lensed thick-rimmed glasses and lives off his royalties in a big penthouse apartment with a sultry Raquel Welch type of mistress.)

Maybe I should forget style and just write what comes naturally, Scots words and all. (Scots, Scottish, Scotch — which of these 'comes naturally'?) If I did, whatever came out on to the paper would be my very own style and I could read it back to myself and find out what kind of a person I am. 'Le style, c'est l'homme même', as Auld Baldy keeps saying as he hands me back my English essays, implying. . . I don't want to think what he's implying.

I'd better go back to my real-life story and make the style so muscular it'll compensate for the deficiencies of my actual physical muscles, if that's possible. So here goes.

On the by-pass I was getting wetter and wetter and colder and colder. Suddenly I had a visual of Mother worrying when she found my cagoule on its hook. But, I reassured myself, she's used to my 'long walks' after hairy scenes with that man she married. She knows I'll be back sometime. Just as suddenly, Mother's image was blasted out of existence by a car roaring up behind me and passing so close the wind and spray nearly knocked me over. It screeched to a halt and the nearside door swung open dramatically. Was I in a TV thriller?

'Hey, Andy, c'moan in,' shouted a hoarse voice.

I didn't know the voice that knew my name. I stood still.

'Fir Chris' sake, Andy, we've nae time tae waste.' The voice was youthful and excited and urgent.

I started towards the tempting warmth and shelter, but hesitated when the driver revved up the engine noisily and unnecessarily several times. The boy who was holding the door open motioned impatiently. I hopped into the smell of leather and cigars and he crashed the door shut as the car took off, the driver screaming the engine through the gears like a maniac.

As the car surged away, I was able to put together what I had glimpsed as I stepped into it with what I could see now in its dark interior, spasmodically lit by flashes from passing headlights. In the back beside me there was a boy of my own age and height. In the front passenger seat there was another of the same size.

(My own age and height. It depresses me even to write the words, but it depresses the hell out of me altogether when people ask me, presumably for purposes of comparative developmental anatomy, exactly and mathematically what they are. Wallow like this, Robb, and you'll lose whatever muscularity your narrative has. Keep it moving.)

In the driver's seat was a boy even smaller than the other two. He could have been eleven or twelve. It took a moment or two for my mind to register that he was the one actually controlling the car, pretty efficiently, at seventy or more, with the wipers barely coping with the waterfall hitting the screen.

The boy beside me sat leaning forward, his eyes moving from the road ahead to the speedometer. As the needle moved upwards I saw that the limit was at 160 m.p.h., so it was a Jag or a Porsche or even a Ferrari. The boy's mouth hung open and his hand hovered round his flies. Every so often he gave them, or the animal inside them, a good tug. The boy in front switched on the radio-cassette, a quadrophonic job, and the car was filled with a Stones track that I like a lot and that harmonised with the rush of the car through the night.

I began to yield to the excitement of the moment, as the car's heater thawed me. My eyes too kept moving to that needle as it rose and rose and rose. Pleasure spread from my solar plexus, or thereabouts, but I kept my hand away from my flies. Honestly, I did. Even when the boy in front twiddled the knobs of the radio and lost the Stones, I was not disappointed for long, as the boy beside me had other excitements for me.

'Get the polis. Kin ye no get the polis waveband?' he kept asking. 'They'll maybe be efter us.'

This seemed to egg on the driver, for the needle rose and rose again as he pushed the car beyond the ton. With an ecstatic jerk my companion turned to me, putting his hand on my knee and squeezing hard.

'We nicked a real hot-rod, eh, Andy?' he asked eagerly.

Monosyllables seemed in order.

'Aye,' I ventured.

His hand slid up my leg knowingly. 'Ye're drookit, man, but we'll be hame in twa hoors an then ye kin have yer wee hairy Mary.'

I took his hand away. 'Poof,' I said, meaningfully.

'Okay, we ken whit you like,' he said, in a puzzled way. It wouldn't be long before he found out I wasn't the right Andy. Then what would happen?

As I write, in my present enforced isolation, I realise that I was no longer worrying about going mad, or being annihilated by a nuclear warhead, whatever I'm doing now, crazily scribbling like this. The situation was insane, maybe the other boys too, but at least I was using all the wits I had to cope. I was doing at least as well as Holden would have done.

The two passengers started to talk, but I could make out little of what they were saying. It was all too allusive, slangy, and adenoidal. (Yes, *my* adenoids have been seen to, thank you. What a wimp I am sometimes!) I did pick up that they were talking about some out-of-the-ordinary school they all attended, various boys there, and who were the hardest men. Andy, whoever he was, came from a separate place called 'the unit' where the least hard men were, so I would have to be careful not to speak out of turn. Keeping mum, I just let the thrusting joy of the forbidden speed carry me along.

The others were so engrossed in talking and the driver in listening that none of them noticed huge quadruple headlights behind us. They were gaining on us fast. I turned to look and the boy beside me saws me full-face in the white glare.

'Ye're no Andy at aa!' he cried.

The headlights developed a blue flashing light above them.

'The polis!' I shouted, without thinking and in a passable imitation of their hoarse nasality. I was instantly forgotten in a babble of viciously obscene language. The driver revealed a bass voice and a determination that the police were going to have to work hard to catch him. He accelerated away and I found myself hanging on to the grab handle, urging him on excitedly and yet afraid of injury or death. (Oh, that mindless exhilaration! How I could use it now, in reality, instead of just writing about it, cooped up in this stinking hole, with the walls, and nightmares about the fission bomb, closing in on me.)

The chase did not last long. Beyond the end of the dual carriageway the police had set up a roadblock of two landrovers with wide fluorescent stripes on their sides. The driver braked, with a long shriek of tyres.

'Haud on, boys,' he shouted, 'we're gaun through the hedge.'

There was a thud, shudder and heave as the car took the kerb, a moment of ominous quiet as we skidded across the verge diagonally, then a literally sickening jolt and smash of glass as the car came to rest on its side. I found myself lying on top of my companion, dazed from a dunt on the head, seeing stars, and hearing a high singing note. This is it, this is how it will be if the fission bomb *misses* you. I couldn't move, but he was trying to open the door below him, but it was jammed, of course. As he wriggled desperately to free himself from me and reach the other door, I passed out.

When I came to properly, after being half-aware of voices and lights and being lifted, I was still in my damp clothes and lying on my back under a smelly brown blanket on a bench in what seemed to be a narrow lobby. Looking up at the ceiling blearily and listening to the shrill resonance that was filling my skull from the inside, I knew, without having to think about it, that this was a police station and not a hospital, and that I'd been in a car-smash and not a nuclear incident. I knew too that I had to be ready for more unpleasant happenings, like being forced by an unholy alliance of police and parents to return home before I was ready for it. I am not, repeat not, a cry-baby who wants to run home to Mummy. I'm going home in my own time.

I turned my head. Almost within touching distance, on another bench against the drab wall opposite, sat three boys. Two I recognised right away as the passengers from the car, both dressed like me in grotty tee-shirts and clarty jeans. They were red-eyed and down in the mouth and they still needed to clutch at their flies every so often. Their bruised and blotchy faces and their skinny tattooed arms made them almost pitiful. I could handle either of that pair, I thought, undersized though I am, and maybe both together. Andy the Hard Man. I still can't recall them as separate individuals because the third boy, the driver, grabbed all my attention as soon as I focussed on him. He was someone byordinar altogether, black-browed and tiny and fierce, his arms grimly folded. His studded Levi jacket was ripped from collar to waist-band, revealing a smooth golden skin and a muscly shoulder and arm. His jeans had style, stretched tight over aggressively jutting knees. He was my age, and maybe older, and not taking defeat easily. Perhaps I wasn't such a hard man, for I didn't want to tangle with him, ever again. He'd had three lives in his hands and he'd gambled with them.

Weighing up the place and the three boys had diverted me from the condition of my cranium, which was still sore and singing away without any let-up. I lifted it, to test my general well-being, and immediately the dark boy leaned over to me.

'Dinnae move and keep quiet,' he whispered.

I rested my head again.

'Whit's yer name?' he asked.

'Andy,' I whispered back.

'Andy whit?'

'Andy Robb.'

'Listen then. Yer name's Andy MacPhail. That's whit us three has jist tellt the polis in wir statements. Okay?'

'Robb the snoab,' one of the others giggled.

The dark boy — I never found out his name — turned on him. 'His name's MacPhail, ya runt,' he said through clenched teeth. Then back to me, 'Ye're a hell of a man, okay? Ye're Randy Andy, that sexy ye cannae wait for it, so ye're a persistent absconder.'

I grimaced cagily, my brain flipping through a hundred options. 'It would be simpler to simulate a memory loss, wouldn't it?' I asked.

'Smart guy, eh?' He clenched a white-knuckled hard-looking fist. 'Jist stop talking Englified and say yer name's MacPhail.'

'Okay,' I murmured, partly because I was in no condition to resist his threat, partly because some of the illicit excitement of the bypass was still with me, and partly because I was going along with whatever would save me from a return to my family and the barrage of stupid questions they are bound to ask me about this escapade, or the stony silence that is just as likely. Mostly, though, I was influenced by the dark boy's animal magnetism and, yes, his beauty. It was an effort to write that last word, but no other will do. Compared to the rest of us, he was a god — one of those ancient ones, half-animal and half-human and all unpredictable power. I had to pay some kind of homage, hadn't I?

The god spoke. His voice was fluty and polite, without a trace of menace. 'Sir, Andy MacPhail is coming round, if you wish to speak to him.'

Right away a police sergeant appeared by my side. My hackles rose, don't ask me why. 'You are Andrew Stuart MacPhail?' he asked in a phoney English accent. Maybe he thought it sounded official.

'Mphm,' I nodded.

'You have just absconded from Balriddie List D School?'

'Could be.'

'Not for the first time?'

'Maybe no.' He was believing me, I could see. How easy it is to keep a lie going, and how satisfying!

'They're not having you back, if that's a comfort to you. Can you stand?'

'I dinnae ken.'

'Stand up then,' he said, whipping off the blanket and yanking me to my feet.

I saw a star or two to accompany the one-note celestial choir, but stayed upright, hate helping me. The sergeant, blithely unaware of anything I might be feeling, pretended to relax into a Scots accent, but it sounded just as phoney as his English one.

'Sit doon. Oor doactor said ye'd be okay, but if ye're no ye kin ask tae see anither when ye get tae the Assessment Centre.' He then read me a short statement, obviously based on what the others had told him, and asked me to sign it. I did so, under the watchful eye of the dark boy, and hating the sergeant even more, for I could see he thought he was pulling a fast one. If he is, I determined, it's one more reason for getting my own back. Somehow. Anyhow.

He turned to the others. 'Balriddie are comin fir ye in ten meenits,' he said, 'Jist time fir a drag.' He handed round a packet of cigarettes. The god took one, lit it with a fancy lighter and inhaled deep into his lungs. Perhaps he's an Aztec deity, I thought, and is propitiated and controlled by offerings of the sacred weed. There was something ritualistic, a fawning on dangerous power, in the way the sergeant had offered him the packet first. (Budding social anthropologist A. Robb in full flight!) I came last of course and refused, indicating my head.

'Randy's feart that fags'll spile his perfoarmance,' one of the others sniggered.

I kept a low profile (why do I use clichés?) and said nothing, for I was wondering what an Assessment Centre was. It sounded sinister, coming from the sergeant, like something from the Gulag Archipelago, or somewhere top-secret where you went to be screened for radioactivity. I tried to guess who would be assessing whom and how it would be done. (If I'm being assessed now I'm not aware of it. The place feels like jail to me.) These thoughts, if that's what they were, were interrupted by hearty voices from beyond the corner of the lobby. The sergeant disappeared.

'It's the twa beardy screws,' said the dark boy. 'Turn yer face tae the waa, Andy.'

I did as he commanded, as I had to, and he covered me to the top of my head with the blanket. I nearly choked with the foul odour, but the touch of his hands had such authority I dared not complain.

'They'll no come in here, but we cannae tak chances,' he said. 'Ye'll mind yer name's MacPhail?'

'Randy Andy, that's me,' I said, seeing a momentary mental picture of the more interesting aspects of Koo Stark.

'Ye're no bad fir an English bastard,' he muttered before turning away and raising his voice. 'Okay, boys, we're wanted.'

I heard the three of them shuffling out and then the hearty voices again, with perhaps a hint of anger in their joviality. Then silence, except for the sergeant shifting his feet. That's what it sounded like, but he might well have been indulging in other practices. I took the blanket off my face and lay for the better part of an hour while the dunt on my head throbbed, accompanied by visions of *A Day in the Life of Ivan Denisovitch.*

How would Holden have coped? He'd have started, I thought, by having a long and interesting conversation with the sergeant, maybe even asking his views on C.N.D. and the police role in a nuclear incident, but that's the kind of thing I'm no good at, especially when I hate someone. He'd have been sorry for him because of his sad serge uniform and his pitifully polished boots, and then sick to his stomach with his phoney-ness. And Iain Crichton Smith, he of the diamond words, what would he have done? Made a poem? 'Those who move others and are themselves stone, Should be hated without ambiguity . . .'

These literary meditations are a load of cobblers. I'm making them up, now, as I write. What I was really doing at the time was trying to comfort myself with thoughts of Raquel Welch. Hardly a literary pursuit. However, her image didn't work its usual magic. I was cold, and sort of shrunken, and the night was still young. There was nothing to do but lie there, fight off the Gulag Archipelago and the fission bomb and try to hear what was going on round the corner in case it had to do with me. The sergeant seemed to have an ever-increasing stream of callers — I hoped they all hated him too.

In the end, my transfer to this place was effected without fuss by police car. The two policemen who escorted me were impersonal but kindly. One gave me a piece of chocolate (warm from his pocket) when I refused the ritual cigarette. The Centre is actually within this City and Royal Burgh where I have lived all my life, but I didn't know of its existence before. It has massive glass front doors and as I emerged from the car I could see a brightly lit hall, like a hotel foyer. My two escorts and I stood for what seemed a long time, after one of them had rung the door-bell. Then two informally dressed men appeared, talking animatedly to each other. The bigger one produced a bunch of keys on a long pocket chain and unlocked the door.

'MacPhail, eh?' he asked the policeman, without looking at me.

'Yes, Mr Scott,' said one.

'Any papers?'

'Just the body.'

'You'll be wanting away?'

Both nodded and turned back to their car. After the big man, Mr Scott, had wordlessly motioned me inside and locked the door he re-started his conversation with his companion, who was a squidgy pop-eyed wee man, the spitting image of Peter Lorre in those old movies, while shepherding me across the foyer and into a bare corridor.

I was pretty confused at this point, I must admit. 'No papers' and 'just the body' and the sound of the key in the lock were echoing in my head. My eyes were dazzled by the bright lights in the foyer and the vivid pattern of the carpet and the huge modernistic prints on the walls and the brilliant covers of the armchairs tastefully arranged round unused-looking coffee-tables. When we entered the dim light of the corridor I could barely see. But my nose was in working order. It certainly was. The smell of that corridor was a mixture of the sweaty fragrance of the changing rooms at the school playing-field and the early morning aroma of cold deep fat from the cheapest of Chinese chip-shops.

To add to my confusion, Mr Scott's deep voice was reverberating down the corridor. Was I supposed to listen to him? 'I don't care what the policy is, Mr Blaikie,' he was booming, 'I'm the senior man on duty and I say that this character's going to be checked in, showered, and bunged into the cooler in five minutes flat. If the duty-roster says I'm on duty all week-end, it also says that I hand over to the night man at ten o'clock, not five past.'

He unlocked what seemed to be a store-room and we all went in. He seized a large crumpled polythene bag and held the mouth of it towards me. 'Pockets,' he said.

I looked at him. I knew what he meant, but this was the first thing he'd said to me and I was still confused by the idea that I was going to be assessed. Perhaps the way I behaved now would be noted down and used against me? Sure enough, Mister Blaikie was fiddling with a wee black book he'd taken from a shelf. I tried to work out how I should act, but Mr Scott was in a hurry.

'You know the drill. Move.' I still looked at him. 'One thing at a time. Into. The. Bag. Mac. Phail. And. It. Will. Be. In your own interest. Not. To. Try. Any. Funny. Stuff.'

Obviously, my options were: conform and be assessed, or reveal my true identity and be sent home, so I dropped my hankie, my C.N.D. badge, my house-key and my 3^1/2p into the bag, feeling quite a sense of loss as I did so. As if they mattered! Mr Scott called them out to Mister Blaikie, who wrote them carefully into the wee black book, now revealed as more-or-less innocuous. The C.N.D. badge was no surprise to them, obviously. Maybe they are used to locking up dissidents.

'Cigarettes,' said Mr Scott.

'I haven't any,' I said. Mr Scott raised an eyebrow, perhaps at hearing my accent for the first time. Was he making a mental note of it?

'You'll be desperate. I'll give you one after breakfast, maybe. It depends, of course.' He was still holding the bag open to me. 'Clothes,' he said.

Take my clothes off? Was this part of the assessment too? I stayed not for an answer but conformed again, responding to impatient gestures from Mr Scott. I stripped everything off, still damp, right down to my birthday suit. The process was accompanied by a series of peculiar coughs and throat-clearings from Mister Blaikie. The store was infernally cold, but I had to stand there, naked and unmagnificient, while Mr Scott checked the pockets of my jeans, inserting expert knowing fingers into them one by one. I began to feel skinnier and skinnier and pimplier and pimplier. As casually as I could I covered my private self with one hand, but that didn't make me, or it, feel any bigger or any more human. I felt like an object with a ridiculous tassel attached to it and hellishly exposed and raw. I was beginning to think that home might not be such a bad place after all when, without warning, it happened.

From the inside 'secret' pocket of my jeans Mr Scott produced a folded and flattened potato-crisp packet. What on earth, I wondered, forgetting my nakedness, is that doing here? It was intimately familiar, somehow, and yet in these surroundings, completely and utterly strange. Not mine, anyway. Nothing to do with me. As Mr Scott peeled off the tape with which the little bag was sealed my mind went numb, so that I was neither surprised nor unsurprised when he gave a long whistle and withdrew from the bag a squashed bundle of grubby papers. I could see sepia and orange engravings. David Livingstone. Africans in leg-irons. Mr Scott counted the papers reverently.

'Potato-crisp bag,' he called out to Mister Blaikie, 'containing ten Clydesdale Bank ten-pound notes. One hundred. One. Oh. Oh. Pounds. Sterling.' Then to me,'All your very own, I suppose? Earned by honest toil and all that?'

'Well, actually,' I began, unable to say anything rational in answer to the man's idiotic question. Where is 'honest toil' to be found these days? I was shivering again forbye.

'Oh, it's *actually* yours, is it? Your allowance from dear old Dad, what what?' I wasn't far short of paralysed with the cold, but I must have nodded. 'In that case, we underlings will enquire no further. Our betters have to earn their salaries too, when they condescend to return to duty on Monday morning. Mister Blaikie, show him what you have written in the book.' Mister Blaikie turned the book to me, but kept his distance.

Mr Scott became sarcastically formal. 'You confirm, MacPhail, that this entry is correct, correctly dated, and in ink?'

My head jerked in a shivery spasm which Mr Scott took for a nod. He proceeded to pull the sleeves of his hairy fake-Icelandic cardigan half-way up his horrible great hairy forearms and with ostentatious care re-folded the notes, returned them to the packet and re-sealed it. Then he held the packet out at arm's-length between finger and thumb, glanced at me, and when he saw I was looking, dropped it into the polythene bag, which he quickly closed with a piece of string.

I was in a dwam, not sure I wasn't dreaming all this, but Mr Scott brought me to by grabbing a pair of pyjamas from a shelf and throwing them at me. I whipped on the trousers p.d.q., followed smartly by the jacket.

'Right, Mister Blaikie,' said Mr Scott, 'you shower him and I'll write him up in the office.' Write me up? My mind was boggling, but Mister Blaikie was wriggling his shoulders and looking at me oddly. 'With these fellows,' he said, 'we're supposed to . . .'

'Are we supposed to work more overtime than we'll get paid for?' demanded Mr Scott. 'The Cuts, Mister Blaikie, the Cuts.'

'It's not that, it's . . .'

'Oho, *that's* your problem?' said Mr Scott and turned to me. 'You won't rape him, will you? Tell him you won't. Go on, tell him!' I managed to convert a shiver into a shrug of my shoulders. What on earth is he going to say in his write-up of me? 'Admitted — one rapist, in possession of £100 and a C.N.D. badge.'

'You are a rapist, aren't you?'

'So everyone keeps insisting,' I said. 'I seem to be type-cast.' That sounds cocky, but I wasn't feeling cocky. Pyjamas are better than nothing, but no real defence. What do I mean? Defence against what? I was wishing the pyjamas had zip-up flies.

'Aye-aye, Mister Blaikie,' opined Mr Scott, 'we're forgetting he's middle-class. Mid-dle. Class. C.N.D. and all that. But it figures, Mister Blaikie. Working-class kids aren't allowed rides in cars, so they have to steal them. Middle-class kids aren't allowed sex, even when they have a hundred pounds to buy it, so they have to steal it: and they're brought up to be *against* self-defence. If I hit him, he wouldn't hit me back. Right, MacPhail?'

I risked shrugging my shoulders again, but Mr Scott wasn't looking. He was going off at full steam — to 'write me up' I was afraid. Mister Blaikie blinked several times, handed me a towel as if it was obscene, and led me to the shower room. His behaviour while I was under the shower was so odd that I can't bring myself to be too specific about it on paper . . .

Perhaps I should force myself to write at least part of the truth about Mister Blaikie's antics. After all, Holden was able to describe the perverts he saw from his hotel window. Mister Blaikie didn't move from just inside the door and stood there going very red in the face . . . I *can't* be more specific. I really can't. This is Scotland, not New York, and I'm Andrew Robb, not Holden Caulfield/Salinger.

Otherwise, the shower was super, hot and plentiful, and I felt almost human as I dried myself and put on the pyjamas again. Mister Blaikie, his face now a dirty grey, composed himself and led me circumspectly away, up some stairs and along a corridor with huge windows on both sides, like the aquarium at Edinburgh Zoo. The atmospheric pollution here was different from that downstairs. It smelled like the old Primary Three classroom used to on a wet day when all the kids were steaming damp and half had pee'd their pants because the headmistress was on one of her rampages and everyone was scared to ask to 'leave the room'. The smell seemed to float on a foundation of floor-polish. Through the reinforced glass of the windows, dimly lit, I could see rows of beds, a tousie head on every pillow that wasn't supporting a skinhead or a punk-head.

I was not exactly reassured by that smell, or those eerie windows, or the sight of all those kids peacefully sleeping. I didn't know if they were juvenile delinquents or mental patients or dissidents of some sort. (Scott and Blaikie weren't wearing white coats or navy-blue uniforms, but perhaps they'd taken them off because they were just going off duty?) There was no telling from the outside of the kids' heads what malfunctioning, if any, was going on inside them. If I was assessed as insane nobody would believe me if I insisted that I was Andrew Robb, a case of identity confusion. It's surprising, isn't it, how many thoughts one can think while walking the length of a quite short corridor.

At the end of the corridor was this room I'm occupying. It's not a padded cell, as I'd more than half expected, it's just an ordinary cell, but the staff have phoney names for it. They call it 'the isolation room' or 'the separation room' or 'the cooler'. It would be more honest of them to call it 'the cell' or to use the accurate name its occupants use — 'the slammer'. But perhaps the staff don't want to be honest. Why should they? They're adults.

Mister Blaikie locked me in and I smelled its unique smell for the first time. It can only be described as a concentrated essence of gents public convenience amalgamated with the pungency of the pavements round a pub on a Saturday night before the vomit has had time to dry. The amalgam is sandwiched between layers and layers of disinfectant and something else, which Holden could have described, but I can't. I hardly notice it now.

I looked around and saw a foam mattress and a blanket on a cement platform: a window with obscure glass through which, in daylight, I can see bars; a ventilator; a toilet buried in a concrete block and with a foot-stud flush; and a judas-hole in the door. Heat, rather too much of it, seems to come from the ceiling. One wall is painted black and a few pieces of chalk kick around the floor so that inmates may draw or write what they fancy, but nobody seems to have bothered. I don't need the black wall because I have this jotter and ball-point that Jimmy brings me.

I should have mentioned Jimmy before. He's the Night Supervisor, a little bald chap with his own ideas, and my link with sanity. My only link with sanity. He came on duty at ten o'clock, I suppose, when the other two went off, but he didn't visit me for an hour or so. When he did I was in the dumps, wide awake and without a trace left of the excitement of the by-pass. My head was hurting like a bastard and full of those Hiroshima pictures of people with their eyeballs burned. I was convinced I was in a mental hospital and I hadn't been able to raise Raquel Welch at all, just when I needed her most. I would say that that woman obsesses me if I wasn't thinking of trading her in for Koo Stark. I'm a madman. I swear it. Being locked up is what I deserve.

Jimmy locked the door behind him and stood looking down at me, making chewing motions. He was wearing a white shirt with the sleeves rolled up, a narrow black tie, baggy black trousers and white tennis shoes. His knotty veiny arms were covered with tattoos.

'Whit's yer name?' he asked, between chews.

'Didn't they tell you?' I replied, with touching faith in 'they'.

'They'll have wrote it in the book, but I dinnae bother wi that. I like tae hear things frae the lads theirsels. Whit are ye cried?'

'Andrew Robb.' Somehow I *had* to tell this man the truth.

'Oh aye. And whit are ye in here fir?'

'I'm a case of mistaken identity.'

'Oh aye. Mphm. Ye'll be wanting a fag?'

'I don't smoke.'

'Oh aye, fancy that.' More chewing. 'Weel, ye'll see me every twa hoors and maybe oftener. But if I keek through the hole an ye're sleepin, I'll jist leave ye. Ye hungry?'

I told him the truth, that the policeman's chocolate was the only thing I'd eaten since dinner-time,

'The bastards,' he said with some venom, and went off. He was back in no time with a piece-box full of bully-beef sandwiches, a packet of biscuits, and an enormous flask of coffee.

'Eat whit ye want,' he said, 'they're ma ain. I've nae dealins wi the kitchen here.'

As I ate, we started the first of the long conversations which, along with this scribbling, make the nights bearable, even enjoyable sometimes. Jimmy sits on a chair he brings while I sit on the bed with my back against the wall. Every so often he goes off on his rounds, checking that all the doors are locked and that the right tally of heads is on the pillows. Back with me again, he leaves the door open so he can hear the bells — one for the front door, one for the telephone, one for the fire alarm, and the only one I've actually heard, which always provokes him.

'They cannae haud their pee at aa, thae laddies,' he exclaims as he slopes off, fetching his keys out of his pocket as he goes. (Subtle, allusive author A. Robb leaves the reader to work out that the boys are locked into the dormitories and have to call Jimmy if they experience micturition.)

On that first night, it seems like weeks ago, I asked Jimmy what an Assessment Centre was and he gave me an old-fashioned look.

'It's jist a Remand Home,' he said, 'but the high heid-yins decidit tae chynge the name. It wis whit they cry a "public relations exercise". The neebours had been complainin.'

This was a relief, but only for a moment. Surely, if I was sane, I'd have known it wasn't a mental hospital or a place for assessing your radiation levels. My head is still hurting. I wonder if my brain functioning has been permanently affected by that dunt? The singing note comes and goes too.

'So there isn't any "assessment" then?' I asked, still anxious.

'I wadnae ken aboot that. The day staff are aye writin reports.' His voice had a certain finality.

I didn't dare to ask more questions, so I was left wondering what sort of report Mr Scott might write about me. From the way he talked it would be hostile as well as inaccurate, like my school reports. I'd have worked myself up into a high old state if Jimmy hand't begun to talk soothingly about his experiences at sea before, during, and after World War Two. I cocked my ears, for here was racy real-life material that would be useful if I ever want to write a sea -story. I was thinking of telling Monsarratt 'Move over!' when Jimmy launched into a description of his ship's visit to Nagasaki not very long after the war. I was thinking that there's no escape from reality, no escape at all, but he must have seen my face, for he moved on quickly to New Zealand, where he'd been to all-night beach parties where the Maori girls were well-built and friendly and played 'Now is the Hour' on their guitars. This was more like the kind of reality I needed just then and I started to relax.

Later in the night I told Jimmy *my* story, giving him my address and even the name of the educational establishment (so-called) which I attend. He believed me, I could see, but was sweirt to do anything about it, which was fair enough, as I'd got myself into the place deliberately, almost. When I pressed him a little it emerged that he could barely read or write, hence his lack of interest in 'the book', in which, I gathered, details of admissions are recorded and in which he is supposed to write down any happening of importance. 'If it really matters,' he said, 'I phone the Officer-in-Charge.'

'Couldn't you phone him about me?' I asked. I was so enjoying Jimmy's yarns and his relaxing company that I was in no hurry to get out just then, but I did want to know how to set about getting out if I began to want to. (Jimmy isn't here as I write this, so I'm all on edge again. What if there isn't a procedure for getting out? If there was a Gulag Archipelago in this country, it would be a secret, wouldn't it, like the network of nuclear warfare places nobody is allowed into? Go back to writing about Jimmy, he's your link with sanity, remember? If this place was part of the Archipelago, or whatever, he'd have given a hint, surely?)

'He's awaa fir the weekend,' Jimmy was saying, 'The Depute's left and there's nae replacement. Scott's Third-in-Charge an he wadnae believe either of us.' That note of finality again.

I had no choice but to give up and hope there was some way out for me, with or without that £100. I refused Jimmy's offer of a 'tranny' and begged for pencil and paper, which he went and fetched. He handed them to me with a solemn warning.

'I'll hae tae tak them awaa in the morning afore the day-staff come on. They think ye could damage yersel or attack folk wi that ball-point. I had tae nick that jotter frae the class-room.'

It's a good fat jotter too, bless him. If I keep my writing small it'll last quite a whilie, and the ball-point is turning out to be a good discipline (as auld Baldy would say) after my usual pencil and rubber.

How it is we've trusted each other so quickly I don't know, but Jimmy now leaves the cell door open when he's off on his rounds. He must think I'm sane. He's in a minority. On my side, I'm absolutely convinced that Jimmy won't let anyone else see this jotter. Which is just as well, for I'm writing like a madman. I've changed to the present tense, too. I wonder why? It gives immediacy, Baldy says, but at what cost? I've been so obsessed that I didn't stop, except for Jimmy's visits, till after five o'clock on Saturday morning. Last night was the same and now it's the wee hoors of Monday morning and I'm still at it. I can't stop. What on earth would I do if I did? Look at the bare ceiling? Think about Raquel Welch/Koo Stark for hours on end? Worry, as always, about the fission bomb? Enlarge the holes in the plaster with my finger-nails, pretending I was digging my way out? No, no, no, I must go on scribbling and try to be rational.

Three things are bothering me now. *First,* school tomorrow, or rather today. I want to be there for a reason, a very special reason, which is now over-riding my reluctance to go home and face my father's wrath and Mother's insistent anxiety. *Second,* those ten-pound notes, if they exist. I can't seem to focus my thoughts about them at all. *Third,* I'm not sure I could take another day here. The nights have been okay because of Jimmy, but the days are hell. The rational thing to do is to try and sleep, but all my attempts are interrupted by an incredible variety of unbelievable happenings, if I may be tautological. (Or do I mean pleonastic? Or just repetitious? I wonder if Jimmy could nick a dictionary too? I'm Andrew Robb and I'm a wordaholic, with irrational lexicophagous tendencies. I need new words like a junkie needs fixes.)

These happenings, they really are insane. They include two-hourly visits by staff in pairs, as ordained by Act of Parliament, according to Mr Scott. Yet Jimmy comes to see me on his own, when he's alone in the building. He must be extra-Parliamentary and sane. But then he would be.

After breakfast I have to scrub the whole cell, bed platform and all, with hot water and disinfectant, though I haven't pee'd or defecated on the floor. The regulation pair of staff watch me, arms akimbo. I usually get my pyjamas wet, but am told they'll dry.

At tea-time yesterday the meal was brought by a middle-aged woman, escorted by Mr Scott.

'Satisfy your curiosity, Miss Porteous,' he fog-horned. 'Have a

101

good look at the answer to many a maiden's prayer.'

'It was you who insisted that I came, Mr Scott,' she acidulated. 'He looks as if he needs a proper diet and a bit of mothering.'

'Haw-haw-haw!' bull-roared Mr Scott and I was left to eat my baked beans off their plastic plate with my fingers. Which did I prefer to be, an undernourished little boy or a sex-fiend? The fiend, obviously. Mothering I need like a hole in the head.

All the time there are noises, some comprehensible and some not. Bawling and banging and stamping. Thrashings-about and whooshings and what sound like throttlings. The last may come from the plumbing — I can't tell. There's no doubt, though, about the horrible screams and even more horrible laughter coming from what Jimmy tells me is the girls' wing, which must be very close by. Worst of all, yesterday the girls found out somehow that there was a rapist in the slammer and started to talk *at* me through the ventilator. Jimmy says they have to stand on the seat in one of their toilets to do it. Some of their remarks are really very crude indeed and made in harsh voices, but others are supposed to be throaty seductive whispers. Luckily the girls' visits to their toilets seem to be rationed, for their talk never lasts for more than a few minutes at a time. If it didn't stop I'd be even further round the twist.

The way I'm writing about those girls suggests I might be some kind of innocent who hasn't even got a girl-friend. I have one, though. Fat Fiona Phimister my siblings call her, and I'm supposed to lose my temper about the adjective, but I don't bother now because she hasn't been fat for a year or so, only kind of stocky, which suits me as she's never grown taller than me. We have a rather special kind of relationship, perhaps a wee bit unusual in this day and age. I can't believe it, but we haven't been 'out' together yet, or held hands like Holden and old Jane, but we do get together at the church youth club discos, which we organise for the under-fourteens, poor infants, and we walk to and from school and church together, now and then, when there aren't too many others about. We both like the Stones, too, just to be old-fashioned. Best of all, our classes are together for Art on a Monday afternoon so in twelve hours I could be sitting talking to Fiona about this weekend. I could pretend to write out a poem in Creative Calligraphy while she fiddles about with a felt pen pretending to illustrate it. Artless Annie couldn't care less, a typical art teacher.

Fiona is the quintessence of sanity, with a mind like a razor and a sardonic sense of humour. She's better fun than any boy I know. That's no great praise, but I have often wished she was a boy, so that we could be pals and go to each other's bedrooms and blether half the night away. I need to know her views on C.N.D. and I never get a chance to ask her properly. My being a girl would have the same effect, of course, but I don't like to think about that, not since my tits got tender some time back and I lost a lot of sleep wondering what was happening. Then I read something about 'hormonal imbalance in adolescence' and, miraculously, they got better. Any way I think about it (including the awful fear that Fiona's bedroom would smell like my sister's) bedrooms are out. Still, we have this unspoken agreement that neither of us will date anyone else (when it comes to dating), or get drunk, or experiment with glue or drugs, without consulting the other.

I've felt quite sane just writing about Fiona, but after finishing that last paragraph, and wishing fervently that Jimmy would come back soon, I've lost control. Mad thoughts are starting to echo from the walls of this place. What if Fiona is like those girls in the toilets? Her sense of humour has been pretty crude recently, especially when she's standing at the school gate with a gang of other girls and giggling as the boys, including me, run the gauntlet. I could hate her then. And I really do hate her when she walks past a gang of boys I happen to be with (I won't insult myself by calling them 'friends') and pretends not to see me. If some smart alec makes a crack about her, as usually happens, she always gives a pert answer, or a dismissive shrug of her backside, or one of those superior smiles which girls are good at.

My 'muscular' narrative style has gone. I'm describing nothing but the chaos inside my head. My 'stream of consciousness', as Baldy would call it, is muddy, stagnant, and choked with rubbish.

How is Fiona spending the weekend? There's another mad thought. A First XV fellow, a real thick-head I'll call Joe (after bloody Joe 'Room at the Top' Lampton) has taken to going to church for no religious reason I can see and sitting near her. Often right in the same pew, for god's sake. Perhaps the 'unspoken agreement' is all on my side. Come to think of it, Joe's been hanging round her at the disco too, all fourteen stone of him. Perhaps she invited him to come because she's bored with me . . . perhaps . . .

The maddest thoughts of all are about radioactivity and allied phenomena of a threatening nature. I keep thinking that this could be an experimental chamber for studying the effects of radiation on actual human beings. Adolescents would be particularly important subjects as they are in a phase of rapid hormonal, bone and glandular development. Well, they are, aren't they? This heat from the ceiling, is it really heat-frequency radiation, or could it be something more sinister? It's certainly having strange effects on me. If I run my hand through my hair, it's hot, and feels as if each and every strand is screwed to my skull. I can't escape the hostile rays, even on the loo, and if I try to hide from them under the blanket it feels as if it was electrostatic and ready to give off sparks at any moment. They keep pressing down on me, and they've found this place on my head where I had that dunt and it's swelling all the time. I can feel the glands in my neck swelling too. Those two-hourly visits, they could be for checking my responses to different levels. . . Jimmy could be an ignorant accomplice, or a very sophisticated plant . . .

Maybe I watch too many TV doomwatch documentaries and read too many sci-fi stories. Maybe sci-fi writers make their millions from just writing down the fears that come to them in the night. If so, I'm definitely a potential millionaire.

Jimmy has left me alone for longer than he has ever done. What can be keeping him? If this is the state I get into in the peaceful night, how on earth will I cope with the unending prospect of more and more daylight hours, when I can't sleep or wake or scribble? Or with the Officer-in-Charge, when he 'condescends to return to duty' on Monday morning? Which is this morning, in a few hours? Unlikely though it seems, sleep is overtaking me . . .

I've woken up again, the ball-point still in my hand. What will the morning bring? A grilling from the Officer-in-Charge? The police? My parents? The same routine, Gulag fashion? Worst of all, more radiation experiments.

Fiona . . . I nearly wrote down her real name. My name's not Andrew either. Why am I here? Holden never had these kind of problems and he ended up in some weirdo place out West, so what chance have I?

Jimmy, I'll just eat the last of your chocolate biscuits and lie down properly and drop off. This blanket is beginning to smell of me, electrostatic or not . . .

Well, I'm out of that place and writing this on the lab bench in the Physics double-period. Routine first half of Monday morning, except that writing up my weekend is far more important to me than writing up last week's stupid little experiment, which has nothing to do with reality, i.e., radioactivity. What happened in that Assessment Centre is in the past, so it's back to the past tense and the most muscular style I'm capable of.

I didn't have much sleep after all, for at three forty-five or thereabouts Jimmy came in lugging a mattress and followed by a boy dressed in pyjamas identical to the ones I was wearing. He was carrying a blanket. I leapt out of bed.

'Get back in there,' ordered Jimmy, dumping the mattress on the narrow patch of floor beside the bed. 'Here's the real Andy MacPhail.' He turned to my alter ego. 'This is Andy Robb. He's been mistook fir ye, he says.'

'You'll let me out, then?' I asked, with indecent haste.

'Na, na,' reproved Jimmy, 'I'm only the night man. The Officer-in-Charge'll sort ye in the mornin.' He picked up this jotter and my heart stopped beating, for its daft contents are to make me a millionaire, but I had misjudged him, for he added, 'I'll drap this at yer hoose, eh?'

I nodded, my heart functioning again, but I still wanted out. The grilling I would just have to take. 'Can't you ring the Officer-in-Charge?' I asked.

'Aye. I'll dae jist that, but at seeven o'clock and no earlier. Aye. And meantime, I'll be checkin on ye baith. Nae nonsense!' He started to shut the door. I realised that our chats might be over, never to happen again.

'Thanks for everything,' I said, unoriginally but with feeling. I didn't want him to leave me, I discovered.

'It's been a pleesure,' he said, and locked us in.

So there we were, the two Andies, staring at each other. We were the same build, near enough, and our hair was roughly the same length and gingery colour, so the mistake made by the Balriddie boys was understandable, but I didn't waste too much time on comparisons. I was worrying about sharing a small cell with a real sex-maniac. Radiation experiments went on the back burner.

It turned out that the sex-mania was the least of my problems. What I had to cope with, first of all, were Andy's complaints. He was full of them. Full, pressed down, and running off at the mouth. He complained of having only one blanket and feeling cold, despite the stifling heat I was experiencing. He resented my having the bed while he had to lie on the floor, and when I let him have the bed he complained it was no softer than the floor. He complained bitterly that the other boys hadn't bothered to come to the rendezvous to pick him up in the stolen car. He cursed the weather, which had forced him to go back to Balriddie and hide in a cellar near the boiler. He was annoyed that this was the first time he's absconded and not reached his home town where, if he'd been picked up, he at least knew the Assessment Centre and the staff in it. He kent naebody here and he didnae like it.

He'd been found, he complained, breaking into the school clothing store for something to make a bed with. What he'd eaten he didn't say, but it can't have been good for him for he had diarrhoea, which was the second of my problems. Every so often he jumped up and sat on the toilet, girning about his guts as if he was the only one to suffer. The stench was unendurable, but I had to endure it. He didn't seem to have any qualms about defecating in my presence, or exposing the whole of his anatomy, the skinny git. (My problem is quite the opposite, of course. I'm prone to constipation. I have a constipated personality too, according to Mother. If I have, how come I suffer from (enjoy?) this galloping logorrhea?)

On or off the throne, Andy's voice was high-pitched and saw-edged and I reached the point where I wanted to scream at him to shut up and maybe listen to *my* problems. However, I reasoned that while he was talking I knew where he was and what he was up to. If I talked, I might relax and he might jump me. He did look sinister in the dim of the tiny blue night-light, which was all that Jimmy had left us. But all he did was girn and girn and girn, like a spiled bairn. Every so often I risked a rational word or two, but that seemed to make him even more infantile. He whined that he would have to go back in front of the Children's Panel (I think that was what he called it) which had sent him away, according to him, for one more-or-less innocent incident with a girl.

'Whit d'ye dae when a girl's beggin ye?' he asked, jumping on to the toilet yet again, and cursing the girl's mother, an auld bag wha was on the game hersel, and wha'd shopped him.

When Andy went on to moan about his faimly I began to recognise some of his problems. He didnae like onybody at hame; his faither was awaa; his mither's fancy-man was a bastard; an his brithers an sisters an the fancy-man's weans aa ganged up on him. He didnae even like his mither much since she tellt the Children's Panel, 'Ach, he's jist like his faither, he cannae keep his hands tae himsel when there's a lassie aboot. He's better awaa.'

He never complained about one thing for long. One minute he was giving me his views on school, which were thoroughly well-founded but incoherent, and the next he was complaining about the lack of money at home. 'It's okay fir you,' he said, 'living in a big hoose, wi plentya money comin in an a joab waitin fir ye.'

A job waiting for *me*? In this town? In this part of the country? In this quarter of the century? He obviously hasn't seen last year's leavers wandering the streets with their ghetto-blasters, wondering why they bothered with so many Highers, and talking about becoming social workers.

And he thinks there's plenty of money coming in! My accent was his only evidence for this, and I'm entitled to use any accent I fancy. Any semblance of rationality I possess abandoned me and I was engulfed by resentment and infantility, just like him.

'You're not the only one with problems,' I blurted out. 'My father . . .' and I told him more about that Principal Teacher of Guidance than I've ever told anyone, even Fiona. She knows without having to be told, anyway. She always *knows*.

'Christ!' said Andy, wiping his bum, 'whit's he like when he's pissed?'

'He never gets drunk.'

'Hoo d'ye get money aff him then?' pulling his pyjama trousers up over his anatomy.

'I don't.' (Well, it's true. I don't. Not 'off' him.)

'Christ!' getting under his blanket again.

There was a silence for a while, during which I pondered the pitiful pittance I receive each Saturday and the miserable clothing allowance I'm given on the first day of each quarter, neither subject to negotiation. Watch my father till he got drunk? I'd wait till doomsday, and beyond.

Andy broke the silence. I wish he'd kept quiet. 'Whaur did ye get yer hunner nicker, then?'

'What do you mean?'

'Ye had a hunner quid when ye were brocht here.'

'What on earth makes you think that?'

'I seen it in the proaperty book when auld Fag-fir-a-feel wisnae lookin.'

'You're a nosey bastard.' (It's the first time I've used that word aloud, except when we read King Lear in class. Honest!)

'An you're a leear wi ten ten-spoats.'

I answered this manifest truth with silence, a reflection of the empty numbness within my head. As a tactic it worked very well, as Andy couldn't thole any silence for long. Neither could I, cooped up in that hole with him and trying to ignore what my nose was telling me, but I could thole it better than he could. He began to talk, in a sad voice, about what it was like to be marked down as a 'sex-offender' by everyone, everywhere he was sent. I'm sure I heard the sadness because I've experienced forty-eight hours of the process myself, from lunatics like Scott and Blaikie and mad craiturs like those girls.

I believed Andy too when he started to speak of the real extent of his sexual experience. At that time of night in that ghastly slammer, and because of the sad way he described it, it didn't sound too thrilling, up dirty closes and in cold empty houses with girls I'm sure were pasty and spotty and smelly and stupid. It didn't only make me sad, it scunnert me. He was no messenger from the old pagan gods, no Hermes bringing me a gift from Aphrodite or Pan. He was just a poor fellow-human with a little technical information I was grateful for and a muckle load of misinformation I could recognise as rubbish, even with my mind at low torque. As a turn-on his talk was worse than the girls' crudities

. . . a thick bearskin rug, the flickering light from a huge log-fire, a fragrant golden Raquel drawing me to her . . . that's how I'm going to be seduced, if I don't go mad first . . .

Back to Andy's chatter. The more I think about it the more fascinating and scunnering I find it. Girls, he implied, stated really, exist to give boys dirty thrills and were to be despised for being willing to do it so readily and so often. Yet they were to be feared too, because their short-term willingness was a kid-on and they had long-term plans for trapping you and skinning you of your buroo-money, if you weren't wise to their ploys.

. . . maybe I'd shrink away if Raquel stroked my hair . . . I don't really like being touched . . .

Girls, continued Andy, were 'snobs' if they did not give the boys what they wanted . . . Really scunnert at myself now, I began to wonder if these weren't my own disgusting views on girls, and on Raquel Welch and Koo Stark too. Somehow Andy's foetid nearness and our shared predicament made it difficult to separate his views from mine. Fiona, of course, is my *pal* and someone else altogether.

(Thank god I've got my little dictionary with me now. I've moved to the library, so I have access to the Shorter O. E. D. too. 'Foetid' is a super word, but not as apt as I'd hoped. I already knew it meant 'stinking', which we both certainly were, only he ponged more than I did, but I thought it was also the adjective from 'foetus' and would hint, in a clever way, that our nearness was like twins in a womb. What a pity! But it's still a word I relish for its nasty nuances. Foetid.)

Andy and I had another silence, which he found so comfortable he fell asleep. I was much less comfortable, and Raquel Welch was fighting Koo Stark for my £100, but eventually I fell asleep too. The time would be 5.30 a.m. at a guess.

We were wakened by Jimmy unlocking the door. 'I've rung the Officer-in-Charge,' he said to me, 'an he's comin across in ten meenits tae get rid o ye. He's no awfu pleased.'

'What time is it?' I asked dopily.

'Five past seeven.'

'Whit aboot me?' demanded Andy in a squeaky voice.

'Ach, ye're jist routine. He'll hae his brakefast afore he has a look at ye,' said Jimmy, chewing away and looking uncertainly from Andy to me. 'I'm awaa. Be seein ye,' he said, and went, leaving me with the realisation that I had lost my contact with a very shrewd and kindly gentleman, who had accepted me for precisely what I am (a mad scribbler with occasional sane interludes) and then given me exactly the treatment I needed, within the limits of the four walls of the slammer and of his duty to keep me there. What condition would I be in without his talks and without this jotter and that ball-point? It doesn't bear thinking about.

Right away, Andy started to work up some resentment, sitting up with his blanket wrapped around him. 'I'll maybe no be here when the Guv comes tae see me.'

'Where would you go?' I asked, pretending I wasn't all choked up about the imminent arrival of the Guv.

'Hame.'

'I thought you didn't like it.' Rational Robb plays it cool.

'I dinnae, but I've got ma pals there, haven't I? You're no refusin the chance tae get hame. Tae yir Dad an aa.'

Somehow I couldn't tell him that it wasn't home I wanted but my one-and-only pal, Fiona. A pal who happened to be a girl wouldn't be in his book.

Andy's mind, if that's what his head contains, changed tack in its sudden way. 'I've tellt ye mair than I've ever tellt onybody. If ye gress on me, I'll come an get ye. An I'll be fir a cut of that hunner quid tae.'

That hundred quid. I'll show him. I grabbed his arm and twisted it up behind his back. We struggled on the bed, his string-and-bone versus my string-and-bone, till I pinned him against the wall. Oh! the relief of action! I gave his arm an extra twist and he grunted. I waited, thinking he would try to throw me off, but he didn't. He couldn't move. I was quite surprised. He's a physical weakling, really. I don't know what the girl, or girls, can have seen in him. Perhaps all the proteins in his diet go straight into building up his what-nots. His genitalia. But they didn't look like much.

'You won't grass on me, will you?' I gritted, like a character in a pulp magazine. Robb the Hard Man Turns on the Heat.

'Naw, ya sexy bastard,' he gasped.

'This is just a friendly fight,' I threatened playfully.

'I ken. That's whit I mean by sexy.'

'You've a one-track mind.' I gave his arm another twist.

'Aargh! Ye cannae deny . . .' gasp! ' . . . that ye're enjoyin yersel.'

'I'm enjoying beating you.'

'That's sexy an aa, stupit.'

I let go his arm, for he was right. I had disgusting stirrings. That's not the truth, Robb, the stirrings were as pleasurable as ever, but their cause was disgusting. Who's a poof now? I wondered, hoping my hormones weren't unbalancing themselves again. How are you supposed to stay sane?

Andy rubbed his arm and grinned at me, the first smile I'd seen on him. 'Got yin tae?' with an unmistakable gesture.

'Naff off,' I said, turning away from him.

'Okay, okay, forget it,' he said, without malice and with due respect. 'Ye're a harder man than me. If I have tae come an get ma cut, I'll bring a shiv. Christ! ma guts.'

As he hopped on to the w. c. for the umpteenth time, his butterfly brain had another change of tack. 'Kin ye no pit a word in fir me?'

'You've just told me not to grass,' I grumbled, 'and anyway who'd listen to me?' I retreated to the farthest end of my bed.

'Educated folk like yersel. The Guv here maybe.'

'But you're going to run as soon as you get a chance.'

'Okay, but maybe I'll no rin sae aften if they lay aff me.'

I wasn't sure I'd have the bottle to put in a word for myself, never mind him, but I was saved from further discussion by the sound of the door being unlocked and then slowly opened. My eyes were pretty well accustomed to the dim blue light, so I could see that the man poking his head in was slightly built, grey-haired and grey-faced. He looked from me on my mattress to Andy on the loo.

'Which of you is ah-mm Robb?' he asked in an English voice.

I raised a finger and he muttered to himself, but my ears are sharp.

'Is sewage really worth all the hassle?' I heard him ask as he opened the door fully and beckoned to me with a steaming coffee mug. I could make out that he was wearing a grubby grey track-suit and scuffed grey training shoes. I threw off the blanket and stood up uncertainly. Why was he talking about sewage? As if in answer to my unspoken question Grey-face buried his nose in the mug and kept it there, like forever. It must have smelled nicer than the effluvia from Andy's rotten guts and from me, sweaty and unwashed and rumpled in the pyjamas I'd been wearing for two days and three nights. Message received, we're the sewage, over and out.

Grey-face lifted his nose and beckoned again. I walked out past him, catching a last glimpse and whiff of Andy, still sitting on the po holding his belly. He grimaced and lifted one hand in a thumbs-up sign, implying, 'Buddies, mind!'

I signalled back as Grey-face locked the door, muttering glumly, 'Lets dispose of the sewage!' He tip-toed off down the blue-lit corridor and past those eerie aquarium windows. My feet were bare, so I didn't have to tip-toe. The heads on the pillows looked exactly the same as when I arrived, as if time had stood still. If it had, the slammer and the radiation-experiments and all that were a momentary dream, a flash of nightmare. Get a grip, I told myself, this man's not the mad scientist who has been irradiating you, but he seems to be mad in other ways.

I've never been so grateful for a double library-period before. There's a good deal of the usual whispering going on around me, but there's no actual *obligation* to find a partner and talk, so I'm scribbling away like mad, full of crazy energy. Underneath, though, I'm exhausted. I'll flop soon.

Barefooting along behind Grey-face I wasn't too successful in getting a grip. In reality, I was panicky and desperate for a pee. Was he the Guv? How could I tell? His back was bowed and made him look weary and depressed and sinister, unlike Mr Scott, whose weekend on duty had made him ever rosier and more cheerful. (Phonies both. Right, Holden?) If Grey-face was the Guv, exactly how was he going to 'get rid' of me, in Jimmy's ambiguous phrase? Back to the police station to 'assist the police in their enquiries'? That sergeant would be keen to pin something on me. The £100 would do for starters. Or was it to be a phone-call to my parents to come and fetch me, followed by a deathly interview, with all sorts of stupid and irrelevant questions asked? And then back home, to those long and hostile silences? That short corridor was certainly the place for panic. By the time we'd traversed it, gone down the stairs and reached the store-room, I was in a fair old froth, my bladder so full I was ready to pee the pyjamas.

Once inside the store, Grey-face locked the door, found my polythene bag and gave me my still damp clothes one by one, wearily ticking off each item in the wee book before handing it over. Needless to say I put them on with the utmost speed.

'Sorry they're ah-mm moist.' he said, 'but the drier's on the ah-mm blink . . . things fall apart, you know . . .'

An apology to the sewage, I thought apprehensively, whatever next?

Keeping quiet is the best plan when adults say they're sorry.You never know what they're up to. He gave me my hankie, my key and my 3¹/₂p. Then he fished out my C.N.D. badge, squinted at it and handed it over. Next, he held up the crisp packet, looking in the approximate direction of my face. 'Jimmy tells me you attend the seat of learning known as . . . ah-mm?' and he named my school.

'Yessir!' I said, acting the perfect schoolboy.

'You'll be sitting A Levels?'

'Highers in Scotland, sir!' It came out automatically.

'Ah-mm, Highers, quite so.' A suggestion of frost reminded me not to get cocky. 'Which "Highers" are you sitting?'

I told him politely, but I'm dammed if I'll write them down here. The Scottish Education Department computer has stored them in its data-bank already. I hope it gets maggots in its mainframe, *and* syphilis in its software.

'Quite the little ah-mm polymath?' I kept my mouth shut. 'This address you gave Jimmy, is it ah-mm?'

'Yessir!' He had my name and address! Jimmy had grassed. Or done his duty. Whichever, I was now standing to attention, overdoing the rigidity out of panic and the need to hold on to my pee. He could look up the phone-book. He could . . .

'Ah-mm, very residential. Very popular with the ah-mm professional classes. Definitely C.N.D. territory. No sewage in evidence.' He paused, then spoke very fast. 'There'll be no need to enquire into this, then?' meaning the £100 inside the packet he was still holding up.

My head jerked like a puppet's and he handed over the packet so quickly it was like a conjuring trick. Almost as quickly, for I was hampered by my agonised bladder, I put the thing away without opening it. I could feel that the notes were still there, though. I'll just lose it somewhere, I decided.

From the store Grey-face took me to an office just off the foyer. It would be his, I suppose, if he really was the Guv. He sat me clammily on a hard chair, sighed, walked to the desk and laid down his mug, now empty. Then he looked out of the window, where a dank football pitch could be seen in the dull light of dawn. He sighed again, like the End of the World is Nigh.

I vowed I was going to write about reality and not phantasy, but if I write down what Grey-face actually said at this point it'll read as if I'd made him up out of my own fevered imaginings, influenced by my screaming bladder. And how can I describe the faint but unmistakable sensation I had that I might be the sane one, confronted with his mournful maunderings?

'New problems,' he was saying, still looking out of the window, 'why did I ever think "never a dull moment"? New problems are as deadly as old problems. This place is a stagnant pool, with raw ah-mm sewage *swilling* in one end and untreated sewage ah-mm *oozing* out of the other. Every so often a filthy great bubble surfaces and bursts and there's a splash and a stink in the papers. Then it's back to festering stagnation again. Why don't I break out? There must be a New Life. . . back down ah-mm South . . . a new squaw . . .'

I stayed on the edge of the chair, ready for anything. He went mumbling on and on, dropping his voice till I couldn't hear him at all. The wastepaper basket was next to my chair and I was thinking of dropping the crisp packet into it when he turned away from the window and spoke audibly, 'Back to sewage disposal.'

'Sir?'

'Will your parents have reported you ah-mm missing?'

'It's highly unlikely,' I answered. Report me missing? You don't know my parents! 'Sir,' I added hurriedly.

His grey countenance lightened for a second or two, then darkened again as he returned to looking at the football field.

'You realise that I have no obligation ah-mm whatso*ever* to inform them of your sojourn in the sewage here?'

'I suppose not, sir,' I said, trying to sound neutral while my hopes dared to rise a little.

'Will you be ah-mm *discussing* where you have been with them?'

'Oh no, sir.' *Discuss* with my parents! That'll be the day! 'We don't communicate at that level, sir.'

His face brightened again and he became conspiratorial, almost chummy. 'I should warn you that the police have no ah-mm glad feelings about your signing that ah-mm . . .' He lowered his voice to a whisper. 'I'd keep out of their clutches if I were you. Otherwise . . .' and he made a lugubrious throat-cutting gesture.

'I'll do that, sir,' I said, my hopes rising further.

Grey-face now picked up a paper from his desk, holding it as if it was impure. He handed it to me and I found it was a hastily typed statement that my being locked up was entirely my own fault and that all my property had been returned to me undamaged. He asked me to sign it, leering greyly. Should I? I couldn't think clearly. I couldn't think period. Fiona, with her analytical mind, would have known straight off what to do. Holden would have used his world-weary wisdom. But me, I'm muddled, even if sane compared to Grey-face. I looked up from the paper and he was drooping there, holding out a pen.

'You'll let me out? I asked, without meaning to.

'Ah-mm, yes, provided . . . ah-mm . . .'

I realise now that he'd probably have gone down on his knees to have me sign, but at the time I was in such a tizzy that I thought I was in the supplicant's position. Obediently, I signed. Suddenly, Grey-face was full of energy.

'Terribly terribly sorry about all that sewage nonsense, my dear chap, but Monday mornings are absolute hell, aren't they?' He thrust some small change into my hand. 'That'll do for your bus-fare.' He rushed me out of the room and across the foyer to the front door. He unlocked it smartly and fresh air and freedom poured over me, reminding me somehow that Andy was still locked up in that black hole. Loyalty matters to me — let the trumpet sound! — and I had half-promised to put in a word for him. This would be my only chance. I stopped in the doorway, mastering courage.

'Sir!' I said, 'Andy MacPhail, sir.'

'NO! NO! NO! A complaint about him would really make my day. What did he do?' No ah-mms now.

'No complaint, sir. I . . .'

Grey-face briskly shoved me out of the doorway and almost closed the door. 'What then, if you've no complaint?' he asked through the crack.

'He's being driven crazy by . . .'

'Good god, man, aren't we all? Don't you want your breakfast?'

'Yessir, but, sir . . .'

'Look here, Robb, I have twenty-five other boys, all saying sir! sir! sir! and not meaning it, and ten fornicating girls, all trying to seduce the boys.' His face was darkly flushed and his eyes glared redly. 'Grey-face' indeed! 'MacPhail's not my fornicating responsibility at all.' He paused, then added, like a rapier thrust, 'Nor is your fornicating hundred pounds.'

I could only stand like a zombie while he locked the door and strode away manfully on the balls of his feet without a backward glance at me through the glass. Eventually I turned away, the 'fresh' air just plain cold and raw and feeling as if it was polluted with radioactive fall-out. Freedom, as it turned out, was nothing but one disaster after another.

It's Friday evening and I've locked myself in my room with no intention of coming out till I have to. I've stocked up on coke and crisps and I've 'borrowed' a can of bully-beef and some bread and butter.

As I said, my release from the Assessment Centre was followed by a catalogue of disasters. They have been so frightful that I'm not sure I can write about them at all. I'm terrified, too, that more may be on the way. So if I'm going to write anything I must discipline myself somehow. De la discipline, camarade!

Perhaps it would help if I made an actual catalogue of the disasters, with annotations and comments. Mother reckons that if you make a list of your troubles you'll find that two-thirds of them don't really exist — I wonder where I come on her latest list? If I'm no trouble to her, I don't exist, do I?

Firstly, I was caught peeing in that bus shelter by Mrs Brown, the dinner lady I've known and liked very much all my school career. When I left the Assessment Centre I was bursting and there was nowhere but this empty shelter with a big graffiti sign saying PEE HERE and an arrow pointing to the corner. Mrs Brown isn't a lady to keep her mouth shut. I like her, but does she like me? She didn't say anything, but she looked really shocked.

Secondly, my family, always a disaster area, but worse than ever now. What they've done, all of them, is to pretend that nothing has happened; that I was not absent for three nights; and that I didn't turn up on Monday morning looking rumpled and unwashed and ghastly. There have been no stupid questions; no stony silences either. Father banters heavily as usual, Mother worries as always, sister criticises and brother is okay except when sister is present and then he joins in her criticisms. Nothing has changed. No one has taken any notice. I have what are called, I think, 'feelings of unreality'. I could use a kid sister like Phoebe.

Thirdly, Fiona. (It's easier to write that pidgin-Gaelic pseudonym than her real and much more beautiful Greek name.) When I met her at school on Monday morning she was furious with me for not being at the disco on Saturday. The kids had got out of hand and they really needed a man (me!) to control them. Joe was there but isn't a man, it seems, despite the latest rumour that someone's named him in a paternity suit. Fiona looked so beautiful in her anger that I now get a pain every time I think of her, a real physical pain, like indigestion, and that's not a joke, it's not even remotely funny. I can barely breath, let alone write, when I remember her dark eyes glistening, surrounded by those fabulous eye-lashes, so long they might be false, which they're not. And she regards me as, insists that I am, a man!

Fourthly (after a long gap when I couldn't write at all), this jotter, my passport to millions, ha! ha! The only non-disaster that has happened is that Jimmy dropped it through the letter-box in a plain brown envelope addressed in shaky block letters. That was on Monday morning. However, I've been owing Auld Baldy an essay for weeks and when he saw it on my desk on Monday afternoon he just assumed it was my essay, grabbed it and took it away to mark. There was nothing I could do but wait till he gave it back this afternoon. Here is his red-ink comment, complete with the alliterations he criticises when I use them:

'I must say I find your use of Scots and slang words scarcely apposite, your obscenities and profuse profanities profoundly distasteful, and your delving into depravity deeply disturbing. I cannot accept this as an assignment for an assessment and must insist that you show it to your Teacher of Guidance. He may be able to help you in ways that I cannot. (Incidentally, the 'diamond words' you attribute to Crichton Smith, whoever he is, are a misquotation from Shakespeare. Always check your references.)'

Fifthly, Holden. With my jotter in Baldy's keeping, I found I couldn't write at all, so I tried to re-read *The Catcher in the Rye* — for the fourth or fifth time I reckon. I tried for three nights running, but I just couldn't read it. Holden isn't like me at all. For one thing, his style is so *consistent,* while I have trouble keeping the same style going for more than a page or two. For another, he likes Hitchcock's *Thirty-Nine Steps,* the phoniest movie ever. For yet another, he's so *cool* about girls, while I have this *burning pain* every time I think about the only girl who matters. Maybe I'm in love. If I am, it's something neither Holden nor Salinger warned me about, the idiots.

Sixthly, Raquel Welch/Koo Stark. I can't raise them at all. Every time I try to, I see Fiona's dark hair swinging as she turned her angry back on me — I smell its clean dark scent too. I suppose it isn't a disaster to have got rid of those two baggages (who have no scent of course) but there's no *comfort* in my thoughts about Fiona.

Seventhly, Andy MacPhail. I feel bad about not being able to help him, but the feeling is wearing off, to be honest. The disaster is that I can't stop wondering what he meant by calling Jimmy 'Auld Fag-fir-a-feel'. At first I thought he was referring to Mister Blaikie, but now I've realised that Jimmy was the only adult in the building when Andy was admitted. Jimmy a queer? I don't believe it! But Andy was street-wise . . . I'm confused. Maybe it's a nickname for Night Supervisors? I may never know.

Eighthly, that money. It's still the same old disaster/mystery. I haven't checked to see if it's still in my jeans because I've stuffed them as far behind the wardrobe as I can and then piled some old magazines on top. Mother may find them at spring-cleaning time. If she doesn't, where will they be?

Ninthly, I've missed that chance of a job in a printer's, which is what I want more than anything else I can think of. I want to start on the shop-floor and work up to executive level as quickly as I can, but the Teacher of Guidance point-blank refused to give me a reference, which the printing firm made a big thing of. He pointed out that there were twenty other chaps with 'O' Grades (and no chance of Highers) in line for the job and it would be a waste of my undeniable but under-used talents, etc., etc. In my present state of mind I haven't the heart to complain to the Rector and I couldn't possibly discuss the matter with my moribund parents, so Highers and Sixth Year Studies and Honours English and graduate unemployment are the prison-house prospects for me. Being a millionaire sci-fi writer is just an adolescent phantasy I've grown out of.

Tenthly, nuclear war. The disaster is that it isn't going to happen quickly enough for me. I'd settle right now for the Four Minute Warning, time to rush out into the garden and gaze at the sky, the flash, and an end to it all. Just to be logical, or maybe not, I've tried to pin my C.N.D. badge to my blazer, with some idea that I should stand up and be counted, but my fingers paralyse themselves. I'm a madman.

Lastly, this diarrhoea. I probably caught it from Andy MacPhail, if it isn't an early symptom of radiation sickness. As it wasn't improving, and the dunt on my head was still hurting a bit, I went to the doctor earlier this evening. To cut a long story short, I emerged from the surgery with a prescription for the squitters, an X-ray appointment for first thing tomorrow morning, and the promise of an appointment with a shrink. I don't want my parents to see even the outside of the shrink's appointment letter, so I'll have to intercept the post every single morning till it comes. The doctor said that my parents needn't know about the psychiatrist unless he insists, and even then I can simply opt out of the treatment if I want to. So I'm in the same boat as Holden. Who doesn't exist. Yes, he does, for I'm hanging on to the Holden in my head and sod Salinger — in his pent-house, or behind his piranha-infested moat, or wherever he is.

What am I going to tell the shrink? That I accumulate money and can't account for it? That I'm prone to inexplicable disasters? That I'm hoping that the ultimate (nuclear) disaster will happen quickly? That I'm wishing I was out of this room of mine, away from the pains I get when I think about Fiona, and back on the by-pass under the leadership of the dark boy-god? With his charisma and my brains we would soon be running a real outfit, dealing in thousands in Swiss bank-accounts and not tens of tenners in potato-crisp bags. Then I could go and find Holden, the real Holden, in Ernie's night-club, if he's been let out of that what's-it place.

Most of all, though, dear shrink, I'd like to settle for the radiation experiments and go back to that slammer, in the middle of the Archipelago. I'd scribble away with half an ear cocked for Jimmy, dear couthy conscientious Jimmy, padding along the corridor with his piece-box and his flask. How much madder can I get than that? You tell me, before we're all nuked.

Fiona Scribbling

Andy,

Why the hell did you try to kiss me in that stupid way? You smelled disgusting, as if you hadn't washed for a week, and you certainly hadn't shaved since the day before yesterday. I like men to have some consideration for me when they take me out and the longer I sit here at the kitchen table and think about your other insensitive behaviour, the colder I become. I am *not* the girl you knew at school and I am *not* available for that kind of kissing . . .

Fiona, that's more explanation than he deserves. Start a new sheet. No, that would be a waste of good drawing paper . . .

Saturday. 4.50 a.m.

Dear Andy,

I've changed my mind about going out with you to Ballyhillock, as I would have to be back in time for . . .

Wrong again. That's about as sensible as telling him the date is with his old adversary Joe, and is the one when you issue him with his weekly ration . . . Why don't you just tell the wimp exactly how you see last night's happenings? That should sort him out . . .

Saturday. 5.15 a.m.

Andy,

That phone call yesterday was a surprise. It was our first contact since you left for Edinburgh University three years ago.

'Fiona?' you asked.

'Hi, Joe!' I answered.

'It's Andy.'

'You?' I snapped, irritated at mistaking your gravelly voice for darling Joe's. 'Who do you want to speak to?'

'Can I come and pick you up?'

Pick me up? Just like that? Who does he think he is?

'Fiona?'

'Yes.'

'Can I come right now?'

What's his hurry? I said to myself, still irritated. If he's made it up with his family, he'll be home for a long weekend at least before he starts a vacation job and I might just agree to have one drink with him when I'm good and ready. If he hasn't made up that quarrel, I don't want to know. He'd be a waste of time. Put him off . . .

'What's the idea?' I asked edgily.

'Let's have a drink at Annie's, if it's as quiet as it used to be. I need to talk.'

Fancy that, I thought. About you-know-who, I bet.

'I'll be round in five minutes,' you said, taking my silence for consent and hanging up. In two minutes the door-bell rang and there you were. You glanced shiftily at my face for a fraction of a second and then away again. You neither spoke nor smiled. My irritation swelled to anger and rose in a lump in my throat, for you hadn't given me time to change out of my really much too ragged painting jeans or to invent a story that would satisfy Mum and Dad and Morag, who are all in Joe's fan-club, especially Morag, the little clype. Though why I should need a cover-story for going out with you I can't imagine. I'm a free agent, a consenting adult, etc. What is a girl supposed to do?

I swallowed most of my anger and answered your silence with silence and jumped straight into your nasty rusty cramped old Morris 1000. God, it smelled rank, and so did you. Unlike Joe, who is always wrapped in several layers of manly toiletries. If you'd started one of those oh-so-boring justifications for having an old car, I'd have demanded to be taken home again.

However, you stayed quiet, and I calmed down enough to be able to take in that you were a grotty student version of the shy, sly, po-faced, skinny, carroty-curly-haired Andy who has been such a contrast to roly-poly dark-haired outgoing me ever since we were small. You were wearing a sweat-stained blue shirt (which *did* match your eyes) and shapeless tan cord trousers. They suited you marginally better than the drab navy-and-grey school uniform you're always wearing in my rather dim mental picture of you, and you seemed to have lost most of your pimples, but you still didn't look like the answer to any kind of maiden's prayer. In fact . . .

5.25 a.m.

Darling Joe,

Please believe me that you have nothing to fear from my going out with Andy. He's like left-over adolescent acne, while *you* are a man, my real man. See you this evening, my poppet, all of you . . .

5.35 a.m.

Andy,

You again! Writing to you about you is like touching a broken tooth with my tongue. Sitting over a beer in the crappy brown and crimson of Annie's I had to use all my social skills to get you to open your mouth. And you were the one who wanted to talk! Still, you did eventually thaw out, though not into the merriest of companions. You asked serious questions about my painting and whether I'd tried any other media at College. You listened (yes! listened!) as I explained that I'm starting teacher-training in the autumn as my modest talent isn't enough to earn me a living as an artist.

'That's all shit,' you said suddenly and earnestly.

'But it's true. I'm not good enough.'

'You're kidding yourself and it's not like you. You want to do something else.'

'I'm not kidding myself. I've *got* to paint.'

'But you haven't *got* to pretend you're teaching art to schoolkids. They teach themselves. Be honest, Fiona.'

'But, Andy . . .' Why did I tell mournful you, of all people? My secret crazy ambition is to be an art therapist in a prison or a mental hospital or both. I saw it on TV and contacted the local hospital and helped out for a term. I didn't tell anyone at all. 'I got such a kick out of shut-in people revelling in the materials. And the way they responded to the colours, it was fantastic!'

You turned your head away and started to mutter, which wasn't

127

good for my fragile temper.

'. . . the way they'll . . . your sexiness . . . fantastic . . . male wards you mean . . .'

'Be serious, for god's sake.'

'. . . being serious . . .'

At this, I became all muddled up with panic, for my sensitive Joe isn't in on the secret and it would upset him. Me working among nut-cases and lifers, he couldn't make it fit. As his wife, neither could I, and he's so comfortable, so safe, and we've made a lot of plans, including a honeymoon surfing in Hawaii. And I'm to design and colour co-ordinate every single item in his office when his father takes him into partnership next year. I don't want to lose him. Back off.

'I don't suppose I'd be any good,' I said, 'and anyway it was only a passing thought. Don't think it matters.'

'. . . you'd be terrific . . . healing sort of person . . .'

'First I was sexy, now I'm healing. Who's talking shit now?'

You flicked your eyes to mine in the shifty way that I remember only too well.

'. . . not inconsistent . . .' you mumbled.

I decided to change the subject. It was more difficult than it used to be to get you to talk about yourself and your plans, but I kept up the pressure and you eventually admitted that you wanted to give up Honours English right now, with only a year to go. This is the problem you wanted to talk to me about. You are longing to be the third partner in one of those tiny Edinburgh firms who print and publish little magazines and Lallans poetry and kinky posters for the Fringe and other rubbish, but you can't make up your mind, your so-called mind. Typical. The other two are urging you to join them and you're sure you could work with them. Your indecision made my anger surface again. Joe knows exactly where he's going and what he's going to do *and* he smells nice.

'Don't mess about,' I said. 'Do it.'

'. . . no security . . .'

'To hell with security, you need experience.'

'. . . no degree . . .'

'Finish it later. Are you still writing your own stuff?'

' . . . doesn't seem to be . . . '

'That's wicked! Wicked! Pack in honours and do what you really want.'

Your face was getting more and more numb, Here's one shut-in person who's not responding to me, I thought.

'Take me home!' I demanded, ready to blast you out of your seat this time if you tried excuses for your car's age, but you said nothing. You're good at that. But of course I wasn't being too healing, was I?

When we arrived Dad and Mum had gone to bed and there was no sign of the Blessed Virgin Morag. Purely out of politeness, I invited you in and you agreed with a half-hearted nod, so we went into the kitchen, as we used to in our teens. You said you'd have cocoa, so I banged about and slopped it into two mugs and made a mess and wiped it up and we were drinking the stuff awkwardly at the table when Morag appeared at the door in all the cool pride of her seventeen years, and her film-star face, and her ravishing figure, and her clothes that always fit.

'Oh, I do beg your pardon, I thought it would be Joe,' she said in her bitchiest voice and posing like a half-witted model.

'Come in and don't be silly,' I said. 'You know Andy.'

'Indeed I do,' she murmured sexily, as if the words were loaded with innuendo. She didn't look at you.

'Andy, you remember Morag,' I said inanely.

'Yes,' you said, squinting in her general direction with inhuman blankness. Unlike Joe, who has to look away and lick his lips and shift about in his seat. All hairy warmth, all manly man, my Joe, thank God.

'I know when I'm not wanted,' said Morag archly, and left us, closing the door behind her with elaborate care.

'She always talks in clichés,' I said.

'She *is* a cliché,' you said, ' . . . hard on the poor girl . . . big sister who's twice as . . . ' you looked into my eyes, almost, ' . . . three times as . . . '

I decided not to hear your meaning and started to chatter about our

129

schooldays, which seemed so long ago they weren't anything to be embarrassed about. You responded really quite eagerly, and after a while we were able to talk about our careers in a rational manner and when we'd exhausted them as a topic we went back to our schooldays. When the blackbirds started to sing and we had to notice the dawn you were in the middle of telling me about that mysterious 'lost weekend' I'd almost forgotten. You just disappeared from home, which you were in the habit of doing, understandably enough, one Friday evening and you weren't seen again until school on Monday morning. Nobody could find out where you'd been and you looked simply dreadful — green and ill and drained. I fantasised that you'd found an older woman and been initiated and sucked dry, like the adolescent hero in a French novel, but when I tried to probe you were so rude that I ended our childhood friendship with a fierce slap on the face, the first and last time I've done that to a man.

When you'd finished telling me about that top-secret weekend and how you'd had your stupid self locked up in the local jail in the same cell as some poor idiot of a sex-maniac, the sun started to pour horizontal rays of pure tangerine through the kitchen window behind your head. They turned your straggly hair and the ginger stubble on your chin into a million unpaintable points of light and I had to get rid of you.

'It's time you went, Andy,' I said . . .

Saturday 6 a.m.

Joe my pet,

I'm full of thoughts of you and your warmth and your cheerful smile and your ceremonial seduction of me every Saturday . . . I don't suppose you've ever run away from anything in your life. You wouldn't be my rock if you had . . . and you *are* my rock . . . there's nothing unstable about you . . . and I love you . . .

Saturday

Andy,

Why didn't you just shut up and go away when I told you your

130

time was up?

'It's going to be a scorcher of a day,' you insisted on saying. 'Let's go out to Ballyhillock and climb the Ben before it gets too hot.'

'Now?'

'Okay, let's have a wee sleep first. I'll come at eight.'

The kitchen clock was saying 4.30, so you were proposing only three hours sleep. In other words, I told myself, he's still as daft as ever. Get rid of him, now. NOW. I stood up.

'Out,' I said

'Packed lunch?' you asked as I shooed you into the hallway.

'Just you come at eight and you'll find out what I have ready for you.' I clenched a fist at you. What did I mean by these words and that action? What did you think I meant? As always, uncertainties multiply when you're on the scene.

At the front door, as you weren't leaving quickly enough, I gave your bony form a good shove and you turned and half-succeeded in kissing me, which wasn't very original of you. It was upsetting behaviour too, for I haven't slept at all, I've been writing all this ridiculous nonsense and thinking that your girl-friends must have been hard-up if they were satisfied with *that* kind of kiss . . .

Saturday 9 a.m.

My Darling Joe,

I'd better be honest with you and tell you that I *was* going out to Ballyhillock with Andy this morning, but there was some doubt about the arrangements and he hasn't come for me. Meanwhile I've had to cope with Mum and I think you're entitled to know the line she's been taking. As you know, she is a very powerful person, even though I have pretended to take no notice of her since I was fourteen or thereabouts. The way you pretend to defer to her is just part of your act and nothing to do with me. Just wait till you really have to deal with her.

When she found me in the kitchen just now she was dragging on her early morning cigarette as if it was the only thing in the world that mattered. She peered at me and all my preparations for a hill-walk.

'Someone new?' she asked. 'Already?'

'Miaow!'

'Miaow yourself! He's overtaking Joe in the fast lane, whoever he is.'

We looked each other in the eyes. An unusual happening, signalling a female-to-female transaction. Our first in years. I've still got the claw-marks from the last one. It was before your time, darling.

'Mum. Stop there, right there, before you say something even sillier.'

'It's someone I know,' Mum said, stubbing out her cigarette half-smoked. Another unusual happening.

'If it was, how could it matter?'

'It could, if it was Andy Robb.'

'Morag's wasted no time, as usual. Not that there's any kind of secret.' (Which there isn't, of course. I'm going to phone you about it in a minute, sweetie.)

'Morag's said nothing to me, but Joe doesn't like bully-beef and tomato sandwiches, does he? Half a chicken, salade nicoise, and french bread for him.'

'We didn't have a definite arrangement. I mightn't bother going. He's a bit of a bore, anyhow. So solemn.'

'Still the same old Andy effect. You look stunning in that dress.'

(I'm wearing that horrible jazzy dishcloth dress you don't like. You know, the one I dyed and designed myself, with the ragged sleeves and hem-line. You were polite about it, but I could see you thought it made me look tarty as well as arty. Don't worry, I'll stick to the clothes you like when I'm out with you.)

'He was supposed to be coming at eight if he was coming at all.'

'An hour late, that's Andy. Where was he *supposed* to be taking you?'

'Ballyhillock was his idea.'

'Fiona!'

There were, and are, all sorts of implications in Mum's tone of voice as she said my name, for it reinforced a suspicion I've harboured for years that I was conceived in the heather out there.

(This is supposed to be a letter to Joe, but I wouldn't dream of telling him that. Yet I must admit I might just say it to Andy, as a sister-to-brother confidence.)

'It's the right kind of day for an easy climb,' I said.

'Joe for security,' Mum pondered, 'and Andy for kicks. I wouldn't mind that solution myself. Especially the Andy bit.'

'I'm not that kind. I didn't think you were.'

'Oh, I could be, I could be. But *you* are making a choice?'

'Mum. Stop making things up. There *is* no choice. Andy's like a brother. You know that as well as I do.'

(But when I tried to phone you just now, Joe darling, you had already left for your cricket match. Why are you always so punctual? You could have been a tiny bit late, just for once.)

'Sticking to Joe avoids a problem,' Mum said.

'Mum. *Listen*. There *is* no problem.'

'Andy may be like a brother to you, but he's far from being Dad's idea of a son.'

Speechless, I looked into Mum's eyes. Something naked showed in them for a moment, then vanished.

'Make up your mind then,' she said, 'Security or fun. Or both, if you're clever enough. Give me two cups of that tea, it'll be too stewed for Andy now, and I'll go back up to Dad. That boy might be too much for my self-control. If he turns up, that is. He was always a bolter, wasn't he?'

Joe, you can imagine how I'm longing for you and your reliability, what with brother Andy letting me down and Mum pressuring me in that perverse way. You and my Daddy are the people I like, big and strong and straight and understanding and predictable and businesslike. . .

Well after midnight.

Dear Andy,

I don't know what on earth to make of yesterday's happenings, the highs and the lows and the in-between uncertainties. I've tried drawing with my charcoal and painting with my acrylics, but neither is a comfort, so I'm back in bed scribbling.

I suppose it was in character for you to be so dour this morning when you arrived nearly two hours late for our rather indefinite date. I didn't reproach you with being late and you offered no excuses. I had to endure Mum's leers and Dad's glowers while I gave you breakfast. In return, I received nothing but grunts and monosyllables and finickiness about food. Why am I doing this? I asked myself several times without getting any kind of rational answer.

Even when we drove off in your ancient Morris you didn't act like a brotherly brother, or indeed like any kind of human being with an inbuilt need to communicate. You drove with fierce concentration, as if every kerb was a precipice and every other vehicle was driven by a maniac. If you had been anyone else I think I would have talked you into relaxing, but what could I say to that profile of yours? So I, yes I Fiona Phimister, stayed silent for the whole drive.

When we arrived at Ballyhillock you parked the car on the level patch of turf just beyond the bridge, where the road changes into a landrover track. You jumped out of the car, swung on the pack and looked around the glen, which was as featureless as ever of course, and up at the Ben, the one our families have always liked because no one else but shepherds bothers to climb it. Then you looked straight at me for a second and spoke your first sentence.

'That dress, is it practical?'

'It's cool, and there's no wind to blow the skirt up.'

What was the sense in offering an answer like that? I wasn't quite in control of myself. Your response was to set off up the Ben as if we were in a race.

The day was airless and increasingly hot, so I could take no pleasure in the act of walking through heather and tussocky grass as I toiled to keep up with you. As the going became steeper I began to be really cross about the pace you were setting. I felt as if you were running away and I was being forced, or manipulated, into chasing after you. My anger about your lateness this morning was simmering away underneath too, so it's just as well you didn't stop and speak to me, or I might have said or done something I don't like to think about. As I said, my self-control was a bit dicey.

When you did eventually flop down on your face on a gentle slope of grass half-way to the summit, I seated myself very properly six feet away and with my back to you. I was beginning to regret the thickness of my odd hockey stockings, one purple and one red, so I rolled them as far down as they would go. But I was careful to pull my skirt over my knees. I was beginning to wonder how long I was going to have to sit like this when I heard the oddest sound, so out-of-place I couldn't make it out at all. I turned my head. You were sound asleep and snoring loudly.

I wish I could write that you looked as innocent and defenceless as a baby and all that guff. You didn't. You looked and sounded like a thoroughly nasty little boy who needed a clout on the ear to teach him manners. Joe would never have asked me to climb the Ben, hill-walking would bore him, but if he had he would have been fussing round me and making me feel fragile and precious. I didn't want you reminding me by your brotherlike behaviour that I'm well able to look after myself, as strong as a short-coupled pony and as tough as an old leather bag. I was also perfectly capable of carrying on climbing after you'd tired yourself out by rushing. To prove it, I actually rose to my feet and climbed upwards for a few steps, but something made me look back at you and bang! there and then, without the slightest warning, it hit me like a blow, a stunning sickening blow between the eyes, that you were my one and only, my very very own nasty little boy. Yes, it happened, it happened, the *coup de foudre*, every soppy teenager's dream, and it had to be you, grotty Andy Robb of all people, as if the world wasn't full of lovely lovely men.

Why am I hurting like this? Aren't I supposed to be the happy liberated child of the sexual revolution, to whom falling in love is all familiar warmth and uninhibited ecstasy? But here I am, like some inhibited, repressed, virginal spinster from way way back in the 1950s who can't recognise the joys of falling in love when she is in the middle of them, and only knows about the falling, falling, falling . . .

Back on the hillside, I turned away from you and the pain you were causing me.

I closed my eyes and by an effort of will changed your image back into my childhood friend, the proverbial spotty boy-next-door I know far too well to have any romantic notions about. That took a while, but when I had succeeded I decided it was time you woke up and we carried on with our brother-and sister outing. If I woke you gently everything would be fine.

I opened my eyes, stepped back down the slope, and was just about to wake you with a touch on your shoulder, when, yes, it happened again. The pain was so excruciating this time that I wanted to kick you awake with my walking shoe, right in your ribs, and shout, 'Wake up! Take some notice! I love you!' But I daren't, of course, for I might have cracked some of those ribs. But oh my darling Andy, I was also desperate to wrap my arms tenderly round you, but I couldn't, for I might have discovered that you didn't want me. I had no real reason to believe you did. How my arms ached, like that girl's in *Weir of Hermiston*, round the emptiness where you should have been!

So I was trapped. There was no way in which I could express my feelings. I had to lie down, as near to you as I dared, and look at the tall clouds, the irrelevant tall clouds, one of which was obscuring the sun, the irrelevant sun. The tumult of my feelings died down, very slowly, to the point where I was able to join you in sleep, lulled by the chirping of grasshoppers and the scent of wild thyme. They were irrelevant too, but comforting.

Oh Andy, we *are* going to see each other tomorrow, aren't we? And you won't have changed, will you? Your eyes will still be the blue they've always been, with that suspicion of a squint? Your freckles still the same semi-transparent Highland-Cream-Toffee colour? Your lips still those two thin red lines, hesitant and wolfish at the same time? Your two front teeth still crooked in that heart-stopping way?

I was wakened from that sleep by a grizzled and dirty old blackface ewe saying 'baa!' to her two middle-aged grey lambs.

136

They smelled sickeningly of mutton and sheep-dip. The day was still warm but had clouded over completely and I was thirsty and headachey and miserable. I looked at my watch. I'd slept for three hours, but you were still unconscious. Maybe you hadn't slept the night before last — I'm sure neither of us slept last night.

I sat up and the sheep ran away, with a bobbing of revolting tails. As for you, you'd slid down the slope a little and lay untidily, with your trousers twisted up into your crutch, revealing spindly legs and socks that didn't match. Your shirt was twisted too, right up under your armpits, baring an anaemic-looking torso and half a bony chest. Only your left hand, stretched out palm downwards, looked like something that might want to relate to me. It was a handsome knuckly hand, quite small of course, its whiteness and freckles set off subtly by the finest of gold hairs, but it didn't justify the rest of you. You'd ruined my relationship with Joe, for whatever happens he isn't one of my options any more, and now it looked as if you weren't going to replace it with anything. The way you were lying there suggested that you didn't want me at all. Perhaps it was me that was doing all the wanting (and oh I wanted you, and I want you now!) and your awkwardness was just the way you were made and nothing to do with a banked-down furnace of desire for me. A bare drab prospect, like the glen in front of me now that the sunshine had gone. A prospect of my sexiness — don't be modest, Fiona — my marvellous talent for sex being doled out in cheap parcels to Joe — but he's not one of your options, remember? — to a procession of strangers, then, one lonely stranger after another.

At this depressing point in my thoughts you woke, stretched, scratched your navel, straightened your clothes and squinted at me blankly, almost as you'd looked at Morag. Dully, I unpacked our picnic lunch and without a word we drank all the tepid orange juice and ate a sandwich each. I was wanting to go home, but I didn't know how to say it to you. I thought of using my Saturday night date with Joe as an excuse, but I didn't want to think about him either. If there was to be loneliness, I wanted to meet it right away, alone.

Before I'd finished packing away the left-over sandwiches you took off downhill, leaving me to carry the pack. I was so fed up I wasn't even angry about being the beast of burden who had to follow you. You stopped to wait for me at the bottom of the glen, the dreariest part of the dreary scene — dull grass, dull green bracken, grey rocks and messy boggy places that had no colour at all. When I caught up with you, you were standing beside the burn, which was the same poor thing as ever, its brown water sliding over slimy stones and between crumbling peat-hags. It looked coolish, though, so I handed you the pack, took off my shoes and stockings and slung them round my neck and stepped in. You watched me with your face more shut that I'd ever seen it.

I paddled downstream, with you following morosely on the bank, till I came to a point where the water slipped over a peat wall into a big dark pool. I had to leave the burn, jump down the wall and squelch back in. I wriggled my toes in the semi-liquid peat at the edge, then inched forward till I found a gravelly bottom, just deep enough for my skirt to trail in the water. The deepest part of the pool, guinness-black and inviting, seemed to be under the fall. I looked round the great bowl of hills and there was no one to be seen except you, standing absolutely still. Should I wade further in, lifting my skirt? A show of thigh didn't seem too appropriate and I clearly remember making a conscious decision against it. What I did do was not the result of any decision I can recall.

'Go away,' I told you, 'I'm having a bathe. I'll not be long.'

You retired into some tall bracken and I made a bundle of my clothes and threw them on to the bank. I lay down on my tummy and eased myself over the gravel to the deepest part. Suddenly, a tiny spring of happiness welled up inside me. I rolled over and found I could sit up to my neck in the water, with the fall dribbling deliciously through its bright green slime on to my hair. Its gentle caressing assured me and reassured me that I was beautiful, Morag or no Morag, so my happiness was nourished and grew and grew and grew until I had to share it. I had to reach out to you, for your silence and stillness were saying that you were alone too, and I couldn't bear that. I'll make it worth your while not to bolt, I was planning, deep down inside me.

'Andy!' I called out, 'come on in! It's heaven!'

I had to call again before you consented to emerge from the bracken, swatting at flies and even more expressionless than when you went in. You gazed at me from ten feet away, then down at the ground, then back at me.

'Tank,' you said, reviving a rude nickname from our primary school days and speaking in a very strange voice, 'we should be living together.'

'You're probably right,' my happiness said, setting alight a catherine wheel of fierce joy inside me before I could control it.

Instantly, your face changed to a white so white that all your freckles showed; then, slowly, to scarlet with white patches by your nostrils; then, slowly, to an overall putty with weird crimson-purple blotches. Your unsteady breathing filled a long pause, while my catherine wheel fizzed and sparkled.

'Would you really?' you eventually asked.

'Would I really what, Stick?' I asked, more defensively, but unable to prevent the old counter-insult from popping up from its long-forgotten corner.

There was another long pause. The silence was becoming unbearable, and I thought the catherine wheel was going to sputter, when your lips moved, and so clearly I could read them.

'You know . . . Live with . . . ?'

'I'll think about it if you come into the water this minute.'

You stayed putty-coloured, hesitated and turned your back. You made a vague gesture with uncertain hands, then started to undress rather slowly, like a toddler who has just learned his buttons. As I watched, not caring if I embarrassed you, I saw something that would have made such a painting — 'Man undressing against a background of bracken fronds' — the kind of early Picasso subject that's way beyond my resources. There's not a scrap of fat on you and all your very visible bone structure is elegant, so it's no use pretending that you're anything but the best-formed, best-proportioned and altogether most compellingly handsome man I have ever seen. (But only with your clothes off, I don't know why. Dressed, you look like a mis-shapen clothes-hanger in an old clothes shop.)

You were stripping down to a pair of navy-blue briefs, faded and ancient-looking and with a hole two inches wide on the point of your right buttock. You wouldn't turn and come to me so I called, 'Your minute's nearly up!' You spun round and with one mad rush were over the mud and into the water beside me, throwing up a splash that half-drowned me and washed even more mud into the pool.

'Super!' you spluttered and ducked your head right under. When you lifted your face, all streaming and a reasonable colour again, you were almost smiling. You put your mouth close to my ear.

'You were going to think . . .'

'I'm thinking,' I said, meaning I've put the brake on my catherine wheel but it's still fizzling nicely.

'Joe . . . ?'

'You know?' I asked, for Joe's ring had managed to get itself left off my finger last night.

'Mother tells me. . . even when I don't want to hear . . .'

'He's *my* business, Andy. But if I agree to your suggestion, that'll be the end of him. Okay?'

'And if you don't agree to my suggestion, that'll be the end of me?'

'Yes,' I said, thinking, oh dear heart, why can't I tell you now that I'll go with you to the world's end? I don't give a damn about Joe. I don't feel guilty about ditching him either. Come to think of it, guilt has never been my thing, has it?

'Oh,' you whispered, before hiding your head under the water again, 'it's a sudden death play-off, is it?'

This time, when you surfaced you looked straight into my eyes with your cobalt blue ones, indescribably familiar and yet strange in their brilliance and desperation.

'I need data to help me make up my mind,' I said. 'Kiss me, Andy.'

Your face was plastered with a mixture of peaty mud, stringy bits of grass and your own long ginger hair, and your kiss was awkward. Tender and sincere, yes. Passionate, potentially, yes. Awkward, definitely. I was just wondering if you needed some lessons in

elementary technique when you moved on to kissing my
birthmarks, first the little ones on my cheek and then the big brutes
on my neck and shoulder. You were telling me, without a word, that
if you loved me it would be because of them and not in spite of them.
Technique hell, I thought, this is something else, and it's confusing
you, Fiona.

'How's the data?' you asked, giving me another dose of the blue-
eye treatment, which confused me even more.

'I don't know . . .' I whispered, as you worked your way back over
my shoulder to my neck. Then you found your way to my mouth
again and kissed me more confidently, but half-way through or
what should have been half-way through, when you put your arms
round me (remember?) I couldn't cope any more. The water, for
reasons of its own, had turned bloody cold and bold bad
experienced Fiona was scared and shivery. No sign of a catherine
wheel at all. I wrenched away from you, blundered to my clothes,
threw them on, and ran barefoot down the glen to the car. It didn't
occur to me to wonder *who* was bolting now?

Near the car I turned to look back and there you were running after
me, with the pack over one shoulder and your shirt and shoes over
the other. At the edge of the turf you stopped.

'What's the matter?' you seemed to be asking.

I was asking myself the same question and not getting an answer.
(Poor Joe. He'd have been sure and I'd have been sure and we'd
both have been comfortable.)

'That cold water's made me hungry,' I snapped. 'Let's eat.'

I took the pack from you and sat down on the grass. After a minute
or so you pulled on your shirt and sat down too, three or four paces
away. I unwrapped the sandwiches and held one out to you, half-
heartedly. When you leaned over to take it, I couldn't help pulling
it back, teasingly. Your face lightened and you moved nearer, till
our knees touched. I let you have the sandwich and you took a bite,
then held it out to me with a tiny smile, your first of the day. I took
a bite. You giggled and suddenly we were having fun of a kind I've
never had before. It really was exhilarating to munch our way
through the sandwiches and the biscuits and the apples, taking

alternate bites at everything. Surely, I thought, he's so happy he'll never need to run away again.

When we'd finished we had a long gaze at each other, something else that had never happened to me before. It ended with us wrinkling our noses. We had to giggle helplessly.

'I love the way you shoogle,' you said, telling me I wasn't wearing my bra, my rather necessary bra. It turned out to be missing and we had lot more fun going back up the glen to look for it. You found it, of course, and were for helping me to put it on. If you'd been any other man I'd taken a fancy to I'd have seduced you there and then, or let you think you were seducing me, but my feelings overwhelmed me again. I so wanted you, all of you. Not just your body and the joy and comfort it promised; not just your permission, which I was sure you were already giving me, to be my sexy self and not Joe's weekend fantasy virgin; but every bit of you, inside and out. I didn't want to be me, Fiona, and my own woman, any more, but me-and-you.

Luckily, you were sensitive to all this (or were you just scared too?) for the fooling with the bra stopped by itself and we walked back to the car holding hands as if we wanted to keep each other at bay and yet stay in touch with the tremors and twitches coming down each other's arms.

In the car we sat side-by-side. What right has anyone to do this to me? I thought, sneaking a look at your profile. He's the Andy I've always known, but I don't really know him, and he's so nervous and jumpy I could almost be his first girl. But that's not possible at his age, old-fashioned though he always was. No, Fiona, he's running away from some other relationship and feeling guilty about it. Guilt could well be his thing, though it isn't mine. He's maybe even married.

'You got another girl?' I asked.

You started the car and made a lot of noise with the gears going over the hump-back bridge and off towards home.

'. . . never had a chick,' you said indistinctly.

'Why ever not?' I snuffled, for I was wanting to cry.

'. . .none of the . . .you know . . . smelt right when I got close . . .'

'Don't be silly.' I was sobbing now.

'. . . not being silly . . . precisely why . . . still a virgin . . . realised it last night in the car . . . you did smell right . . . all warm and painty and . . . making peat smell sexy now . . .'

'Oh, Andy,' I whispered, trying to dry my eyes on your shoulder, 'you know I'm not a virgin?'

'Enjoyed yourself?' Not a mutter or a mumble now.

'In a way.'

'Yes or no?'

'I've had fun.'

'That's okay then. You'd have been letting yourself down if it had been a duty or a martyrdom or to prove something. If we live together you'll be able to teach me plenty.'

Oh, my innocent innocent Andy, it's not as simple as that. Nothing's *all* fun. There are disappointments, and nasty smells, and chauvinist pigs, and other people feeling guilty, and sour mornings after. On the other hand, this conversation with you is *not* possible. It just *can't* be happening. Men don't speak to me the way you're speaking. They waffle and tease me and kid themselves. And I don't answer the way I'm doing. I wrap up half-truths for the silly sausages and tease them back. I wonder what I'm going to say next?

'I can't teach you much, Andy.' The point of your shoulder, on which I was resting my cheek, was the sexiest single thing I had ever come into contact with. I was trembling as I bit it, quite gently. 'You're the one who has really turned me on.'

'Cross your heart?' you asked incredulously.

'Cross my heart and hope to die!' I answered, making the childish motions before biting you again, a little harder this time. I was not going to be overwhelmed again.

'Tankie,' you said, slowing the car down to a crawl, 'you'd better name the day. And stop that biting.'

This started the kind of internal dialogue that belongs in a teenage comic-strip weekly rather than in my more-or-less grown-up head. 'Live together' and now 'Name the day', what does the man mean? He wants to marry you, stupid! But what he is saying could mean anything. Listen to the music, then, and hear him telling you to name

143

your conditions, like the old-fashioned gentleman he is. He hasn't told you he loves you. He doesn't have to. You haven't told him either. But he knows I'll go with him anywhere, any time. He's trying to order you about and stop you biting, which is what you want to do to him right now. He can't order me about, I'll see to that. If you don't make concessions, he'll run away, he's a bolter, remember what Mum said. I'll give him time, and reassure him, and make him so happy he won't want to run. He's never been happy, he doesn't know what happiness is, that's what scares him, he'd rather stay unhappy than commit himself to anything or anyone. But I'm good at making people happy. Maybe happiness isn't his thing, just as guilt isn't yours. What about Joe? What about him? You'll need to kick the habit of that huge hot furry body of his. Will I? You know you will — he keeps popping up in your head when you're not expecting him and he's taking his time about going away, even when you tell him how disgusting he is compared to your lean and alabaster Andy. But what will Dad say? Oh dear, what will he say? Dad matters.

'Let's go to the Registrar's Office first thing on Monday morning,' I heard myself saying, 'and take the first slot he can offer us.'

You didn't answer. You were pretending to concentrate on your driving.

This wasn't the plan, I thought, for deep-laid plans had been mysteriously appearing in my head, only to be displaced by even deeper laid ones. No, I was to gentle you along and make you so happy and sure of yourself that things would take their natural course — a sweet and sensible plan. But here we are following a deeper plan and challenging each other brutally to make a commitment. It's barely two hours since our avowal (a funny old-fashioned word for a funny old-fashioned happening), since you lit up my catherine wheel, and we are naming the day already. But this deeper plan will be counter-productive if he bolts — I'm sure he's going to, any minute now, and that will be him gone for good, unless there's an even deeper plan I don't know about yet.

As if in answer to my thoughts, you pulled off the road on to a wide grass verge near a high hedge with a field gate in it. You switched off the engine and we directed high-voltage silences at each other. I don't know how long this went on, but eventually you put your head on the wheel and gripped it with white-knuckled hands. I put my arm round your neck and tried to pull your head on to my lap, but you weren't having it. You pulled away from me with a rough jerk, opened the door, got out of the car and slammed the door shut again.

'I won't be a minute,' you said, and vanished.

So I had to sit there with my arms aching again. I sat and sat until the stale-beer-and-vomit smell of your car began to make me sick and I had to get out and sit on the bonnet, but facing away from the hedge.

After twenty minutes or so I was exhausted by sitting so tensely. I stood up, quite convinced you had bolted. I still didn't dare to look at that gate or even the hedge. A pick-up truck full of teenage boys came cruising along and they whistled and waved at me. I couldn't respond normally by sticking out my hip and waving back. I glowered at them, as if I was you.

It must have been more than half-an-hour after you bolted that I decided to look over that gate. The field was enormous and empty and bare, except for cowpats. The hedge went all the way round and was bushy enough to hide a hundred Andies, a thousand runaway bastards. I went back to your car and sounded the horn, loud and long. I waited. No result. I sounded the horn again, even longer. Still no sign of you. I started the engine and revved it up madly, sounding the horn at the same time. Nothing, nothing at all. How empty the country is, even on a Saturday afternoon!

I stopped the engine, left the car and went to the gate again. Emptiness. I opened the gate, went back to your car and drove it through. To hell with farmers, I thought, as I left the gate open behind me.

Well, I can hardly believe it now, but I drove that car of yours right round the field, it must have been at least a mile and a half, scanning the hedgerow for your ginger mop and blue shirt and seeing not a sign. There were a few false alarms, which turned out to be blue plastic fertilizer bags and tangles of orange binder-twine. Otherwise, not a thing.

When I drove back out through the gate there you were, sitting all hunched up on a pile of road-chippings with your head on your arms. How I remembered the handbrake I shall never know.

'Where have you been?' I wailed. Yes, I wailed, and barely recognised my voice. That other Fiona, the one who was me up till last night, she never *wailed* for anyone or anything in her whole life. There's a new Fiona now and I'm not sure who she is, wailing like that. *She* has something to lose, of course.

'Don't ask me! ' you said, not raising your head.

'But Andy . . .' I could feel tears coming. Again.

'Just don't *ask* me!'

Tableau: man hunched on a pile of chipppings; woman standing over him, tears streaming down her face; old banger with its engine idling. We seemed to hold it in freeze-frame for hours, while the sky darkened ominously. We might have held it for hours longer if a landrover hadn't stopped beside us. A farmer leaned out.

'Shut that bluidy gate!' he yelled.

You jumped to your feet, ran to the gate, and shut it as if the devil was after you.

'Bluidy toon-folk!' said the farmer and drove away. We were left looking at each other in yet another of those silences. How long it would have lasted this time I don't know because, as you must remember, rain started to pelt down in great warm summery drops. We had to jump into the car and wind up the windows. We didn't look at each other; in fact, we both gazed straight ahead while lightning did its flashing act and thunder did its rolling and all the windows of the car steamed up. I'm indifferent to thunderstorms, I'm neither deliciously scared nor sexually stimulated, so I wasn't driven to fling myself at you for a Dido and Aeneas scene. We just sat and sat until the sky cleared and the rain slackened. Then, for a change *you* broke the silence.

'Shall we move on?' you whispered.

I nodded, and we wiped the windows and you started the car and found we had a flat front tyre, the result of my trip round that field probably. We got out and looked at it, the rain now just a drizzle but still capable of wetting us.

'Can you change a wheel?' you asked.

'I've never tried.'

'Neither have I. We'd better put our heads together.'

'Where's the jack?' I asked, since you were telling me that I was supposed to be competent as well as tough and that problems exist to be shared.

'I've no idea,' you said, opening the boot. 'I've only had this jalopy three days. My flat-mate's off abroad for a long spell and I swapped him my typewriter and my radio for it, so now it's all the worldly goods I have, if you still want to be endowed with them.' You pulled out a rusty jack.

'I'll see if there's a hole for that,' I said, taking it from you, and ignoring the 'worldly goods'. I want a statement more specific than that.

'Okay, I'll heave out the spare.'

By the time you had the spare out and were bouncing it to see if it was inflated I'd fitted the jack and was trying to wind it up. It was stiff. You kissed the back of my neck, now dripping wet of course, and put your hand on top of mine to help with the winding. Our arms became entangled.

'Hey!' I protested, for concentrating on being competent under that kind of provocation wasn't easy, 'don't we loosen the wheel-nuts first? I was sure I'd seen Joe doing that to his shiny macho sports car. Joe, him again. He'd have had me watching him, sitting on a rug, or his blazer, under a plastic mac or a brolly. I was so much happier squatting by the roadside loosening alternate nuts with you, while we got our hands greasy and our whole selves wet. When we went back to the jack you slid your hand along my arm.

'Sorry!' you said, looking at the black smears you'd made. For answer, I held out my arm to you, whether begging or commanding I don't know, and you turned your hand over and stroked the inside of my forearm with the back. This raised my happiness to a level so intense it was almost an orgasm. I wasn't even brought down to earth by that nasty moment when a lot of rust flaked off the bottom of the car and it looked as if the jack was going to bore its way up through the bodywork instead of lifting it. However, it held, and you took the wheel off and I fitted the spare and we wound down the jack and tightened alternate nuts.

On a day of tremendous ups and downs this was our highest peak. Just to emphasise it, the rain died gently away. Thinking about it now, I'm beginning to wonder if I've ever really had an orgasm. What I was feeling about you there by the car coinciding with a sexual climax would add up to an ecstasy I've never even begun to experience. (I'm starting to hurt again. I haven't *something* to lose, I have *everything* to lose. If you don't come for me in the morning, I'll die.)

'Could you manage that on your own?' you asked, meaning change a wheel.

'Of course, Stick,' I replied, for I was so high, on you and on love and on happiness that I was sure I could lift the car with one hand and change the wheel with the other, 'but we're going to do everything together, aren't we?'

You were more down to earth. 'You'll be using the car more than I will,' you said. 'I can walk to the printing shop, it's just round the corner, but your hospital or whatever will be miles away. You'll need it to cart your materials, won't you?'

We're making plans, I noted, even though you haven't said 'yes' to Monday morning at the Registrar's, but I wasn't going to spoil my happiness by raising that issue. (Don't let me die.)

'You're right,' I said, and we put away the jack and the punctured tyre and started off towards home through familiar farming country that smelled of rain-washed clover and looked like paradise. Even the caravan sites and petrol stations were bright and clean enough to be out of an American Mid-West painting. I was just revelling in it all when you spoke and changed everything by being down to earth again.

'What about Joe?' you asked.

'Andy, I said he was *my* business.'

'I bet you have a date for tonight.'

I looked at my watch.

'In twenty minutes. So what?'

'He'll have to be told, and it *is* my business if . . .'

I didn't answer, and I wasn't happy at all when you stopped the car at the next telephone box and gave me another of your loaded silences. I did say I didn't give a damn about Joe and I did mean it when I wrote that I didn't feel guilty about ditching him, but I wasn't in the mood for hurting anyone, and Joe was to be hurt, poor chap. I'm sure his feelings for me are real enough. What could I say to him? My mind was so blank that not a single phrase occurred to me. Then you leaned over and breathed into my ear.

'I love you,' you said. The magic words at last, and timed as if by an expert.

'I love you too,' I said and gave you a kiss and left the car for the phone-box as if I'd been fired from a gun. Luckily, Joe himself answered the phone.

'Graham speaking,' he said.

'Joe. . .' I hesitated.

'Fiona, I though I'd cured you of using that nickname.'

'Graham, listen . . .'

'You know you learned it from that wet Andy Robb. Room-at-the-Top Joe, always-on-the-make, remember? I loathe it.'

'Why make a fuss? Listen to me!'

'He's back on the scene, isn't he?'

'I said *listen!*'

'I saw him myself last night, in a car that wouldn't pass an MOT. Looking furtive, like he always does, as if he was casing some joint with a view to a felony.'

I was speechless and nearly slammed the phone down, but luckily I looked through the phone box glass and saw you sitting at the wheel, gazing straight ahead with your neck stiff, as if you were desperately trying not to intrude while longing to look at me. Your hair was just as I had left it when I rumpled it.

'Hang on,' I said to the phone and put my hand over the mouthpiece and knocked on the glass. You looked at me and smiled your angelic shifty smile and we blew each other kisses and my catherine wheel started fizzing again. I took my hand off the phone and spoke to it.

'You still there?'

'I never hang up on you, do I?'

'Graham, it's all off.'

'What's that? Explain yourself.'

'I'm not going to marry you.'

Silence. I had to put in another coin, wondering if there was a real live man at the other end of the line. When something dies, it dies. And I'm cured of huge hot furry bodies too.

'Not him?'

'Afraid so.'

'I'm not going to give up without a fight.'

'Who on earth are you going to fight?'

'I'll break his neck.'

'And then what?'

'I want to see you, anyway.'

'No way, Graham.'

More silence.

'Well, you were always straight. As straight as he's bent. But you're a bitch all the same, and you can give the ring to the Thrift Shop. Keep out of my way, both of you.'

I put the phone down gently, thinking, well, he's a gentleman to the last, handing me an excuse to break off right there, with the fault on his side. And I'm not angry with him about the Thrift Shop, or for calling me a bitch, not now anyway.

I'm in such a welter of raw feelings about you, not knowing whether I'll see you this morning, that I can't think about Joe/Graham at all except for a dim picture of him in a drunken sleep, waking every so often and muttering 'bitch'.

I *must* carry on with this writing-therapy, even though I've felt like stopping every few minutes and I feel like stopping now. Sometimes it helps me to clarify my ideas; sometimes it just adds to the hurting; sometimes it seems to be a magic that brings you near to me for a few moments so that I can face up to the reality of who you are.

I left that phone-box and joined you in the car and you drove on again, squinting at me out of the corner of your eye. You looked so scruffy and your car smelled so foul that I couldn't even speak. The catherine wheel had died.

'You told him?' you eventually asked.

'Yes,' I answered.

You had the sense to keep quiet, but that didn't make me feel better. When we reached the outskirts of town, your scruffiness became unbearable.

'Have you some decent clothes to change into?' I asked.

'This is my only outfit.'

'Those are embarrassing,' I said, pointing to the peaty smears where you'd pulled your trousers over sopping briefs, and the blacker marks where you'd wiped your hands after the wheel-changing.

'Who is going to be embarrassed?" you asked.

'Me, in front of my people.'

'I don't think I want to meet them.'

'Andy!'

So we had that quarrel and your driving deteriorated badly and since we were back in town amongst the traffic I was terrified as well as angry. We were both choked up and when we arrived home and I wondered if you were just going to drive away and leave me standing. However, you came into the house and stood glumly while I fetched Dad's old dressing-gown.

'Every stitch is going to be washed, dried and ironed,' I said, pulling your shirt up out of your trousers. You submitted and I pushed you into the bathroom with a towel. When you came out after what sounded like a long shower you point-blank refused to enter the sitting-room, or even to sit in the kitchen, so I had to induce my family to come through one-by-one to the scullery where you were squatting on our kitchen steps, picking your nose and watching your precious clothes rotating in the tumble-drier.

Morag said, 'I wish you every happiness, I'm sure,' or some other stupidity. You gave her blankness, the complete hole-in-the-air treatment I've learned to dread.

Mum, true to form. looked at you as if you were scrumptiously edible, rumpled your damp hair and said, 'Nice work, Andy!' After looking confused for a moment you leapt to your feet and — I can't believe it! — gave her funny stiff bow from the waist and sat down again without speaking.

Dad, even though I'd had a very thorough session with him while you were here in the shower, growled at you. 'I thought Graham was too good to last,' his tone and stance and gestures implied. 'Fiona always had a yen for the things the cat brought in.' You hunched your shoulders, nodded glumly and said nothing, yet again.

A big part of me was agreeing with Dad, and I was ready to hit you, good and hard, for all the trouble you were making. How on earth am I going to control you? Will I ever get the chance?

('I won't be your friend any more,' I used to call out angrily as you pedalled away on your tricycle to the forbidden back lane where the dustbins and the witch and the wild dog were, and on you would go, your shoulders hunched with determination. I had to follow, for it was only me who could face up to old Mrs Linkletter's senile ranting and give her back as good as she gave. But when the big black dog bayed and slavered and snarled you were the brave one and I needed you to escort me past. As for the dustbins, I could never stop you eating any tasty titbits you found — remember that half-empty box of raisins and the tears I shed as you popped them into your mouth one by one?)

When your clothes were ready you insisted on ironing them yourself, while I did a few needle-and-thread repairs. The domesticity of what we were doing so close together in the tiny scullery seemed to warm us a little and we smiled at each other, almost shyly.

Once dressed again you looked so smashing that my catherine wheel lit up again and I simply had to kiss and make friends. I fetched my hairbrush and gave your fiery topknot a brushing so comprehensive that you looked not just smashing but incandescent. (How I need to remember you like that!) You had no choice but to warm up and kiss me back and make some sort of apology for your behaviour, blaming it on the fact that you were starving. I rushed to the fridge and found a bowl of left-over salad. I added chunks of cheese to it and buttered some bread and sat on your knee and we fed each other without bothering about knives and forks.

We were so happy and relaxed we had to be sleepy, and since we weren't quite ready to sleep together we had to sleep apart. I got off your knee and you stood up to go. Here I come to the really bad bit. Perhaps I'll stop here. No, I must go on. You let out that you weren't staying with your parents as you'd told me last night but in somebody's empty flat. This started the next quarrel.

'But you're a liar, Andy.'

'Maybe I am.'

'Why can't you go home?' I demanded.

By this time you were out of the scullery and edging through the kitchen.

'Because of my father, of course.'

'What about your Mother? Surely you can be civilised for her sake.'

'Nothing is civilised when my father and I are in the same house. And Mother doesn't help. She provokes us by trying to bring us together. Just as you're doing now.'

'But you *have* to tell them about us. Surely you can't make a quarrel out of that?'

'Oh yes we can.' You were working your way down the hall. ' "I don't see why a decent church-going girl like Fiona Phimister should throw herself away on you of all people." That's what my father would say. And Mother would sit there looking white and miserable because she believes the worst version of your reputation as the Art College whore, even if my father has different ideas. I could no more talk sense to them than they could talk sense to each other. I'd go mad and start shouting.'

You were half-way out of the front door.

'If we have a son,' I exclaimed, not responding to the 'Art College whore' bit because I didn't hear it till much later, 'I'll want him home regardless of any stupid feud you may be having with him. And what's more, he'll need all the grandparents available.'

This wasn't the plan, I wailed to myself, this wasn't the plan at all. Children, they're the plan behind the plan behind the plan.

Mentioning them at this stage is crazy. He'll bolt for good now.

You didn't, though. You turned to face me (we were out by the car now) and looked straight into my eyes.

'If we have children, they'd be far better off never seeing that pair. So don't crowd me.'

You jumped into your car, slammed the door, and rattled away, leaving me with all these feelings I've been trying to wrestle into some kind of order.

Right now, I'm too tired to write another word . . .

Sunday 6.30 a.m.

I fell asleep almost as I wrote that last sentence and now I've wakened from nightmares about heaving emerald-edged ice-floes, and igloos with stifling smoky-brown interiors, and little yellow babies so slippery with grease I can't keep hold of them, and dog-sleds with phantom drivers disappearing towards desolate horizons. They are colouring my conscious thoughts so much I can't very easily decipher what your last words to me really meant.

The one thing that's certain is that we haven't made any arrangement to see each other, or even to phone each other, today, or tomorrow (why did I suggest the Registrar's?), or, let's face it, ever. On the other hand, you did imply that there is a 'we', and that we had a future. The 'if' applied to our children, who are an if anyway. So you must be coming or phoning some time — make it soon! — unless you're lying scared on the floor of that empty flat, looking at the ceiling miserably and contemplating marriage to me, demanding pushy me, and deciding you can't face it when you haven't even settled on a career. You may even be on the way back to Edinburgh.

I'm scared too, Andy, but not so scared I wouldn't come looking for you if I knew where you were.

I'd have said I know you better than I know anyone, and here I am not knowing you at all. I wonder what your flat is like, 'just round the corner' from the 'shop'. I have no idea at all, only fantasies. Perhaps it's so ghastly you're ashamed of it; perhaps you've run off to Edinburgh to clean it up before I can see it. I hope there's room for a big double bed, and I'll need space and light to paint and somewhere to put the pram, the toy-boxes, etc., and you'll need a place to sit hunched over your writing where the babies won't be wakened by your typewriter. Wishful dreams!

Behind the dreams are the nightmares, still exerting their baneful power. The narrowing strip of sea between the grinding ice-floes is a threatening dark bottle-green, reflecting an even darker green sky. I'm, drifting again. Pictures like these aren't me at all. I paint direct from life.

I can't stand this! I'm going to get up out of bed and *act*. I must find you because, wherever you are, you're alone and unhappy and I can't bear that. I never could . . .

Wee Andy, Wee Drew, Melanie Klein, and Significant Others

'**O**h, stop that noise, stop it, stop it stop it . . .'

I can hear some of what Fiona is saying during the pauses for breath which our son, our first-born, takes between insane screams of rage. The rest I have to lip-read as I look up from the stove, at which I am concocting goulash for our supper.

'. . . oh, get a hold of it and sook, get a hold of it and shut up, for god's sake, shut up, shut up. I know it looks bad but it's all you're going to get, oh, oh, oh, that Melanie Klein, she's right, she's *dead* right, he's wanting to kill me, he's wanting to splatter me over the walls, belt up and calm down, sod you, or ye'll be oot the windae afore ye ken whit's happened . . .'

Her voice is edgy, without her usual soothing tone of ritual impatience. I am edgy too, my responses to Wee Andy's raging being more complex than they usually are and certainly not soothing. I am wishing I was back at the office, where people don't actually scream.

'Cool it,' I say into the goulash pot, but not loud enough to be heard, 'cool it, both of you.'

'. . . here, have it you little swine, it won't bite you, it *can't* bite you, it's only my left tit and it's always the fullest and you were dead keen on it this afternoon, go *on*, get a grip and sook or I'll run like two rivers, oh, oh, please *please*, sook-sook-sook, oh yes-yes-yes, that's it, that's it, go on, oh, oh, oh, the blessed silence, oh, sook hard, harder than that, oh, that's my boy, my bonny bonny boy, sook-sook-sook, my boy-boy-boy, Mummy's boy, Daddy's boy, Granny's boy, oh, the harder you sook the bigger you'll grow . . .'

Her voice tails off into silence and I can hear Wee Andy applying himself to his rhythmical task. I have to say something.

'Augustine,' it comes out primly, from the depths of my complex feelings, and in the general direction of the goulash, 'wrote something about bawling too loud for milk being a baby's first sin.'

'Augustine who? Don't let that goulash burn. That's the biggest load of rubbish I've heard in a long time!'

'I'm stirring it. Augustine, as in Confessions of, and it can't be all rubbish. This gas won't go any lower. If that character wants to murder you, like you said, that's a sin in anybody's book.'

'Are you going to peel those potatoes or just boil spaghetti? If his bawling was a sin he'd be feeling guilty now, and he's not. Just look at him. He's looking straight into my face, which is more than you ever do.'

'Potatoes are worth the trouble. He *ought* to be feeling guilty. Bawling is far too mild a word for the noise he makes.' I empty some potatoes into the sink.

'Poor, poor you! Poor, poor Daddy!'

'Where have you hidden the peeler? That Melanie woman and Augustine are probably saying the same thing. It's definitely sinful the way he murders my ear-drums.'

'Stop intellectualising. And being sorry for yourself. You'll put him off his feed. He's a horrible man, isn't he, Andrew Sooky Robb Junior?'

Junior is too busy to take any notice.

'Stick, you need a warm-up.' I continue to peel. 'Come on, warm-up drill. I have a spare arm.'

'Yes, Tankie. The goulash'll burn.'

'Turn off the gas.' I hesitate. 'Hey! don't lose your grip, sook-sook-sook! Come *on*, Daddy-oh!'

Fiona is sitting on the emperor-size futon on which most of our family business and entertaining of friends is done. There's nowhere else in the studio for a nursing mother to sit. I walk across the bare boards to it, still self-conscious about the bare feet Fiona insists upon indoors. I squat down quite near her, but find it difficult to look directly at the mother-and-baby-dyad. She's right, she's always right, I'm shifty-eyed.

'I've turned the gas off,' I say.

'Help me to get this tee-shirt right off,' Fiona says, 'it's in the way. Oh, he's really *pulling* now.'

I do as I am asked, commanded, careful not to distract Wee Andy from his exertions. The tee-shirt has two damp milky spots on the front, adding piquancy to its boldly printed slogan 'Mothers Do It'. Our son is now sucking as if he knew his life depended on it, pressing both little fists into Fiona's breast and, yes, looking into her face with an expression so full of concentration it is unnerving. I might as well not be here is the message I always receive when he does that. I am, though, it seems.

'Take off that silly business shirt.'

This achieved, there follow attempts at affectionate interaction, the warm-up drill, which are not too successful. We are still edgy, I don't understand why. The attempts are interrupted by Wee Andy showing signs of having finished the milk in Fiona's left breast. He spits out her nipple, screws up his face, belches, and waves his hands and arms about.

(Why doesn't the English language have a nice warm cuddly word instead of 'nipple', 'teat', 'tit', or 'titty'? OED has nothing but 'the small prominence in which the ducts of the mammary gland terminate', while Webster offers only 'the protuberance through which milk is drawn'. Yuck! CSD doesn't come up with anything couthy. And there isn't an English or Scots word at all for that dusky rose-red ring on which Wee Andy has been chomping his gums, according to Dr. Spock. It has to be the Latin 'areola', the only word on the subject with any music or poetry to it, even though it sounds like a record label. I'm sure Fiona would have some kind of Kleinian explanation. Meanwhile I'll have to stick to 'nipple', suggesting a grease-point, in preference to those other names, which suggest rubber goods or music-hall jokes.)

Wee Andy has another go at sucking, seems to find no joy, and spits out the nipple again. I am mortally afraid that he is going to upset the Augustine in me once more, but he doesn't make a sound, just looks about him enquiringly. Maybe he has learned that there are *two* breasts and is confident that there is more joy to come — it's time he learned something. He is smacking his lips now, in what looks like the expectation that his unsmiling lust will be satisfied.

'Stop squinting at him like that,' urges Fiona, 'I can't change him over till you move.'

'He's a greedy little pig!'

'I bet you'll have a second of goulash.'

Of course, I'm starving, that's why I'm edgy. We had a working lunch at the office, consisting of a pie so revolting I couldn't finish it and tepid coffee from a dirty mug, and when I arrived home Fiona was still at her easel and simply pointed with a charcoal to the makings of the goulash on the draining-board. Why is Fiona edgy too? Because I'm edgy? No, it must be something else, not too important, or she'd have told me.

We have been re-arranging ourselves and Wee Andy starts his rhythm again. He goes back to staring into Fiona's face too. Our warm-up drill, *la rencontre de deux epidermes,* is a little more successful this time, but I can feel the hard-edged bone in her shoulder, warning me all is not Eden.

Wee Andy's eyes are darker every day, but they still have a bluish haze. He resembles my Mother more than anyone.

'How shocked Mother would be if she saw the three of us like this!' I say. 'She's sure breast-feeding isn't really natural, and as for semi-nakedness like this, she'd think we were acting like savages.'

'I love her too. His hair's going to be black after all, look! She's had a hard life, especially raising you. You're forgetting the tatties.' She pushes me away.

I force myself to my feet, re-light the gas under the goulash, and pick up the peeler. I set to work again realising that, despite Fiona's edginess, and my own, one strand in the complexity of my feelings is happiness. It can't be true. Happiness isn't my thing, as some fraught character in an Iris Murdoch novel has to say. But here it is, quite unmistakable and winding its way through all my other feelings like a gold thread. Happiness, bonjour!

'I wish you didn't have to go to the prison,' I say. 'That enough tatties?'

'Don't start that again! I don't really want to go out tonight, but I must, so don't make it difficult. We'll never eat all those. Maybe I'll try him with the left-overs, mashed. Don't forget the salt. Oh, Stick darling, *look* at him!'

I look and see that Wee Andy is playing a game, a new one. He is spitting out that nipple (be specific, Fiona's nipple, in which you have a strong proprietary interest), brushing his lips across it, grabbing it, and spitting it out again. It's a game all right, but a serious one, for he isn't laughing or smiling. Neither am I.

'Oh, I could breast-feed for ever!' exclaims Fiona, 'I get such a bang . . .'

I lay the pressure-cooker on the stove with extreme care, twist on the lid and position the valve precisely on its seating.

'Don't forget the salt,' I am telling myself, 'don't whatever you do, forget the salt.'

I have forgotten the salt, of course, so I have to untwist the lid, add the wretched stuff, and twist the lid back on again.

'That's it! He's finished. What a shame! Come and burp your son while I get ready for the fray. Once more into the etcetera.'

I take the warm little bundle who is my son and squat cross-legged on the futon. That word 'son'. Tankie keeps on using it and using it, as if she had a point that needed to be hammered home, but after all these months I still don't feel like a father to this creature. I feel like 'that wee Robb boy with the red hair', or 'Stick', or even Holden Caulfield. (Who would think of Holden as a potential father?). Yet I seem to have learned to hold him properly, even when I'm sure I'm going to drop him. I have certainly learned to be aware of the milk and gas fermenting away inside him. He starts to girn, so I put him over my shoulder and he goes quiet. From the outside I may well look like a competent late twentieth century father. (I'm wrong about Holden. He is fatherly to Phoebe, and that's the bit of him I can never relate to. He goes all soggy about her. Mind you, I don't have a kid sister. My sister is older than me and as a girl specialised in knuckle sandwiches. Perhaps I have a problem hereabouts.)

Meanwhile my son and I are watching Fiona washing herself at the sink. She splashes and towels and I hear her muttering, 'Just as well I didn't rush him, they're not oozing.' She takes a clean pair of jeans from the row of hooks that serves us as a wardrobe and changes into them, all brazenly golden. Then she pulls on her amplest Oxfam shirt.

'Bra for the prison,' I girn, it's my turn for girning. 'Remember what the Governor said about *owing* it to the prisoners not to be provocatively dressed.'

Fiona makes a half-hearted *moue* at me — a pale version of her sexy lass-wi-the-muckle-mou act — finds her bra on another hook and wriggles into it. Without her usual care she throws her arty oddments into her canvas holdall. Wee Andy and I twist our necks this way and that to keep an eye on her.

Fiona has attended to the hissing pressure-cooker and is now brushing her hair, her waist-length sable hair, in front of our 25p Oxfam mirror. The impatient ages-old grace of her movements is almost more than I can bear.

'You have a most gorgeous mother,' I confide to my son.

'Gug-gug-gug,' he says, and it sounds as if he was agreeing with me. He gives a resounding belch.

'I love you both too,' says Fiona. By now she has served out the goulash and potatoes and picked up a fork.

'And *we* love *you,* we really do. Shall I bring him to the table?'

'You've used a lot of garlic. I'm glad you said that out loud. He's one of the family, isn't he?'

With this reassurance all round, I bring Wee Andy to the table, sit him on my left thigh and pick up a fork. He doesn't make a nuisance of himself, just gazes fixedly at the bright colours of Fiona's painting things — her palette and pots and jars and tubes and brushes — which occupy the other end of the table. I am able to eat at a civilised pace, but Fiona is in a hurry and finishes well ahead of me.

'Car keys,' she says to me. Instantly Wee Andy turns to her voice. His face crumples, he stretches out his arms to her and begins the rhythmical 'oof-uh! oof-uh! oof-uh!' which I recognise as the prelude to a real mind-bending scream of anger.

'Who the hell do you think you are? You're not allowed to leave me!' is his unmistakable message as the scream launches into its crescendo. Fiona ignores him and picks up her holdall. The noise reaches its maximum and I don't know if my ears can bear it. There are tears all over his face.

'Mummy! You'll have to hold him!' I bawl at Fiona.

She grabs him with her free hand and he stops his noise immediately, even though she has him round the waist under her arm like a parcel. I find the keys at the bottom of my trouser pocket and hand them over in exchange for the 'warm little bundle', who arches his back and starts to scream again, fortissimo and without prelude or crescendo. He strains his body towards his mother, as if he wants to do a space-walk to her. I grip him tightly

Mother is still intent on ignoring him and all his messages and rushes out, slamming the studio door and clattering away down the stairs. I try to listen for the sound of the car starting up, it's not a reliable starter, but the raging drowns everything.

'Hey! hey! hey!' I protest, gripping the bundle even tighter, and jogging it up and down in the way I've learned by watching Fiona, 'She'll come back. Mummy come back, Mummy come back, Mummy come back!' This does not have the effect it has had in the past. He is getting too quick in the uptake altogether, reacting to 'Car keys!' like that. And now he won't be pacified. His rage bores its way through my ears and churns up the contents of my skull. Mad thoughts and impulses career about inside it. Will he scream his way into convulsions? His little body is becoming more and more rigid and his face more and more purple. If he does have convulsions, I'll have a blackout too, I'm sure, and we'll both be unconscious together, two humanoids alone in a studio that has been metamorphosed into a malfunctioning spacecraft, out of touch with mission control, all communication channels zero-zero-zero.

I can see the stars wheeling and spinning through our high-tech velux windows. I can see myself laying down the little roaring bundle on the futon, going out through the door, down the stairs, and away across the comforting darkness and silence of the Park to the pub, where I could join someone sane in a peaceful drink . . . Or, madder thought still, I could jump on that bus that goes past the jail, leap off at the right stop and hammer at that little wicket door with the barred window . . . I regain consciousness and find I have in fact left the studio, but have only reached the stairhead. I am still holding the dreadful bundle. His noise is reverberating in the echo-chamber formed by the close. The banister is perilously near. I can see right down to the concrete floor of the basement, where the rubbish congregates. Was I about to knock on old Mrs Maclean's door and hand the bundle over to her? Once, in some other emergency, she pacified him by dipping her nicotine-stained spit-moistened finger into her sugar-bowl and giving it to him to suck. Even in my present state I can't face that.

There is a perceptible change in the nature of the noise, if not in its actual loudness. I could swear he's *listening* to that sonorous echo and trying the effect of changing the pitch, but he's not for stopping. Not many of the occupants of the close are as tolerant as the old witch. Some already suspect us of maltreatment, judging by the looks we've been having. I go back into the studio and close the door. This does not please the savage bundle. He stops listening to himself and directs all his noise at me again. Perhaps he's punishing me for not following Mummy. I certainly feel *punished*.

There must be a procedure for rescuing this space-craft out of orbit and spinning to destruction. There must be a magic formula. Nothing less than space-age magic will do.

Without conscious thought I sit down on the futon and jog the bundle gently on my knees. This merely adds a useless rhythmical element to the noise. Then I start to sing, yes, I actually sing, but not tunefully:

'This is the way the leddies ride,
    Jimp an smaa, jimp an smaa . . .'

The bundle's screams tail off. They diminuendo to a kind of whistle through his gums, accompanied by a whimpering sound. I start to bounce him a little faster:

'This is the way the gentlemen ride,
    Gallop awaa, gallop awaa . . .'

His breathing slows down, he opens his eyes and looks at me. He twists one side of his mouth into a kind of smile and becomes Wee Andy again.

Where has this magic formula come from? Fiona never uses it and my parents would never have sung it to me — Scots equals rude to them even now — but my Granny, whom I can't remember, used to look after me and my two siblings for long stretches when Mother was ill. Family folklore insists that she spoke broad to us. She left us each two hundred pounds, all she had to leave, but here is her real legacy. Now I am bouncing Wee Andy from side to side as well as up and down:

'This is the way the cadgers ride,

Creels an aa, creels an aa . . .'

He chuckles delightedly, swinging his arms in an attempt to keep time with the song and the bouncing. I have a faint warm sense of my Granny, a scent of old lady and scones and raspberry jam and security. Her great-grandson and I have regained a tenuous link with mission-control. The stars outside the window have stabilised.

'Ye'll jibble him, man,' I can almost hear my Granny warning, and I'm quite sure I've heard Fiona saying 'Don't over-stimulate him.' I taper off the jogging, without having to think about it, by going back to the gentlemen and then to the ladies. Wee Andy doesn't mind when I eventually stop, and soon I'm able to rise to my feet and walk him up and down. He is as relaxed on my shoulder as he was previously rigid, and mutters something like 'la-la-la' into my ear.

I would be relaxed too, if I wasn't desperate for a pee. I lay the fellow down but he starts his 'oof-uh! oof-uh!' prelude again, as if he didn't trust me to come back, so I pick him up again and take him with me to the shared toilet on the stairhead. He looks over my shoulder contentedly while I relieve myself, but when I pull the ancient chain the sound of rushing water is too much for him. He wets my bare chest and stomach copiously. He is wearing 'leak-proof' plastic pants, but Murphy's Law must be at work.

I lay him down on the futon, remove the wet nappy and put it in the bucket. He smiles encouragingly. I contemplate his miniature privates and try to work out where I last saw clean nappies. People who say babies are beautiful, I decide, are talking sentimental claptrap. Women can be beautiful, oh yes, yes, yes; girls, even little ones, yes, yes; boys and men, sometimes, yes; but babies, how ugly they are, all head and belly and disproportionately tiny limbs, and everything that should be shapely swallowed up in rolls of fat.

What's more, I ponder, since the monstrosity is content to lie and grin at me, babies are not only ugly, they seem to be *strangers*. The family-member we waited for during all those months, he has turned out to be somebody else, somebody I don't know too well even now. Just when I'm relaxing he produces another unexpected aspect to his personality. To prove it, he blows a raspberry at me without stopping his grinning. He's enchanted with his own cleverness, chuckles, and blows another. He's going to be a cheeky brat, I foresee. He chuckles again, in agreement with my thoughts. But even that chuckle is not the family chuckle I should have expected, it's his own chuckle and a totally new phenomenon. Weirdest of all, he must *know* that he is a stranger, otherwise why does he need to be assured and re-assured over and over again that he *is* a family member, that Fiona *is* going to feed him, that we are *not* going to abandon him, and that screaming with purple-faced rage is simply not done in the best-regulated Scottish middle-class families — not out loud anyway.

He interrupts these subversive thoughts. 'Da-da-da!' he vocalises, looking straight at me. It's the first time he has made that noise. It *is* only a noise, isn't it? Babies have to be *taught* words, don't they? They can't just *invent* them, complete with unsettling meanings?

'Da-da-da!' I say back to him, under some compulsion I do not understand at all. Shouldn't he be copying me, when I'm good and ready to teach him words like that? But here I am, my feelings all complicated again, and copying him. Where does this prick of tears come from, for god's sake?

'Da-da-da!' he gurgles again relentlessly, implying that there's no way back for me, only forward to more and more of fatherhood and its responsibilities. (But 'breast-feeding for ever', no!). My gold thread of happiness is still with me though, just discernible.

I fetch a clean nappy from Fiona's hidey-hole and wrap up those privates. When I'm on form, as I am tonight, I do a neater job than Fiona. I pull on the plastic pants and make sure they fit properly. Son is most co-operative — dreamy would be a better word. 'Da-da!' I say to him in a besotted manner, but he isn't interested. Chastened, I walk him up and down until he falls asleep and I can tuck him up in his pram, which almost fills the tiny slice of a room that was left when we knocked down the internal walls of my flat to make the studio. That's the end of him for the night. He's a 'good' baby and his next feed is due at six in the morning.

Suddenly, I'm alone. I go to the sink and wash up. I sponge the fellow's urine off my torso. I find a bar of chocolate and eat half of it. I inspect the nappy-bucket and decide that its contents justify my dragging out our ancient found-on-a-skip twin-tub from under the draining board and setting the suds to swishing. I find my brief-case, but I'm not at all ready for the work it contains. (The chasm between what I do at work and what I do here at home is unbridgeable. What fun my jokey competitive colleagues would have if they could see me now!)

I remember that giving my son a bath is one of my duties. Nothing would induce me to wake him, but I can justify my inaction — cowardice I mean — because the other day I heard some expert complaining on the radio that twentieth century babies are bathed too often for the good of their skins. I did remember to put baby-oil on his tender parts? Of course I did.

The space-craft is losing contact again. The stars are wheeling away giddily. There's no company but that unconscious android, gone away to wherever sleeping androids go. Wandering about, I notice the other half of the bar of chocolate and finish it off, though I don't really want it. It converts my saliva into saccharine sludge. I switch on the radio but can't find a programme that speaks to my condition; nothing in our stack of cassettes is any better.

Time is passing quickly for something that moves so slowly. She should be home by now. They do keep her sometimes, using flimsy excuses. I am thinking bleakly that life without Fiona is unthinkable, supposing she never comes back, and there's no certainty that she will, when there is a knock on the door, Mrs Maclean's knock, tremulous and demanding. I open to her and cigarette smoke pours over me.

'Yer leddy-friend on the tellyphone,' she announces hoarsely, meaning Fiona.

'Oh-yes-thanks!' I mutter, and rush past her across the stairhead and into the nicotine fog that fills her tiny dark-brown hallway.

'It's me,' I say into the reeking mouthpiece of the witch's old black instrument. Fiona's voice anwers, from far far away.

'I won't be home for a bit.' Pause. 'How is he?'

'Fine, fine. But you're out of breath.'

'I know.' Another pause. 'Did you remember to give him his bath?'

'Yes. What's up? Not a riot?'

'No. Just problems. I'm with the A.G.' A third pause, a painful one. 'Kiss my boy for me, I need you to.'

'How long'll you be?

'God knows. See you,' and she makes what could be a kissing noise and rings off.

I listen to the phone whining for a while, then put it down and re-cross the stairhead. Mrs Maclean is standing in our doorway filling the studio with smoke while pretending to keep an eye on it. She and my dear mother-in-law get on like two houses on fire.

'Dis she still love ye? ' she demands in her eldritch voice. 'If she disnae, she'll jist rin awaa.' She's convinced we're not married, that no couple under thirty is married these days, but I'm in no mood for her delusions.

'She rang to say she'd be late, thanks.'

'Thae young weemen are aye gallivantin . . . nae wunner that bairn . . .'

There's one thing to be said in favour of the old beldam, she's not offended if you take her firmly by her skeletal elbow, lead her back into her flat, and just leave her there still blethering away.

'. . . if ye were mairrit noo, she'd have tae bide hame, she couldnae leave ye on yer lane wi that bairn . . .'

I shut the studio door and open the windows wide to get rid of her smoke and start to wander round and round again, just as I was doing before she knocked, only now Fiona's ambiguous words on the phone and those pauses and my feeble replies are echoing and re-echoing in the black hole that inhabits my skull. I pass and re-pass her clothes hanging on the wall. I have to stop beside them, grab two hooks to steady myself, and drink in the scent of them, of her, the milky mother sexy scent I have to share with those thumping crooks. I will our words out of their mad orbitting, arrange them in order, and think about them as carefully and logically as I can.

Logically, there are only three possible sources of the problems that she spoke of — the 'chaps' in her class, the Prison Officer who supervises it, and the Assistant Governor who 'takes responsibility' for it.

The A.G. first. She told me once, after he had been particularly interfering and obtuse, that he's a psychopath, and that the only way society can cope with him and his like is to enrol them in the army and the prison service. Otherwise they'd all have to be locked up and more psychopaths found to replace them. It's the archetypal vicious circle, she said, but so long as the prison service consists of psychopaths beating the hell out of each other behind good high walls nobody is going to complain . . . Little comfort for me there.

He makes passes too, of course; as a psychopath he can't stop himself, presumably, but somehow I got the message over the phone that that wasn't one of tonight's problems. She said 'with the A.G.', implying a general distaste and not 'I'm fighting off rape'. But if so, why was she out of breath?

Keep calm. Stay logical. The Prison Officer next. The ones that aren't psychopaths are just like school Jannies. I wish they'd give me more of the Jannies, she said, but the psychopaths are good at wangling a soft job like supervising me. She can handle them, though — one complaint from her to the A.G. and they'd be in trouble, and she lets them know it in words of one syllable. Logically, hang on to logic, it's probably not the P.O. But the sod has had a good long sniff of the scent of her, while I'm having to make do with the scent of her clothes. There's even less comfort in this kind of logic.

So it's on to the 'chaps' in her Art Therapy class, who have been defined, logically, as 'problems' by society's whole apparatus of courts, police, etc., etc., and probably by their mothers too. Fiona's problems must, logically, derive from them.

It dawns on me suddenly that Fiona has been sending urgent unhappy messages all day, all week, but I've refused to listen. I didn't really *hear* all that edginess I've been describing, I've been putting it in now, with hindsight. Awareness is not my thing. I've

171

been too taken up with contemplating my gold thread. And now something unpleasant has happened, and it has come as a surprise to me when it shouldn't. She knew she was going to walk into problems. Of course she knew. But what kind of problems?

I have given myself cramp holding on to these hooks, so I let go and start to wander again. There's a cold draught from the windows, so I shut them. I daren't look at the stars. I nearly knock over Fiona's easel which has a pile of sketches clipped to it. The top sheet is blank. 'Variations on a Theme by Wee Drew' she said, and refused to show them to me. Uncharacteristic behaviour.

Wee Drew? One of her chaps, of course. She doesn't tell me much about them, only a name now and then, as she makes a point of confidentiality, but tonight Wee Drew appears in my imagination, a fully-formed monster, six-foot-four and a rapist with a long string of offences to his name. He needs to be protected from his fellow-prisoners, of course, because his speciality is raping married women in front of their children. Rape is okay (okay?) but not in front of the children. His speciality in Fiona's art-class, though, is tiny 'professional quality' Christmas cards in spidery ink and delicate washes. I need those cards to highlight the monstrosity of him.

Those 'Variations'. Normally I wouldn't look under the blank sheet that's hiding them, even at my most delinquent, but tonight is different. I look at them, one by one.

All of the sketches, all of them, are of the outside of a curtainless top-floor tenement window, seen from above as if from a helicopter, the windows beneath it brilliantly and dizzily foreshortened right down to the street. Behind the window, in most of the sketches, is a bare room, the distorted receding perspective of the floorboards even more brilliant.

I spread them over the floor and the futon and the table. I even pin a few to the walls. They bring Fiona and meaning a little nearer. They bring back that sturdy attacking stance of hers as she wields charcoal or a pencil — such a contrast to her more relaxed and sensuous movements as she uses a brush, her hand and wrist and forearm and elbow and upper arm all flowing in one continuous line, like a violinist's. I'm glad she's a painter and doesn't look for her meanings in collages or constructions or welded metal. How long will she be? God knows, she said.

Menacingly, the monster of my imagination re-appears, seated in the corner of the drab prison class-room, with the Prison Officer strategically placed between him and the others. His enormous legs barely fit under the table on which lie his Christmas cards. His face is the shape and colour of an over-size brick. His features look as if they had been gouged out with a pneumatic drill. He is leering at Fiona, thinking that she has a baby at home. In a hoarse voice he asks her . . . My imagination seizes up. I can't see any more. Darkness.

I open my eyes, yes, they've been closed, and have another look at the sketches. The overall effect of all those windows is vertiginous — I can't see the connection with the leering monster. Maybe the connection is to be found in Fiona's variations? I have a closer look all round. Some of her rooms are claustrophobic with furniture. In others the bare boards dissolve into infinity. One is a monk's cell, with nothing but a bed and a crucifix. Several have a table with roughly-dressed men playing cards, empty beer-cans everywhere. The biggest group is surrealist; each room has a framed text hanging on a nail on the back wall, stating in ironic cross-stitch 'A Room is a Womb', while other weird and unrelated objects lie about on the boards, as if waiting for a meaning to give them life.

A meaning? They can't possibly have a meaning. Nothing has any meaning. *Meaning is Fiona being here.* Kiss my boy for me, I need you to.

I go to Wee Andy's room and he is sleeping with a gentle smile on his face, the very epitome of trust.

He smells of her milk and of the processes by which he digests and eliminates it. Meaning is Mummy being here, indwelling, immanent. She must be, everything inside him came through her breasts. She's inside me too, the Fiona in my head, so I, Da-da, must have a meaning of some kind. Meaning is Da-da being here. That sounds far-fetched, almost transcendental, but here I am, the one who got in touch with mission-control, the one who persuaded him that the world was safe enough for sleep. I kiss him gently, careful not to wake him.

I close the door gently on him and notice that the twin-tub is overdue for a change of water, so I set the nappies to their rinsing. Before I can return to considering the vertigo of the variations I hear unsteady footsteps slowly mounting the stairs. Which of our friends would want to call on us, stoned, on this night of all nights? Mrs Maclean never has callers after tea-time.

I listen apprehensively as the footsteps reach our door and a key is put into the lock. The door opens and Fiona enters. Her hair is dishevelled, her shirt is torn, and she has the unmistakable beginnings of a black eye. She lays down her holdall and carefully closes the door. Speechless, I hold out my arms to her and she is just about to come to me when she sees her sketches all over the place.

'Hands off! ' she says. 'Get all those things out of my sight!'

'You said there wasn't a riot . . .'

'There wasn't. Not a big one. Move!'

She goes to the sink and splashes her face while I gather up the sketches and start arranging them neatly on the easel. She won't let me finish. With her hands still wet she bundles the lot together and takes them into Wee Andy's room, where there is a low door into the roof-space. Quietly, for she's not so distraught she's going to wake the fellow, she opens the door and dumps the lot on the sooty joists. Then she closes the door and snibs it as if she had no intention of ever opening it again.

We tiptoe back into the studio, where she collapses on to the futon.

'What happened to your eye?' I ask brusquely.

'Nothing much. You've started the nappies. Goody.'

'Did you remember the soap and the disinfectant?'

'Yes-yes-yes! I have a right to know.'

'You've washed the dishes too. What right?'

I nearly blurt out, 'A husband's right!' but think better of it. 'A lover's right,' I say.

We direct a silence at each other, in Fiona's phrase. She takes charge of breaking it, as usual.

'I want you to hold me, and not make love to me. Then I *may* tell you. Switch off that bloody machine first.'

So we lie on the futon and I put my arms round her and smell the prison on her hair and clothes and have a close-up of that eye. She sees me inspecting it.

'You're to be angry if you want to be,' she says, using one of her methods of diverting my anger. Sometimes this one works and my adrenalin disperses itself. Sometimes it doesn't, and I'm angrier than before, deep down, in fiery shades of red and black and orange. Sometimes, of course, I run away. Just now I can't, because she's holding me tight.

'Who did it then?' I demand. 'I need the actual name and exact whereabouts of the bastard who hit you.'

'I don't *know* who hit me. So please don't ask me that again.'

'So he was crafty as well as violent?'

'Oh Stick, I'm so glad you're angry, it makes me feel safe, but I can't tell you exactly what happened, can I? You know that.'

'A poetical truth will do.' I grit my teeth. 'The minute you're ready, actually ready.' I can hear myself stylising my responses, acting the part of an angry husband/lover, but what is the alternative? Fiona is hot and dry in my arms, her whole body twitching and trembling every so often. My own body is dry too, it might be made of bamboo. Our holding each other seems like a ritual that has lost its meaning. Let's not start on meanings again.

'Shut your eyes,' Fiona says, 'I don't want you staring at my bruise like that.'

Well, I wasn't exactly *staring* (I'm shifty-eyed, remember?) but I comply and the darkness behind my eyelids is a kind of relief. I'm not letting her go back to that jail, I think, there's too much danger involved. I am about to say so, but Fiona speaks first.

'Remember the chap I call Wee Drew?'

'Six-foot-four and a rapist?'

'Where *do* you get your ideas? He's five-foot-nothing and a fetishist, actually. Wee girl's knickers. He never harms the girls, though.'

'Physically, you mean?'

'You're interrupting. He doesn't harm them emotionally, either. He nicks the blessed things off clothes-lines and warms them in front of the fire and then he . . .'

'Spare me the details.'

'*Please* let me talk it out.'

'I'll try,' I say, thinking that Wee Drew must be one of the forty per cent whom Fiona reckons shouldn't be in prison at all. I'll try to be judicial as well as quiet.

'Weeks ago he asked me to sketch out that window of his, the one you've been so busy looking at. He told me exactly what he saw in his head and I put it on to hardboard with charcoal. If it wasn't what he wanted he made me change it. Every week he said that next week he was going to pack in his simpering pencil drawings of the Virgin and Child and use the acrylics I gave him to "colour in" the sketch. I so wanted him to have the release of colour, but he began to act as if I was pressuring him, and we both backed off. He was saying things like, "Eh, Miss, ye're awfy like ma mither, ye're that guid tae me," or even, "I wish ye wis ma mither, Miss!" At the same time I started to "help" him with his soppy Virgins. We were both avoiding.

'But I couldn't let go of that window. It grabbed me where I live, somehow. You should know. I tried so hard to work out what the poor sod's message was, and yet every window I sketched seemed farther away from the truth than the last one.

'Last week there was "an atmosphere" in the class, the kind nobody mentions because though you can cut it with a knife you can't define it, and nothing you say or do disperses it. Wee Drew wouldn't speak to me. He sat for the whole time with his Virgin and Child turned face down. The other chaps all painted away, but they were much too quiet and they kept looking at the P.O. He spent the time yanking at the crutch of his trousers as if it was cutting him in half. That's why I didn't want to go tonight. I was scared.

'And, of course, it was tonight that everything happened. Wee Drew started to paint the minute he sat down and he didn't stop, or look up at me, for a second. He's a genius. He did what I'll never be able to do if I live to be a hundred. In no time at all he painted in the tenement and the window and the empty room, using the colour of the hardboard for a deadly dull background. Then he painted a little boy, about four I suppose, bawling with his mouth open in the far corner of the room. You can almost hear him making that horrible hoarse rhythmical noise that a kid makes when he's worn out with crying for too long. And then, shut your eyes again, Stick darling, you mustn't look at me, and then he painted a great ugly ugly woman with huge ugly boobs leaning out of the window holding a naked baby boy as if she was going to drop him into the street, hold me tighter, I need you to . . .'

I hold her tighter. I feel the dryness of her lips on my right eyelid, then on my left.

'He used every possible clashing colour that would heighten the impact. Keep your eyes shut. Here's the bad bit. The woman is a caricature of me. Keep quiet, keep still. She has my hair and my eyebrows and all my other features and my body made gross and obscene and she's wearing my striped shirt, the identical one to mine, this one I'm wearing now. Tonight was the first time I've worn it to the prison and I'm sure he never looked at me and yet there it is to the life. It was nearly time-up when I realised all this. I was standing behind him while he fiddled about putting finishing touches with a fine brush.

' "But that's me you've painted!" I said, I couldn't stop myself, I could kick myself. He stopped painting, threw down his brush and started to shout, at the top of his voice, "Ya fuckan bitch, ye kin jist fuck aff hame tae yer fuckan man an yer fuckan wean! Lea me alane! Fuck aff!" and so on and on.

'I tried to talk him down and I'm sure he would have stopped for me eventually, but the P.O. started grappling with him, I can't think why, and I stepped in and so did everybody else and there was such a rammy. Some idiot hit me or shoved me against a table or something and that's how I got this black eye. Oh Stick, was I glad you reminded me to wear my bra because someone tried a squeeze and I bit his hand hard. I bet he'll be flashing the bite-marks round the jail tomorrow, poor sod . . .'

'Tankie!' I protest, 'I can't stand any more . . .'

'That's the worst over. Please listen to the rest. Please! Some of the chaps actually rallied round and protected me, yes they did! — forty per cent shouldn't be in prison, remember? — but the others were having a go at the P.O., nothing too much, just enough to remember them by. Wee Drew was hiding under his table and nobody bothered with him. I think they all forgot him, but he managed to kiss one of my feet and my sandal is still wet so I think he must have been crying.

'Then everything started to settle down and some of the chaps were apologising to me, some were really sorry but the rest were only bothered about their parole chances. The P.O. was straightening up his uniform and had just put on his cap again when the A.G. arrived with hordes of reinforcements. He ordered people about and took me to his office and I insisted on phoning you before I answered a single question. Then I told him a lot of, well, lies really, and the P.O. backed me up. He's one of the jannies, not the psychopath I had last week, and he's a bit soft on me. To cut a long story short, there isn't going to be an enquiry and Wee Drew can keep his picture in his cell if he wants to and I can have my class again next week. I insisted I was fit to drive the car and I came home as fast as I could to my Rock of Gibraltar and I feel safe now, even if I am a failure and no good at anything . . .'

'You weren't a failure at ordering me about, remember?' I girn out loud. To myself I am saying, 'You're not having that class again, if I can help it.'

'Oh, I'm never a failure at that, but I *had* to get those charcoals out of sight. They were a failure of insight, no, they were a defence against insight, which is worse, and I'll never make a therapist and I was going to be such a good one to make up for not being a real painter, I'm just a mucker-about, I got so hung up on that empty womb because mine's empty and I want to be pregnant again, it's one thing I'm good at, no, don't let go of me, I need you, especially now. I should have *seen* all the insecurity symbolised by that window, I should have *felt* it, because insecurity is basically not trusting Mother, and I'm sure Wee Drew's mother really did threaten to throw him out of the window. Maybe he actually remembers that tenement foreshortening away from him, down-down-down, right to the street, or maybe he watched and bawled at the back of the room while she threatened to do it to his wee brother, I'm sure it was on his file that he had a wee brother, he certainly didn't have a father. Oh, I should have *known* he was idealising me as his *good* mother and been ready for trouble, and (do you remember?) I actually threatened our Wee Andy with "oot the windae" before I went off and I never really *heard* myself . . .'

I try very hard to follow Fiona as she carries on with her Kleinian speculations, but I fail. I fail intellectually that is, but I'm sure I'm still in touch with the drift of her feelings, 'quick and in mine arms', demanding reassurance and security and telling me I'm the one and only person who can give them to her — I wish I was sure I was a Rock of Gibraltar and not a quaking bog. Now I'm hearing her saying something I can understand, almost.

'. . . and so the poor little sod had to break out and swear at me.'

'I'm not quite with you . . .'

'I've *told* you. He was just learning to trust me enough for me to be his *bad* mother as well as his *good* mother. It was true for a moment, that one moment, until society stepped in — and I couldn't stop it all on my own, could I? — I'm simply not clever or strong enough, so society grabbed its chance to insist that he was all bad and I was all good, and he had to wet my feet and kiss them, yes, I became the Virgin Mother again and . . .'

I lose her for the second time, though I think I have a glimmering for a moment (now, much later, as I write) that Wee Andy is learning that his mother Fiona has a bad side to her. She's irregular and unpunctual with her feeding, isn't she? And she bullies him into sucking, thrusting her engorged breast at him in a way I certainly find unsettling. ('Engorged'. What a word! I found it in Dr. Spock, my 1955 U.K. first edition, Oxfam 10p. It's gross enough to put anyone off anything, even off a Good Mother.) And she is beginning to use a nagging tone of voice when she finds his nappy soiled . . . but where does 'society' come in? I'm bemused.

Back on the futon Fiona is relaxing and her body has lost its dry heat and regained its usual dark sexy humid warmth. She stops talking and sighs and I think she's maybe ready to make love. I risk opening my eyes and am confronted with that bruise. There are dark purple-red knuckle-marks on her cheek-bone and just below her eyebrow, and the black and yellow stain is spreading over her nose and up towards her temple. The white of her eye is bloodshot and her fabulously long dark eye-lashes have been flattened and disarranged.

'So bad mothers have to be given black eyes?' I demand loudly.

'It's inevitable, isn't it?'

I find myself shouting, 'And what happens to people who give *good* mothers black eyes?' Rage engulfs me. 'You're not going back to that place, ever! I won't have it!'

'Ssh! You'll wake him! I couldn't stand it!'

'I've bloody well had to stand it while you were out on your do-gooder nonsense.'

'Oh Stick, you're his father. Who else . . . ?'

I roll away from her and stand up. I'm to be angry if I want to be. The red mist in front of my eyes is real, it's not a poetic fancy, I remember it quite clearly, in fact it's coming back now as I write about all this.

'First thing tomorrow,' I bawl, 'I'm going to that jail to see the Governor, I'm going to write to our M.P., and you have no right to leave us and expose yourself to . . .'

'Please don't shout.'

'You should be thinking of us for a change, and I'll shout if I want to . . .'

'Oh no!'

There is an unmistakable and ominous 'Oof-uh! oof-uh!' from the direction of Wee Andy's room. The noise is forcing its way through, round, and under the door.

'Oh!' whispers Fiona, 'oh! oh! you'll have to see to him. I couldn't cope. I can't cope!'

The contradictory feelings I am experiencing should lead to immobility, they should cancel each other out, but no, I am capable of action. I stride across to my son's room. A board creaks loudly, horror-movie fashion, and he must hear it, for he unleashes the full force of a raging tempest of noise, surely the loudest his lungs are capable of. I open the door and it pours over me. I fight my way furiously all the way through it to his pram and pick him up. I'm to be angry if I want to be. I carry him back to the futon with the intention of dumping him in Fiona's arms, but when I reach her she is cowering in a strange curled-up position and her hands are over her ears. Wee Andy sees her and reveals that he is capable of even more than 'the loudest his lungs are capable of'.

The shock of seeing Fiona of all people, admitting defeat is so great that I have to change my mind about handing her the bundle. Instead, I rely mindlessly on a routine gesture by putting him against my shoulder facing away from his mother and patting him gently in case there is a bubble of wind to be dislodged. However, his stomach remains rigid against my collarbone, he continues to bawl and to twist and turn to see Fiona, and no wind emerges. I resist the routine temptation to give him a few hearty thumps. Fiona is lying completely still, my feelings, and probably Wee Andy's, and the studio, and the universe, revolving round her distress.

All these emotions have one thing in common with sex, they make the lights too bright, so I carry the squaller round the studio and switch off our various spotlights, etc. We both relax slightly, and he reduces the decibel-level noticeably, but he still wants his mother. As our eyes become adjusted to the darkness we can see her, lying in a parallelogram of moonlight. She still has her hands over her ears. I tiptoe over to the nearer velux window and hold Wee Andy up so that he can see the moon. Miraculously, he is distracted. He gazes steadily while he reduces his noise to the whistling and whimpering stage. Then he goes quiet and his breathing returns slowly to normal. I look over my shoulder and Fiona has taken her hands away from her ears. Wee Andy puts his thumb into his mouth and starts to suck. He seems to fall asleep.

I do my best to glide across the studio to Wee Andy's room . With one hand I pull back the bedclothes in his pram, then with the utmost gentleness I take him in both hands and am about to lay him down, but he isn't asleep. He removes his thumb from his mouth and opens his throttle. With a conjurer's sleight-of-hand I have him back on my shoulder and am cuddling him as if the thought of laying him down had never occurred to me. He shuts his throttle and sucks his thumb again.

I carry him back into the studio. Fiona, in her patch of moonlight, is now sound asleep, her limbs and hair spread in all directions and one whole golden shoulder showing through the rent in her shirt. She gives a little snort and her body twitches, two sure signs that she is down in the deepest depths of sleep. I should know, I'm the only one in the world to know that, but the knowledge is not much comfort to me right now.

I kneel beside Fiona and let Wee Andy see her. He carries on sucking his thumb. Tentatively, I hold him as if I was going to lay him on the futon close up against his mother, in the Doctor Hugh Jolly position between us which he often occupies. When he has learned to trust us, he'll *want* to sleep on his own, or so the theory goes. He is making no complaint now. I lay him down and watch intently as he sucks his way to sleep. Then I take off Fiona's sandals, loosen her bra, and try unsuccessfully to loosen the top of her jeans, all without waking her. I knew she was in the deepest depths. I fetch the duvet from its kist and spread it over the pair of them. I pull down the velux window-blind on their side in case the moonlight bothers them. I creep under the duvet without undressing. Neither of them has had a wash, so I'm certainly not going to take the trouble.

I lie on my back with my hands behind my head. Soon the moon will reach me through the window on my side. With all these routine caring gestures finished, I am alone with my feelings again. The quiet breathing and the two fragrances emanating from my wife and son are no solace, nor is the moon's cold progress through the cold night sky. My mouth feels foul, so I have to rise to my feet cautiously and brush my teeth without creating any noise of rushing water. I take the chance to put on my vest and shirt. My socks and shoes follow. I take my jacket from its hook behind the door and slip it on. I look at my watch — thirty minutes before the pub closes. I open and shut the door with extreme care and tiptoe down the stairs. I don't let the street door slam.

In two minutes I am walking across the empty spaces of the

monochrome park at a smart pace, blind anger fuelling my legs. What right has she to be doling out permissions for me to be angry? I am entitled to my own anger and to do what I like with it. Am I supposed to take responsibility for everything, absolutely everything, all on my own? It'll serve her right if she wakes up and finds me gone, preferably with that baby bawling its head off. And so on, and on, and on. My anger is so repetitive it should be boring, but it isn't. It goes on and on, getting more and more righteous and more and more enjoyable.

By now I am circling the empty fountain in the middle of the park. All the park benches are empty, no sounds are coming from the shrubberies, there are no sordid events, nothing for the Sunday papers, except inside my head. The gold thread has disappeared entirely from the strangling knot of my feelings.

Each time I complete my circuit of the fountain I can see the scarlet neon pub-sign beckoning to me through the monochrome trees, but my steps are no longer crunching the gravel like those of a macho man on his way to sink a pint or two with his macho mates. Wee Drew's 'ugly ugly woman with huge ugly boobs' is surfacing from the dark depths. I am running away from her. I always know *when* I am running away, I rarely know *why*. I break away from my circling round the fountain.

Right at the edge of the park I have to stop running. I have caught a whiff of beer and cigarette smoke. If I once enter that pub tonight is the night I'm bound to be button-holed by Ex-Sergeant Smythe, ex-public schoolboy, ex-P.T. buster, ex-Twenty-First Highland Division. He has a nose for the defencelessness of misery. 'I made 'em *sweat*, old boy, I made 'em *groan*, but they loved me, they loved me, they knew a *man* when they saw one!' — his wife left him years ago for an Italian, would you believe it, sir, a Wop — 'I worshipped that woman and she turned out to be a haw, but those Jocks now, *they* loved me!' The pub-sign is beckoning me to maudlin self-pity, years of it, if that is what grabs me. Contradictory feelings keep me where I am, immobile.

The cold is reaching me, I should have worn a sweater. The pub will be warm, but so will Fiona and Wee Andy under the duvet.

They'll smell nicer too. I turn away from the pub and face towards home, but I'm still unable to move.

Fiona warm under the duvet, but defeated, lying in the foetal position with her hands over her ears, opting out of coping, abandoning me to uncontrollable storms of infantile rage. She used to be afraid of large dogs, she's still not too keen on them, but otherwise she's always been Fiona the Brave, who copes with dangerous people and situations I have only a glimmering of. Just try to compare my colleagues and their petty rivalries with her violent crooks and her psychopathic prison staff. Remember her in the labour ward too, gritting her teeth and hanging on with white-knuckled fists and then producing Wee Andy as if she was shelling a singular gory pea. In seconds she had the slippery little thing in her hands and was fondling it . . . I passed out and was dragged away by the heels, so I'm told. I pass out now, shivering, but stay upright. I worship that woman.

When I come to, a decision has been made at some level and I am walking home with a hesitant step, laden with guilt. Irrational guilt, of course. Rationally, a man is entitled to a drink in a pub after a hard day at the office, *and* having done his duty, and more than his duty, to his wife and family. Not one of my married friends does more than I do. My guilt is definitely irrational.

I reach our street eventually and see that everyone else has acted responsibly about their District Council refuse bags. I soft-foot it upstairs and find mother and son sleeping just as I left them. The other parallelogram of moonlight has moved across the floor and is illuminating them. Quietly, I seize our refuse bag, collect Mrs Maclean's from outside her door and take them down to the pavement's edge. I sneak back upstairs, undress, and creep under the duvet again, close up against Wee Andy. I'm not sure if I'm queuing for a return to the womb (and there's no guilt there, is there?) or being the Rock of Gibraltar under a fleecy cloud. (Rocks don't feel guilty, do they? Of course not, they wouldn't be rocks if they did.) Wee Andy smells okay. Missing his bath can't have done him any harm. End of guilt on that score.

Despite all my precautions Fiona has heard me and lifts her head.

'Where have you been?' she whispers sleepily over the hummock that is Wee Andy.

'Putting out the rubbish bags,' I whisper through my teeth.

'Clever you. I need to undress.'

She lifts the duvet carefully, stands up and takes off her clothes. The moonlight changes her gold to alabaster. She comes round to my side of the bed and with a classically graceful upward reach of her arms she pulls down the velux blind, but not before I've seen her eye, the purple and crimson and yellow now jet-black in the cold light. Before I can say anything she is settling back in bed.

'Night, Stick darling,' she murmurs.

At this precise moment Wee Andy interrupts by snorting and twitching in his sleep, exactly as his mother does. However, being his own man and no carbon copy of anyone, he also gives me a sharp blow in my ribs with his bony little knee. His rolls of fat don't seem to soften the impact at all.

'You okay, Tankie?' I ask, but she's asleep again. She'll be okay. She'll be herself in the morning. Anything else is unthinkable.

Wee Andy twitches again, turns towards his mother and gives me another dig, with his hard little heel this time, right in the solar plexus. 'That's nothing to what Mummy got at the jail!' seems to be the message. I deserve punishment, of course, but I'm not sure that he's the one entitled to hand it out. (Ask Melanie Klein. You must learn that you are his *bad* father too, my friend.)

Afraid that my son may be aiming to add 'yin wi the heid' right between my eyes, I withdraw out of range. I'm thankful for our enormous futon and its matching duvet. They were Fiona's idea, of course, and her parent's wedding present.

The far edge of the futon is a lonely place, though, I'm in for a sleepless night if I can't creep closer to Fiona. Making love will have to wait till she's slept away the effects of that rammy, and till I've stopped being unmanned by guilt, I know, I know, but I need her warmth and nearness more than I can ever remember. Wee Andy is positioned between us, armed cap-à-pie, a formidable obstacle.

If he's really sound asleep, I ponder, I could lift him over to the other side of his mother. But no, he might kick out and wake her and she needs her sleep. We *all* need her sleep, if she's to be herself in the morning. I decide he must go back into his pram. I plot and plan and mentally rehearse and re-rehearse every move. I'll fold back the duvet, lift him imperceptibly, carry him to his pram as if he was one of those unstable trays of eggs, and lay him down so gently he won't know a thing. Then I'll tuck him up with ghostly fingers and tiptoe back to bed. There I'll snuggle up to Fiona's back, put my hand in its usual place on her smooth round hip, and sleep the sleep of the guilty worshipper. (But I deserve her more than those crooks.)

Everything goes according to plan, except that Wee Andy's eyes open just as I am laying him down. I can see their ominous glitter in the glow from the tiny sky-light. I wait for his little spine to stiffen into that angry arch, but it doesn't. I pull the covers over him and tuck him in. They tuck you up, your Mum and Dad . . .

'Mum-mum-mum!' he mutters, just audibly.

A part of me wishes he'd said 'Da-da-da!' A bigger part of me agrees with him that 'Mum-mum-mum!' is the right thing to say when you're awakened, very gently, from sleep.

'Mum-mum-mum!' I whisper back to him. Meaning is Mummy being here, even when she has a black eye.

I stroke the silky fuzz on his head. He puts his thumb in his mouth, but doesn't bother to suck. I wait beside him until I have goose-pimples all over and his thumb has fallen out of his mouth. I wish Fiona and I had never made our agreement not to wear pyjamas. I feel defenceless as well as cold.

The rest of the operation conforms to the plan, except that I have to warm my hand between my legs before I dare to put it on Fiona's hip. When I do, she sighs heavily.

'Daddy-oh!' she says out loud, but without waking. I let myself drift away on an ebbing tide of feelings. I wish I had her black eye. I really do. Then I'd *know* she's going to be herself in the morning, bustling, feeding, organising . . . meaning is . . . Fiona feeding . . . mum-mum-mum . . . anything else unthinkable . . . mum-mum-mum . . .

Suddenly I hear Wee Andy bawling. I wake and find the studio silent. The noise must have been a half-dream, half-nightmare, but a hi-fi one, faithfully reproducing all his resonance. Muzzily I recall other babies, their kitten-like mewings and asthmatic chokings and donkey-like brayings. (We're in the young-parent mafia, so I've heard a few.) I decide that my son's voice, even in a half-nightmare, has a clear musical trumpet-like note that I wouldn't change for the world. Soppy old Da-da-da. Just wait till he opens his throttle again. Who'll *cringe* then?

Folk Not
Listening Mostly

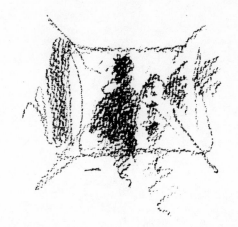

Tuesday. Six p.m.

ah, Mrs Robb, how nice to see you yet again, we really are grateful, you know, for you are a breath of fresh air blowing into this prison, of fragrant fresh air if I may say so without your misinterpreting my motivation, and everyone in the place, and I do mean everyone, Mrs Robb, looks forward to your very welcome arrival and regrets your departure, regrets it very much, the officers, I can tell you, being quite competitive, they are actually jealous of each other, they really do compete for the privilege of supervising your class especially since you don't insist any more on their active participation, on their actually putting brush to canvas or should I say hardboard in the present economic climate,

but of course I keep such petty rivalries under control, I allow no arguments though I do, of course, as you know, allow room for discussion, for the reasoned presentation of an officer's own views, the Governor gives me a free hand in relation to the officers, I'll give him credit for that, though at times, and I'm telling you this in confidence, Mrs Robb, at times I feel it is *too* free a hand he gives me, for I take all the responsibility without an appropriate increase in my salary, without appropriate remuneration,

and as for the prisoners, well, I needn't tell you, you are in close and friendly contact with them and you know how much they appreciate your interest and your efforts and how the word is passed along and so many of them apply that we have to have a waiting list,

I'll just escort you to the classroom, no, I must insist, I just feel happier if you have me as an escort, and there's no reason to hurry, no reason at all, but I must say, Mrs Robb, I must say that your delightful presence and your wonderful contribution only serve to point up the dreariness, the *dreichness* if I may use such a word, of the prison service scenario, too many prisoners, I could show the figures, too few officers, the figures would shock even you, no new resources and no prospect of any in the foreseeable future, the year 2001 is the target date for the modernisation of our toilet facilities

Tory and Labour governments, I have seen them come and go, come and go, during my years in the service and they are both the

191

same, or so similar they might as well be the same, and I am sure an Alliance government would be no different, our remit would be the same, take them in, lock them up, slop them out, feed them at the required statutory intervals and let them out again, so that this place, if I may say so, Mrs Robb, if I may give my honest opinion, and I know that I am at risk of repeating myself or perhaps even repeating someone else, this place is a huge stagnant pool, with raw sewage *swilling* in at one end and raw sewage *sluicing* out of the other, and every so often a huge foul bubble forces its way to the surface, like something out of Dr Who, like a special effect from Dr Who, then it bursts with a plop and a stink or perhaps something more than a plop, and unpleasant happenings take place which we in the service have long predicted, and there are stories in the media, you must have seen them or read them, mostly lies of course, almost entirely lies, or facts so distorted they might as well be lies, and top brass comes from St Andrews House and asks a lot of questions without ever visiting the galleries or witnessing a slop-out and a confidential report is written which no one ever sees except its author and the appropriate Minister of State and if things are desperate, if political pressures are considered overwhelming, the Secretary of State for Scotland, the great panjandrum himself, and meanwhile in this place stagnation sets in again, take them in, lock them up, let them fester, and let them out again,

yes, thank you, Mr Ah, Mr Ah, Mr Ah, I know Mrs Robb's class is waiting, there is no need to stand there, I do in fact *know,* but it will do them good, just to wait, just to learn to postpone their pleasures for a little while, that is what this place is all about, is it not, Mr Ah, Mr Ah?

pardon that intrusion, Mrs Robb, I was just about to extend the analogy, the poetical analogy, for I have something of the poet in me, as you will have noticed, being who and what you are, and to say that I would be better off managing a sewage plant, the stink would be about the same and shit, if you will pardon the expression, does not answer back, or require lengthy reports to a Parole Board composed of well-meaning and worthy but entirely ignorant persons, 'wets' is the current term I believe, or write to its solicitors

192

making unfounded complaints for onward transmission to the powers-that-be, and I think it is a measure of the faith I have in you, Mrs Robb, that you are the only person outside the service to whom I would actually say all this,

and to return to my analogy, the attraction of a sewage-plant is that its end-product is detectably, I think I may say unquestionably, more salubrious than the raw input, that the sewage has been well and truly rehabilitated if you take on board my meaning, Mrs Robb, and I am informed that any proper self-esteeming sewage plant manager will publicly drink a glass of his clear effluent, there is rehabilitation for you! for who would trust the effluent from this place? you will appreciate that I am speaking metaphorically, of course, that I am using a metaphor, so don't look so disturbed, my dear Mrs Robb, you must know that I am not completely heartless, I am only too aware that the 'effluent' I am referring to consists of people, of living human beings, but it is sometimes hard to remember that when there are so many of them and one has to spend one's working life in the odour of their waste-products and some of our recidivists have been cycled and re-cycled through the system again and again and will, you must admit, only be rehabilitated posthumously, like a Russian politician, Mr Stalin for example, who was a bank robber, I believe, a villain,

ah, ah, yes, here we are, I suppose I should let you go, for of course your class is waiting inside, but I think I am entitled to *my* share of your time, your very valuable time, for there are no Art Therapy sessions for Deputy Governors, oh no, nothing like that for us, for nobody, except perhaps you, and you are exceptional believe me, nobody thinks that we need that kind, or indeed any kind, of rehabilitative help, and you can hardly blame me if I feel sometimes that I am not fully three-dimensional, not a rounded-out person, but just some kind of cardboard cut-out, or a flat-screen image, like one of those mannikins in a video-game, and that's a sobering thought, is it not? especially if you extend it to everyone else here, to all the officers, and the prisoners, and to the Governor himself, for if we have no depth, no third dimension, then we have no life, we are just puppets jerking on a string, and it is therefore hard for any of us to see the point of our existence in the circumstances, it's just nose to the grindstone and what is the point? what is the point?

but I am becoming maudlin, you must forgive these mournful poetical outbursts of mine, my dear wife would tell me they are something to do with the male menopause, you must excuse me again, 'the mid-life crisis' is a more gentlemanly phrase, but I shouldn't be burdening you with my troubles, I really must let you go,

mind the step, Mrs Robb, mind the step, it is highly polished, and if isn't, I'll have them, I'll have them, C.P.O. and all,

Tuesday. Seven p.m.

no thanks, I'll jist stick tae the ootside seat, a wumman ma size needs hauf the passageway eh? sit ye doon, it's jist as weel ye're no a big man an we kin stretch oor legs in the front seat here or we'd be sittin in each other's laps aa nicht,

that wis a richt Thatcherite kind o bus queue, wis it no? yin big scrum an deil tak the hinmost, nae workin class solidarity and sense o justice, in fact it's a classic case o setting the workers against each ither jist tae exploit them, oh, thae seats are that narra, Mister, Robb is it ye cry yersel? aye, I see it on your brief-case, Mr Robb, de-regulated coaches like this are hell, pack them aa in, shut the doors, an awaa doon the motorway tae Lunnon like the clappers, profit, profit, an niver a thocht fir fowk, Mary, we're movin, haud on!

I widnae be on this kinda coach, but me an the girls has nae money left in oor Fightin Fund, ye'll hae heard o the Lulu Lingerie sit-in? aye? weel, I'm the Convener o the Shop stewards there, Jean Hegarty I'm cried, ye'll have seen ma name in the papers, the Glasgow Herald cried me 'the couthy marxist' an that's no a compliment, an efter fower months we've still got a hunnerd per cent solidarity, an solidarity is whit maitters, an here I am on a bluidy de-regulated free-enterprise entrepreneur-capitalist coach, bit its three pun cheaper an ivery penny has tae come oot o the girls' ain money and their men are gettin fed up,

oh, thae capitalist bastards, when they come up tae see the factory an the machines an the 'work-force' it's British Airways Executive

Class an a Daimler wi a chauffeur, bit when I gang beggin tae Lunnon tae see them it's a de-regulated coach an the Tube, an I ken fine whit I'm gaun tae hear when I get there, a hail lot o posh and Yankee accents repeatin 'profit, profit, profit,' as if they didnae ken there's fowk involved, an faimlies, an jobs, an I'll hear masel talkin posh so that the stupit gowks kin 'comprehend my actual meanin',

bit I have tae dae it fir the sake o ma girls, ma lassies, oh, Mr Robb, from the meenit we heard that the factory wis tae be shut doon and the machines roupit, ye cud *feel* the solidarity, mind you, we had oor secret weapon, like Golda Meir said, the auld bitch, 'nae alternative', there are nae ither jobs tae be had, fir weemen that is, an damn few fir the men, sae solidarity is the only hope, ye ken whit it's like when aabody's singing their herts oot? weel, it's like that aa the time, an aa the bad things that happened jist brocht us girls closer and closer, an the bad things were bad, I kin tell ye,

first it wis the Union tellin the men tae pack it in an tak the redundancy money and the rats daen it, and then the company weldin the gates and cuttin aff the electricity, it took us three days tae start the emergency generator, there wisnae a mechanic wi enough balls tae climb the railins, eh, we need wumman mechanics, trainin them's a top priority, but the company were feart tae cut aff the gas in case we were stupit an left it on an caused an explosion,

an then the cludgies gettin blocked, we niver fun oot if that wis sabotage or yin o oor ain lumpen lassies trying tae flush doon a sanitary towel, but we cleared it wi'oot a man-plumber, we'll hae tae train wumman-plumbers an aa,

an then twa o the lassies gettin sick, yin had a miscarriage an ye kin imagine the mess that made, an d'ye ken whit? eight o us were liftin her that gently ower the railins an the ambulance wis waitin an she wis greetin fir us tae pit her doon an let her bide! that's solidarity fir ye! the worse things get, the solider oor solidarity is,

oh, Mr Robb, ye should see the girls growin up an raisin their consciousness, it gies me such a lift when young lassies that niver thocht aboot anythin but boys an discos an punk hair-dos learn tae think dialectically an argue logically an then staun up an speak oot fir fechtin on, even when the Union his ratted, chauvinist pigs! an the siller's rin oot,

an the aulder weemen, they're raisin their consciousness tae, an forgettin aboot bingo an *Dynasty* an aa that rubbish, I'm tellin ye a lee, we hae a vote ivery time *Dynasty* is on the box an yince, aye jist the yince, the vote wis against switchin on, fir we had tae decide whit tae dae aboot the kids, some o the aulder yins, teenagers ye ken, were oot o hand wi only their glaikit faithers tae control them, an the police and the Social Work Department were usin the situation tae try tae brak oor solidarity an feenish the sit-in,

oh, there are bastards iverywhere, we had tae release twa o oor best comrades tae wheech the kids intae the Youth Club and keep them oot o mischief an learn them some sense, an explain the dialectic o the sit-in, sae we were fechtin, and we're still fechtin, on three or fower fronts, aa at the same time, bit's worth it, oh aye it's worth it,

na, I dinnae really mind fowk watching *Dynasty*, fir it's *proof* that capitalism's in its decadent phase, ye jist hae tae *look* at Joan Collins and her fancy claes tae see that it cannae last, aye, we laugh oor heids aff at the rubbish on the box, *Reporting Scotland* is the funniest, specially when it's reporting oor sit-in, an laughin keeps us aa girls thegither, if ye couldnae laugh ye'd greet, an we keep the canteen as clean as oor ain hooses, aye, cleaner, fir there are nae men an weans tae muck it up again, an we have the machines aa clean an ready tae stert production jist as soon as we have an agreement,

listen, Mr Robb, nearly aa oor smokers ha gien it up, aye, me an aa, an we're peyin fir cigarettes oot o the Fightin Fund fir the twa-three auld yins that cannae, pair sowls, an that's solidarity fir ye!

ye'll mibby be wonderin whit ma role is in aa this, weel, it's Jean this, and Jean that, an whit'll we dae noo, Jean? an I keep tellin them I'm the Convener and no the boss and they'll hae tae think fir theirsels an if they cannae they dinnae deserve tae keep their jobs, an when they say 'bit ye're like a mither tae us, Jean,' I tell them a real Mother aye wants her dochters tae grow up, aye, bit the truth is, I *am* a Mither tae the young lassies, it wad be unrealistic tae deny it, but tae the older weemen I'm really a pal, I cry them my girls, bit they're really the best pals a wumman ever had, it's like haein fifty dochters an a hunner pals, oh, it's better than haein dochters, an I should ken, fir I've had twa o ma ain an they've ratted, yin's a computer programmer fir the Ministry o Defence an the ither's a Procurator Fiscal, naethin bit agents o the capitalist state, 'if the police reported to me some of the things you get up to, Mum, I would *have* to prosecute',

I wunner whaur me an ma man went wrang, we were that keen fir them tae hae an education an be in the forefront o the struggle, bit no, they're baith as bourgeois as ye like, gie me ma girls at the factory ivery time!

I niver thocht I would learn tae love that canteen, bit it's a holy o holies noo, the place whaur it aa happened, solidarity, it's exhilaratin, ye ken, hoo else could I staun up tae the bastards I'm awaa doon tae Lunnon tae negotiate wi?

I kin see ye're ready fir sleepin, Mr Robb, bit I'm feart I'll no sleep fir wunnering if thae cowboys hae serviced the brakes on this coach, they'd skip it if it was save a few pun, bit ye're a man that needs his sleep, I kin see that, wis there iver a man that didnae? they're aa expert sleepers, men,

the tyres! I wunner if they've got proper tyres, or if they're daein a cost-cuttin exercise on them tae, market forces! the only market forces that wad mak them chynge wad be if ower many fowk were killed in accidents and aabody stopped usin cowboy coaches,

aye, sleep, man, sleep, ye've nae worries, I kin see that, wi yer wee brief-case,

hey, driver, ye're no sleepin, are ye? I thocht it micht be catchin, are ye a Union man? na, I didnae think ye were, ye shud be ashamed o yersel, na, na, mind yer drivin an I'll keep quate, if that's a possibility,

Tuesday. Eight p.m.

ah, Mrs Robb, I have been lying in wait for you, I have to admit, I have been a bad boy, I took time off from my desk and peeped into your class, or thought I would peep without really prying, but actually I watched you for quite a while, I couldn't help myself, the prisoners know they can be watched and I am sure you do too although you are pretending you do not, and I was most impressed, I became quite mesmerised following your progress round the room, for it is obvious that you are still without any disciplinary problems, and that is no mean feat in these permissive times, and it is more than can be said for some officers,

and I notice that the prisoners' paintings actually reflect your command of the situation and when I say 'command' I intend no slight on your womanliness, quite the reverse,

and I do not think I am being too fanciful, too poetical, when I tell you that the prisoners' work demonstrates a commendable restraint, just like your own paintings, a commendably peaceful tone, and there is no sign at all of that trouble we had when I was Assistant Governor here all those years ago, what with prisoners making lewd remarks to you on the one hand, or wanting you to be Mother to them on the other, or throwing paint about and swearing at the supervising officer and uttering threats and so on, and every man-jack thinking he was Mister James Boyle and ready for transfer to the Special Unit,

ah, but we were younger then, we had youth and vigour on our side, and we had the *smeddum*, as my old Grandad used to say, I think I must inherit my poetical side from him, yes, the *smeddum* to take such things in our stride, but now I see that everything is under control and running smoothly, just as it should be at our time of life,

and I do enjoy our chats, I really do, and I have been wondering but no, a lady like you would not want to, you are married with two grown-up children, just as I am, and you would not want to, I mean a dry stick of a D.G. who will never be Governor and has been faithful to his wife, God bless her, for forty years, yes, for the same four decades as she has been faithful to me, no, I could not aspire to, but I see we have reached my office and perhaps you will come in and have a cup of coffee, real coffee, with me, I have one of these really efficient machines and we could carry on with our chat,

no? but you have noticed my flowers, haven't you? yes, my wife fetches them from our garden every day no matter what time I have to leave for work and regardless of the weather, it is not often I have to remind the dear old girl, she has a handicap, a progressive one I'm afraid, which precludes us from, but I do have to remind her sometimes, for I firmly believe that a carefully chosen little vase filled with the freshest of flowers neatly arranged shows people that I am not an automaton, I am not just George the auto-pilot who runs the jail when the Governor is 'not available' or is having one of his 'statutory breaks', but a three-dimensional human being with feelings like everybody else, with feelings of my very own and capable of appreciating art and poetry and being quite lyrical and poetical on appropriate occasions,

and I do enjoy a discreet drink in a discreet pub and perhaps a chat, a little intimate tête-à-tête, in surroundings more conducive, these strip-lights in this corridor are really very bright, are they not? they are quite obtrusive,

oh, well, I mean, we are all getting older and have learned to keep control, I suppose, to maintain a seemly control of our impulses, after all, years ago, if I may return to the subject, when I was only an Assistant Governor and newly trained and full of new ideas, you were the terror of the prison, my dear Mrs Robb, and your class seemed to be the focus of so much discontent and negative behaviour, yes, really negative anti-authority behaviour, but what with the Inspectorate backing you up and my own little-publicised support, you stuck to your guns and over the years you have won through and become an integral, fully integrated, part of the prison structure and of the rehabilitation programme,

and I know I was complaining and a shade pessimistic earlier on, but when I see the prisoners painting so quietly and with such concentration I begin to hope, yes, hope rises eternal, and I am tempted to ask if I might join your class myself, for these autumnal scenes they are all painting, why, I am sure I could instil a little more poetry into *my* version of autumn, for the prisoners' work is just a little dull, is it not? just a little lacking in verve, though saleable enough I suppose, in one of those art shops alongside that print of the lady with the orchid, now there's an idea for you, Mrs Robb, we could have them nicely framed in our workshops and they could actually bring in money and money is not to be sneezed at in these days, is it? after all, everyone is short of cash and there would be something for S.A.C.R.O. and the Howard League to latch on to if they would just take time off from writing to the papers and have a look at what is actually happening, what is really going on in the Scottish Prison Service,

I suppose I had better let you away, and return to my desk and continue with my own work, such as it is, such as it is, but I will be looking forward all weekend to seeing you next week, for I really want to raise a question, no, it's not to do with selling the prisoners' pictures, I am due to retire in the not too distant future, it is a year or two away to be truthful, and both my daughters have emigrated, ah, I know both your children are abroad too, it's something we have in common, isn't it? and I never see my grandchildren because my wife's condition makes flying impossible, and though some of them are old enough to make the journey to see us themselves they don't bother to come to this backwater, so the prospects are, my social life is very limited indeed and I would like to have, I need something to, I thought perhaps you might advise me about,

ah well, you must be going, you must of course, you have been very patient, very patient and kind, and perhaps you know, my dear Mrs Robb, being the person you are, perhaps you *do* know how fortunate you are being free to go home to your studio, and do what you like best and what you are best at and only lock yourself up here voluntarily and of your own accord, and these are the key words, voluntarily and of your own accord, for only two hours twice a week, and perhaps you should forget what I said about joining your class, though if you ever run a class elsewhere I would be the first to enrol, but otherwise let's forget that little indiscretion of mine,

mind the steps, you know as well as I do that officers and prisoners alike take great pride in keeping them clean and properly polished as a mark of their respect, good night, then, and thank you again, I feel quite cheered, really quite cheerful,

Wednesday. Eleven a.m.

come in, Andrew my dear chap, come in, come in, marvellous to see you, have a good trip? they tell me the shuttle is quite civilised these days, a credit to British Airways, and the Picadilly Line brings you straight to Russell Square, doesn't it? we're neither of us in the limousine class, are we? and how is Edinburgh this weather? *snell* east winds in your 'draughty parallelograms' as usual? I can't imagine how you survive that climate,

coffee? my secretary makes an excellent cup, no? then we'd better get down to business, this used to be an occupation for a gentleman, but no more, I fear, there isn't time for the politeness and leisurely chats of yesteryear, time, there doesn't seem to be enough of it for anything,I'll come straight to the point, these figures of yours aren't good enough, my dear Andrew, they are actually stagnating, you and your people must be in a frightful rut, just when we must have growth, real growth, we may have to take over the marketing from you and hold your stock in the Swindon warehouse where it can be properly controlled computerwise, we can't afford a narrow regional approach, the Scottish market is far too small, and as for those Scottish things of yours, my dear chap, they don't sell, even in Scotland, now be honest, they don't, do they? I mean, the figures show it,

no, we need more imaginative thinking, we must latch on to the latest developments, mustn't we? so it's just as well you've come up to see us and learn what they are, but you mustn't feel too bad, you know, most of the other regions are just as stagnant, not an idea in their heads we can use, not one, with the possible exception of where-is-it, the name escapes me, Bristol, yes, Bristol, I knew it wasn't too far away, but of course I can travel round the other regions and knock their heads together every so often, but Edinburgh is really too far away, as you must know from personal experience, Andrew,

not that I have anything against Scotland, far from it, I go there regularly as a matter of fact, I fly to Inverness and motor to a friend's place in Wester Ross, I do enjoy the scenery, I walk actually, and there is peace to catch up on some reading, no, I must make a special point of going down to Edinburgh, I really must see the place and put you and your people in context, perhaps the Festival when there is something worthwhile on, though I gather that is becoming even rarer,

I'm digressing, personally my dear Andrew, I would give you all the freedom you want, but I am more and more constrained by Head Office policy guidelines, they have been running the rule over us and they want action on all fronts, and that includes Scotland I am afraid, cost-cutting plus plus plus, really aggressive marketing, massive increases in turnover and even more massive increases in profits, preferably calculated and presented in dollars,

and they won't listen to one's ideas, one is over-ruled at every turn so that one has reached the stage, and I'm telling you this in confidence, Andrew, one has reached the stage where one is beginning to believe that one has really run out of ideas, and you must know that one has been an ideas man ever since one came down from Oxford, but these people are so dismissive, one feels as if one was some kind of provincial, the English way of doing things is comical and what is most degrading, one begins to caricature oneself and one's Britishness to make them laugh and be more amenable, lucky you being Scottish and not having these problems, one must do it the American way if one is to be considered seriously, they are always on the phone, and they drop in unannounced en route to Frankfurt and I'm sure the telex is chattering away right now, get moving, get off your ass, and other even cruder expressions,

I don't know whether this is their usual behaviour or whether they are afraid of a take-over, the Japanese are really spreading their wings, aren't they? and there are Australians with access to Arab money sniffing about, I'm talking too much, unwise of me, the message is clear enough, Andrew old man, to someone of your intelligence, there is no provision for any redundancy payment in your contract, you insisted on being independent and self-employed so you know what to do, don't you? just ring me any time you're in trouble and I'll see you next time you're up,

and meanwhile I've laid on a little series of refresher sessions for you this afternoon, creativity, productivity, new product awareness, marketing, 'taking care of our people', that's the *in* phrase, I gather 'personnel management' is out as a concept,

oh, and before you go, Head Office are insisting that next time you are up you attend an E.E.T. Group, executive evaluation and training, something from California, the interface between personal development and the microchip, that sort of thing, I'm off to California for mine next week, and I can assure you that I am as apprehensive about the 'evaluation' aspect as you seem to be, judging from the expression on that 'dour' Scottish face of yours, I'm hoping I survive, wish me luck,

well, all the best, I do *value* these sessions of ours, my regards to Mrs Robb, Fiona, it is Fiona isn't it? and to your, 'bairns' is it you call them? to your 'bairns' too, of course, sorry I can't have lunch with you,

Wednesday. Six p.m.

Fiona Robb speaking.

It's me.

I know that.

I thought it was going to ring for ever. What on earth were you doing?

I was on the loo. Thinking.

Thinking of what? How's Birkie?

The vet says he's okay. It's either a new house or California.

What would I do in California? It wasn't a coronary, then?

No, just old age and asthma. We've to carry him up and down the stairs in future. Lucky he's a King Charles; if we'd had that stupid Boxer you wanted . . . What you might do in California would be your affair.

But what would *you* do over there? Old age is coming to us all, I suppose.

Could we communicate without the platitudes, please? I'd paint, of course, as I always do, but . . .

Poor old Birkie! But what . . . ?

Don't be soggy! He's enjoying life. He's wagging his tail right now. I'd be able to keep an eye on Jennifer.

She wouldn't say thank-you. Unlike Birkie.

I know that. But I'd be there. She's pregnant.

Andy, you still there?

Yes, I think so.

What's all that clatter? And the wailing?

I'm in a Greek sandwich bar, near the coach departure point. I think it's Greek. The wailing's the music. Jenny, she's quite . . . ?

Quite sure.

The usual?

No, she's going through with it. The father's the President of something, the line was bad, and he's anti.

Our first unterminated . . .

So far as we know. Wee Andy *is* entire. And hetero.

You really want to be there?

No. Yes. No. I want to paint. Jennifer's beyond help, but California might get me started again. A change of light.

The baby won't be beyond help and Jenny sometimes listens to me.

Okay, *you* go to California. I'll stay here and buy a cottage with a decent studio. All on one floor. And a garden for Birkie.

I've run out of coins. Ring me back?

I might, if you give me the number.

You've rung back.

Say something creative for a change. The hi-fi is on the blink.

Try switching it on and off half-a-dozen times. What have you been doing all day?

I've been looking at a canvas. And wanting to crucify that D.G. I could hammer in the nails personally. How can I get inspiration from Maxwell Davies if the thing cuts out all the time?

We can afford a new hi-fi, surely. You're not letting him get . . . ?

But I am, I am. Last night he gave me an interminable version of his twice-weekly drone, his repetitive 'poor me' play for sympathy. Only this time he included as a novelty, even his novelties are boring, a rudimentary pass. I seem to have lost the knack of avoiding the one-dimensional sod, or shutting him up, or losing him. That bloody hi-fi, it's started again on its own.

I don't like the sound of that. Switch it off at the wall. A rudimentary what?

A pass. A proposition. A sex-u-al ad-vance, idiot. Which I can handle if he tries it again, which he will of course. The only thing to be said in his favour is that he *knows* he's one-dimensional. What is really bugging me is that I'm stuck, I've been stuck for months, years, as you should know but don't, and all the chaps in both my classes are stuck, they might as well be painting by numbers, and what is he doing? He's congratulating me, week in and week out, on my exemplary control and commendable restraint. Crucifixion would be letting him off. The hi-fi has stopped again. *Everything bloody well stops*! It's all right, Birkie, I wasn't shouting at you.

Oh dear.

What a helpful remark! I suppose you've been whooping it up with your spaced-out old pal what's-his-name? A gang-bang in the Garrick Club or something?

You don't want to hear.

But I do, I do. Anything for a laugh.

He threatened me.

The man has a repetition-compulsion. Just like my D.G.

I know. He made the same speech as always, the provinciality of Edinburgh, the non-existence of Glasgow, I think it's a dirty word no decent Englishman can bring himself to use, troubles with our Yankee masters, the lot. What's new is that I am commanded to attend a kind of T-group for executive evaluation.

How boring! That sounds as if it went out with the hippies. Why is everything and everybody so one-dimensional?

Don't ask me. I'll be back in the morning. I hope I don't have to share a seat with that woman again. She said she was going back tonight. Meet me with the car?

Of course, of course. But who's the woman? I'm intrigued, almost.

An enormous earth-mother of a Shop Stewards' Convener. She squashed me right up against the window and talked all night, full of herself and the Lulu Lingerie sit-in.

The hi-fi has started again. I know about her.

Of course, you always *know*. Switch. It. Off.

I heard her being interviewed on Radio Scotland. Mrs Jean Hegarty. I'd say she was articulate, charismatic, and heading for tragedy — bang! or her own radio show — whimper! Correct?

I said you always know. Have you switched that thing off yet?

Yes-yes-yes! *You* should write her story. She sounds three-dimensional. Make a *point* of sitting next to her.

She'll find me, there's no need to make a point, I'm accident-prone. But I'm also desperate for sleep, after last night. I could just about edit her story if she taped it and I could switch her off and on. *You* should make a point of modelling a head, a self-portrait.

Whatever for? I haven't handled clay in years.

On general principles. If you're stuck. Get away from one-dimensional people and two-dimensional canvasses and right into three dimensions.

That sounds far too slick. Are you commissioning this head?

Yes. I suppose so. Yes.

You mightn't be able to afford what I ask. And it could be ghastly, a Hammer Horror thing, the way I'm feeling.

I could have it in my office. I have some money to spare. I wish you'd done the kids when they were small.

Not redundancy money? I could do the kids from memory.

No, I have some stashed away somewhere. You know me.

If it isn't redundancy money I might do it. The price would be a trip to San Francisco. And I'll take an advance to buy a new hi-fi.

When can I have it?

When it's finished, if I ever start. And you've handed over the money. Meantime I'll start looking in the papers for a new place.

But I though you were going to San Francisco?

You're a real thickhead sometimes. The deal is for a *trip*. You'll want to stay in the new place and look after Birkie, won't you. *You* can't afford to retire early.

Oh, I see.

The hi-fi has started again.

I thought you'd switched it off.

I can't reach it from here, thickhead.

You haven't called me thickhead in years. I'm glad you're not actually emigrating.

I'm not glad about anything.

But I'm supposed to be the mournful one.

It's coming to us all, remember?

I've half a mind to retire, all the same.

Not if you're going to get in my way. Mind you, that clay, it might cheer me up. I could pummel and shape some *sense* into it.

You could put me out in the garden with Birkie. How is it that we can only talk on the phone? Face-to-face we . . .

We'll have to be able to. Otherwise . . .

Otherwise what?

Oh, there are hundreds of otherwises. I have to carry Birkie downstairs for his walkies. I might just decide I liked California, mightn't I? I'm hanging up. See you, thickhead. That bloody thing, it's stopped again.

Wednesday. Seven p.m.

oh dear me, it's you Mr Robb, it looks as if we're sharing this front seat again, oh Mither, it's got nae wider, has it? oh, Mary, we're aff, he's wastin nae time, is he? oh, he's gaun tae be worse than the last yin, did ye see that red licht? he cut it fine, oh, we're in fir a nicht, I kin see that, an me that likes ma bed, ma ain bed, Holy Mary Mither, Lunnon traffic's jist free enterprise aff the rails,

oh, ye'd think I wis a fearty, Mr Robb, a wee lassie wettin her breeks, the wey I'm bletherin on, and near tae greetin, bit I wisnae this mornin, I kin tell ye that, I kept at them an at them, an I pit ma pints aboot productivity, an I pit ma pints aboot a nae-strike agreement if there wis nae victimisation, an I pit ma points aboot a leevin wage, an I pit ma points aboot consultation, an I pit aa the ither pints that we'd agreed on, me an the girls, bit it wis nae use, nae use at aa, they had an answer fir iverythin,

whit am I gaun tae tell the girls? whit am I gaun tae say tae them? oor machines, aye, the yins we've got polished and ready tae switch on, they're nae use, they're obsolescent aaready, even though they're American an split new, the Japanese are selling better yins tae the Taiwanese at hauf the price, an wi their wage-levels they cud turn oot millions o the product at a quarter o the price we cud,

d'ye ken whit thae Yanks said tae me, Mr Robb? they said if *we* would buy the Japanese machines, aye, us, the workers, *buy* the machines, or persuade the Scottish Development Agency tae gie us a loan tae buy them, an if we would tak a twenty per cent wage cut, an move the factory, an the work-force, an the hail jing-bang, doon tae the Sooth o England tae be near the major markets, then mibby we'll be competitive, 'and that's a big may-be, Mrs Hegarty,' they said,

if I believed aa that I'd hae tae shoot masel, wouldn't I? there's a con-trick, a capitalist conspiracy o some kind, thae specifications and quotations and market projections they showed me, they cud aa jist be forgeries, naethin bit lies, hoo kin I tell? we havenae got the expertise on oor side,

oh, I ken thae bastards better than iver noo, smooth as ye like an twice as dirty, an ye shud see *their* solidarity, the wey they raise their eyebroos at each ither an signal by liftin their pens and shufflin their papers and lookin at their watches, an the wey they pretend tae disagree and then mak it up wi each ither an present ye wi a united front, oh, ye ken Thatcher wad back them tae the hilt whether they wis richt or wrang, she's aa fir that kind o solidarity,

oh, whit chance have we got against the power o the state an aa the capital they've amassed oot o oor labour, the Labour Theory of Value, I cud see it iverywhere in their offices, ivery single thing frae the drinks cabinet tae the chandeliers an frae the fancy carpet tae the secretary's Gucci shoes, aa made by a workin man or woman, I cud gang on fir iver on that topic, it's yin o ma favourites.

aye man, ye're a guid listener, ye'd have tae be, sharin a coach seat wi me, I'm thinkin ye're a white-collar union man, ye seem tae unnerstan ma problems, ye're no frae NALGO, are ye? ASTMS then? no? ye're pleyin yer cerds close tae yer chest? aye, ye'll be a guid negotiator, ye'll forgie me, bit I cannae stop masel bletherin, I feel sae trapped, in a capitalistic coach that's gaun far ower fast an in a seat that's ower narra fir me, I'm trapped, there's a con-trick an

I cannae get tae the bottom o it, mibby ma intellectual equipment is obsolescent and inadequate,

Holy Mary, he's intae the fast lane again he's jist blinnin on, Mither o God, that wis close, oh, we're in the clear again, it's nice when ye kin see a clear road in front fir a whilie,

ye'll be thinkin I'm a devout left-fitter, Mr Robb, wi a name like mine an the wey I seem tae be cryin tae the Virgin, bit I'm no, I'm an auld-fashioned materialist, aye, a dialectical materialist, an I ken fine that religion's the opiate o the people, it aye his been, bit there's mair tae it than a bald undialectical statement like that, religion cannae hae existed fir thoosands o years an no mean somethin, an whit I think is that religion's a *feelin*, an it's the dialectic o feelin that the rulin class exploits, an that's whit maks them real bastards, charismatic Pope an aa, bit jist because the feelin's exploitit disnae mean that it disnae exist, wad ye like a sweetie? I'm no supposed tae eat them at aa, go on, have yin, have twa, I've lost a stone since the sit-in sterted bit I loss ma self-control when I'm awaa frae ma girls an I bocht this bag in Lunnon, mibby if ye tak twa ivery time I tak the yin, we'll feenish the bag, go on, ye havenae got a wecht problem, that's obvious,

oh, this clear road's giein him the chance tae dae mair than ninety again, oh, oh, I cannae stand it,

oh, I'm jist a wee lassie greetin fir ma Mammy tae come an haud me close an mak me feel safe, no the hauf-deid donnert auld body she is noo, bit ma big strong Mammy, the wey she used tae be, an the only name I've got fir the feelin is Holy Mary Mither o God, an the pair Protestants havenae even got that, nae wunner they're sae soor, bit nane o the theoreticians o the movement his anither name fir the feelin, I cannae greet fir the workin class or fir solidarity fir they're neither o them ma Mither, they're aboot freens and comradeship,

an I wisnae awfu nice tae ma Mither, oh, I wis cruel tae her, an look at the names I wis cryin her the noo, hauf-deid an donnert, an I wis cryin Protestants soor an them exploitit fella-workers, sae I'm a sinner an I'm guilty am I no?

an there's anither feelin the bastards exploit, oor guilt, aye, we're the ragged troosered philanthropists an we feel bad aboot hatin them, through my fault, through my own fault, an we beat oor briests an we try tae love them when we should be hatin them,

I'm jist stertin tae think aboot hoo ma feelins aboot ma faither fit intae the dialectic bit I'm shair the rulin class wad exploit them tae, gie them hauf a chance, ma faither wis awaa maist o the time, workin or lookin fir work, or on union business, an I think I must have identified wi him unconsciously, fir he wis a materialist, ma Mammy wis religious, but she believed in leevin it, no shovin it doon folks' throats,

there's no much traffic, is there? it's aamost peacefu, even though we are daein eighty, it's the time o nicht fir thinkin aboot thae things, ye cannae help it,

I wis at a class yince an d'ye ken whit the leader said? he said 'at the intersection of dialectical materialism an Freudian psycho-analysis, there ye'll find Comrade Jean Hegarty, fightin her ain battle fir enlightenment', but I dinnae like that 'intersection', it maks me think o twa lines convergin an then divergin an I need jist the yin line, the yin theory tae relate the means o production tae the dialectic o feelin,

aye, they exploit oor identifications aa richt, they gie us brave auld blue-eyed Grannies like the Queen Mother, an pretty wee Princess Di, though she's no sae wee, is she? an couthie uncles like Ronald Reagan, an he's nae mair a couthie capitalist than I'm a couthie marxist, but hoo onybody ootside a mental hospital can identify wi that Thatcher wumman beats me, there's naethin in ma conceptual framework tae accoont fir that, an aa jist tae mak shair we keep in our places an dinnae face up tae the realities o the class-structure, an exploitation, an de-industrialisation, an deliberately engineered structural unemployment, an American colonialism, an Japanese industrial pre-eminence,

an that's whaur me an ma girls is at, trapped in historical processes that we tried tae chynge but cudnae, the movement's that weak, an folk that shud be oor allies are sittin on their erses and twiddlin their thumbs, whit am I gaun tae tell the girls? hoo kin I jist say, 'it's feenished!' for whit'll we dae wi'oot jobs? sit in oor hooses an smoke oorsels stupit, we'll aa be feart tae gang oot in case we meet each ither an mind the wey we kidded oorsels, oh, the sweeties are feenished, I'll just hae tae manage,

I'll no be able tae look onybody in the face, it's no ma faut bit I *feel* guilty, why didn't I smash their faces, their big fat smooth capitalist faces? jile wad be better than a cauld hoose, na, I cudnae sit doon, that wadnae be Jean Hegarty, ye'll see, I'll be organisin the dinner-ladies, they're the only workin-class folk left wi jobs, except fir the clerical officers at the D.H.S.S. and they're scabs, an the barmen in the pubs, we've nae high-tech industries in oor toon, we're no posh like thae new toons,

I'll jist tak ma shoes aff, ma feet are aa fired up, I seem tae notice them when I havenae a sweetie tae suck, dae *your* feet no get fired up?

mibby the dinner-ladies winnae hae me, mibby it *will* be sit in the hoose an look at ma man's photy on the mantelpiece, there must be millions o weemen daein jist that, it's five year since I lost ma man, he wis a wheen aulder than me, ye ken, despair, that's whit killed him, whit hae I din wi ma life? he wis aye speirin, whit's gan wrang? I thocht it wis jist the illness, it wis lung cancer tae be honest, fir he smoked aa his life, bit at the back o the cancer there wis despair, I ken that noo, aye, sittin here talkin tae ye it's come tae me, he jist packed it aa in, he wis niver gaun tae work again an the warld wis a mess an there was naethin tae be din aboot it, naebody wad listen tae him, an he deserved listening tae, it wis different in the thirties when he wis a lad an learnin aboot politics, aathin's a mess, aathin's sick, the speed we're gaun at, he touched a hunnerd the noo, I cud see it on the speedometer, it's sick, aabody rushin, look at thae headlichts comin at us an thae rearlamps in front o us, jist like lemmings headin fir the sea, that's an apocalyptic fallacy, an unfair tae lemmings an aa, bit it's hard tae resist, wi the Bomb an aa the sickness ye see iverywhere,

d'ye ken the only building that's properly maintained whaur I come frae? it's the jile, they're aye giein the doors an the bars an the spikes anither coat o paint, or they're pintin the mortar in the waas wi new cement, or they're whitewashin aathin they kin reach, while

211

the cooncil hooses that were built fir law-abidin folk is faain doon,
or damp as hell, an ivery factory is a ruin or a hole in the grun, it's
sick, I'm tellin ye,

an look at me, whit have I been daein? tryin tae persuade the
Baby-bra Corporation o Atlanta, Georgia, tae buy oor factory, Lulu
Lingerie wis bad enough, bit *Baby-bra*! the English poof that wis
in cahoots wi the Yanks, I'd sooner had the Yanks by theirsels, d'ye
ken whit he said? 'it's the *frisson* of paedophilia that sells the
product, Jean,' so I tellt him, I wis past carin, I kent we'd lost by
then, I tellt him, 'ye'd be better chyngin that name tae Boy-Bra, the
soupçon o transvest-ic-ism wad mibby sell even mair o the
product,' bit the bastard pit me doon, ye kin niver beat that kind,
'you *do* mean transvest-ism, don't you, my dear Jean?' so I tellt him
I wisnae his dear Jean, I was Mrs Hegarty tae him,

whit were we daein, me an the girls, whit did we think we were
daein? raisin our consciousness jist tae pander tae the exploitation
o sick petty-bourgeois fantasies like that, our solidarity jist a tool o
thae agents o American imperialism, somethin they cud use an
chuck awaa when they'd sucked it dry,

I keep reachin in ma bag fir thae sweeties, they're no there, we
feenished them, didn't we? but the coach'll be stoppin at yin o thae
service areas, an we kin hae a cup of tea an gratify ma oral cravins,
tae use a concept frae psychoanalysis,

weel, if there's nae job, there's nae job, an we'll hae tae mak the
best o it, 'living on Social Security doesn't hold the terrors for me
that it does for you,' I said that in my poshest accent when they were
threatenin me, aye, that's whit we'll be daein onyway, me an the
girls, an the men tae, when they've feenished their redundancy
money, fechtin the D.H.S.S. fir ivery penny o oor rights, an I'll bet
ye onythin ye like that it'll be the weemen an the lassies that'll be
in the forefront, the men dinnae hae a bit o spunk left in them,
they're aa castratit, if ye'll excuse the expression,

hey, hey, dinnae greet, man, dinnae greet, the warld's no comin
tae an end just yet, unless this coach, oh Mither o God, now and at
the hour of our death, he's made it, we're back in the middle lane,
aye, use yer hankie, aye, gie it a guid blaw,

oh, I'm treatin ye like a wean and you a grown man wi a brief-case,

cheer up! cheer up! anythin fir a laugh, I'll tell ye somethin funny, they took me intae this big boardroom, designed tae overawe workin folk, an they slappit their brief-cases on tae the table an stertit tae spread oot their papers, ye should hae seen their faces when I slappit ma Co-op plastic shopping bag on tae the table and stertit tae spread oot *ma* papers,

oh, I'm firgettin! whit use are ma papers tae us noo? oh, I'll just greet tae, ye silly wee man, aye, an I'll haud yer haun, fir I'm needin somebody tae haud mines, Mr Robb, an I'll jist keep quate and I'll no ask ye whit ye're greetin fir, it cannae be aa that different frae whit I'm greetin fir, the girls, ma lassies,

'No, it is impossible; it is impossible to convey the life-sensation of any given epoch of one's existence — that which makes its truth, its meaning, its subtle and penetrating essence. It is impossible. We live, as we dream — alone . . .'

Joseph Conrad
Heart of Darkness